T0340630

The publisher and the University of California Press Foundation gratefully acknowledge the generous support of the Joan Palevsky Endowment Fund in Literature in Translation.

Against Demagogues

Against Demagogues

WHAT ARISTOPHANES CAN TEACH US
ABOUT THE PERILS OF POPULISM AND
THE FATE OF DEMOCRACY

NEW TRANSLATIONS OF THE
ACHARNIANS AND THE *KNIGHTS*

Robert C. Bartlett

UNIVERSITY OF CALIFORNIA PRESS

University of California Press
Oakland, California

© 2020 by Robert C. Bartlett

Library of Congress Cataloging-in-Publication Data

Names: Aristophanes. Plays. Selections. English. | Bartlett, Robert C., Against
demagogues. | Aristophanes. Acharnians. English. | Aristophanes.
Knights. English.
Title: Against demagogues : what Aristophanes can teach us about the perils
of populism and the fate of democracy, new translations of the Acharnians
and the Knights / Robert C. Bartlett.
Description: Oakland, California : University of California Press, [2020] |
Includes bibliographical references.
Identifiers: LCCN 2020008276 (print) | LCCN 2020008277 (ebook) |
ISBN 9780520344105 (hardcover) | ISBN 9780520975361 (ebook)
Subjects: LCSH: Aristophanes—Translations into English. | Aristophanes—
Criticism and interpretation. | Democracy in literature. | Populism in
literature. | Justice in literature.
Classification: LCC PA3877 .A2 2020 (print) | LCC PA3877 (ebook) |
DDC 882/.01—dc23
LC record available at https://lccn.loc.gov/2020008276
LC ebook record available at https://lccn.loc.gov/2020008277

Manufactured in the United States of America

28 27 26 25 24 23 22 21 20 19
10 9 8 7 6 5 4 3 2 1

Contents

Abbreviations

Budé	*Aristophane*. Vol. 1. Ed. Victor Coulon and Hilaire van Daele. Budé ed. Paris: Les Belles Lettres, 1995.
Henderson	Jeffery Henderson. *The Maculate Muse: Obscene Language in Attic Comedy*. 2nd ed. Oxford: Oxford University Press, 1991.
Henderson, *Acharnians*	Aristophanes. *Acharnians*. Trans. Jeffery Henderson with introduction and notes. Focus Classical Library. Newburyport, MA: Focus/R. Pullins, 1992.
Henderson (Loeb)	Aristophanes. *Acharnians, Knights*. Ed. and trans. Jeffrey Henderson. Loeb Classical Library. Cambridge, MA: Harvard University Press, 1998.
Mitchell	*The Knights of Aristophanes*. Ed. T. Mitchell with notes critical and explanatory. London: John Murray, 1836.

Neil	*The Knights of Aristophanes.* Ed. R.A. Neil. Hildesheim: Georg Olms, 1966. Originally published in 1901.
OCT	Aristophanes. *Fabulae.* Vol. 1, *Acharnenses Equites Nubes Vespae Pax Aves.* Ed. N. Wilson. Oxford Classical Texts. Oxford: Clarendon Press, 2007.
Olson	Aristophanes. *Acharnians.* Ed. S. Douglas Olson with introduction and commentary. Oxford: Oxford University Press, 2002.
Sommerstein, *Acharnians*	*The Comedies of Aristophanes.* Vol. 1, *Acharnians.* Ed. A.H. Sommerstein with an introduction, translation, and commentary. Warminster: Aris & Phillips, 1980.
Sommerstein, *Knights*	*The Comedies of Aristophanes.* Vol. 2, *Knights.* Ed. A.H. Sommerstein with an introduction, translation, and commentary. Warminster: Aris & Phillips, 1981.
Wilson	N.G. Wilson. *Aristophanea: Studies on the Text of Aristophanes.* Oxford: Oxford University Press, 2007.

Introduction

On Reading Aristophanes Today

O democracy! Are these things to be tolerated?

—*ACHARNIANS* 618

This volume contains new translations of the two earliest extant plays of Aristophanes, the *Acharnians* and *Knights,* together with explanatory notes and interpretive essays meant to aid readers coming to the plays for the first time.

It is reasonable to wonder at the outset why this author and these two plays deserve our attention here and now. As for Aristophanes (d. circa 386–380 B.C.E.), we can begin from the contention that he is not only the greatest Athenian comic play-wright but also among the world's greatest comic writers simply. For although only eleven of the roughly forty plays he wrote have come down to us, they are so filled with wild comic invention, zany plots, and unforgettable characters, both lovable and loathable, that they have easily earned him a place alongside Rabelais, Molière, and Shakespeare. In brief, Aristophanes is an unsurpassed master of comedy and its devices—mockery, blasphemy, parody, and the scatological among them. As a result, anyone interested in the peaks of world literature, and in enjoying them, would do well to turn at some point to Aristophanes.

Still, this contention runs the risk of making of Aristophanes an impressive antique or a giant of the past and only of the past. Hence it may not quite do justice to the fact that Aristophanes' plays can still speak forcefully to contemporary audiences, as I hope the *Acharnians* and *Knights* will confirm: there remains something remarkably fresh about them. This is ultimately traceable to the fact that Aristophanes the comedian was also and above all a thinker of a very high order. In fact Aristophanes sought nothing less than what he himself calls wisdom (*sophia*), a wisdom that, however much it may be rooted in a specific time and place, also transcends time and place in the direction of the permanent human condition and hence the permanent human problems. Aristophanes boasts not only of his unrivaled "novel conceits" (*Wasps* 1044), of the madcap inventions and comic twists that enliven his plays, but also of the "subtle things" (*Acharnians* 445) that fill them. In the revised version of his *Clouds,* Aristophanes famously complains that the audience watching its first performance failed to grasp that it—the play on which he had expended the most labor—was also his "wisest" one: Aristophanes prides himself above all on his wisdom (*Clouds* 522-26). Or, as the Chorus in the *Assembly of Women* puts it, speaking for the poet, "The wise, on the one hand, should judge me by remembering the wise things [in the play], but the laughers, on the other hand, should judge me with pleasure on account of the laughter" (*Assembly of Women* 1155-56). Everyone can see that the plays of Aristophanes are filled with jokes of all kinds, but it is good to remind ourselves that there is also material in them intended for "the wise," actual or potential.

This much, then, in support of the possibility that Aristophanes, the supreme jokester of antiquity, deserves to be taken seriously by us—and more seriously, perhaps, than we may be inclined to take comedians of any age. But to pursue this possibility, we must see what the *Acharnians* and *Knights* in particular help make plain, that the thoughts of concern to Aristophanes, while ranging far and wide indeed, were, for all that, remarkably political: Aristophanes deserves to be known not only as a great thinker but also as a great *political* thinker. It is said that Dionysius I, tyrant of Syracuse, once wrote Plato asking the philosopher for instruction concerning the democratic polity of Athens. Plato responded by sending Dionysius the works of Aristophanes.[1] The tyrant's reaction upon receiving Plato's mailing has not, unfortunately, been recorded. But if Dionysius did read those works, he might well have come to see the good sense behind Plato's gift.

Aristophanes' claim to political wisdom or to political judgments of unusual sobriety rests in part on his understanding of justice. In the *Acharnians,* the lead character, Dicaeopolis, turns out to be none other than Aristophanes in disguise, and at one point he turns to address the audience. He asks them not to take it amiss if he will "speak about the city, while writing a comedy. / For when it comes to what's just, comedy too knows it. / And I'll say things terribly clever, but just" (*Acharnians* 499–501). Similarly, the Chorus of the *Knights* praises Aristophanes on the grounds that the poet "dares to say the just things" (*Knights* 510)—even if doing so comes at some cost to the poet himself. In the *Acharnians* the Chorus describes Aristophanes and his political wisdom this way: "But now don't *you* ever let him go, since he'll make a comedy of the just things! / And he affirms that he'll teach you many good things, so you'll be happy, / Not flattering, or setting out the prospect of pay, or fooling you through and through, / Nor acting nastily nor sprinkling with praise, but teaching the things that are best" (*Acharnians* 655–58). The knowledge of what is just and what is best or most

---

1. "Life of Aristophanes" sec. 40, in *Poetae Comici Graeci,* ed. Rudolph Kassel and Colin Austin (Berlin: W. de Gruyter, 1983), 3.2: 3.

beneficial, then, characterizes the political wisdom of Aristophanes, and so it is that he can "make a comedy" of the city, and even of justice, while also benefiting Athens.

The Athens of concern to Aristophanes was of course a democracy, a direct democracy. His plays feature scenes in or about the democratic Assembly, where all citizens were entitled to gather, to speak, and to vote (*Acharnians, Assembly of Women*); the smaller Council or *boulē* made up of five hundred citizens charged with (among other things) setting the legislative agenda for the Assembly (*Knights*); and the courts, the frequent haunts of the famously litigious Athenians (*Wasps*). Aristophanes is concerned with political affairs domestic and foreign, not least the ruinous and seemingly endless Peloponnesian War, which broke out in 431 B.C.E. and lasted until Athens' surrender to Sparta in 404 (*Acharnians, Peace, Lysistrate*). It is said that Athens bestowed on Aristophanes a special honor in recognition of the sound political advice he conveyed to the city in his *Frogs,* where he urged a reconciliation between democratic and oligarchic factions in the wake of the democracy's restoration in 410 subsequent to a short-lived oligarchic coup ("the 400").[2] Instructive here are the remarks of G. W. F. Hegel, among the most discerning readers of Aristophanes in modern times. According to Hegel, Aristophanes was "no ordinary joker and shallow wag"; "everything has to him a much deeper basis, and in all his jokes there lies a depth of seriousness." Accordingly, "when Aristophanes makes merry over the Democracy, there is a deep

---

2. See, e.g., *The Comedies of Aristophanes: Frogs,* ed. Alan H. Sommerstein (Warminster: Aris & Phillips, 1996), 21–22 and 216. According to the prose "hypothesis" that accompanies the Greek manuscript of the *Frogs*, "The play was so admired on account of its parabasis that it was even produced again, as Dicaearchus asserts."

political earnestness at heart, and from all his works it appears what a noble, excellent, and true Athenian citizen he was."[3]

What then of the two plays of concern to us? That they belong together is easy to demonstrate, for they are linked by their proximity in time—the *Acharnians* was staged in 425 B.C.E., the *Knights* in 424—and by their favorable reception: they were back-to-back hits, each winning first prize in their respective festivals. More important are their kindred themes, for both are strikingly political. And it is this concern for politics, for the conduct of democratic politics in particular, that makes the plays so accessible today. The *Acharnians* is a comedic plea to end the Peloponnesian War. The play's lead character is an old Athenian farmer named Dicaeopolis (= Aristophanes), and when Athens proves uninterested in peace, he resorts to striking a private treaty with Sparta, the enemy. This is the comic conceit at the heart of the play, that a "private" peace is possible, and it sets in motion the rest of the play's action.

Now the most vocal and persuasive advocate of war in Athens at the time—and hence Aristophanes' greatest foe—was the demagogue Cleon (d. 422 B.C.E.).[4] We learn in the *Acharnians* that Aristophanes had previously tangled with Cleon as a result of the poet's comedic takedown of him in the play produced the year before, the *Babylonians* (now lost).[5] This recent conflict in no way prompted Aristophanes to soften his attack or, still less, to retreat.

---

3. G.W.F. Hegel, *Lectures on the History of Philosophy,* trans. E.S. Haldane (Lincoln: University of Nebraska Press, 1995), 1:427–28.

4. As part of the background to the *Knights* and its portrait of Paphlagon, i.e., Cleon, the appendix in this volume reproduces a speech Cleon gave to the Athenian assembly, the only such speech recorded by Thucydides in his *War of the Peloponnesians and Athenians.*

5. Consider *Acharnians* 6, 377–82, 502–5, and 659.

Far from it. For in the *Knights* Aristophanes even more directly attacks Cleon, who was then at the peak of his power, this time going so far as to portray Cleon as a central character named Paphlagon (roughly "Blusterer"). This Paphlagon is a wheedling and cynical manipulator of the Athenian democratic multitude, always concerned above all with his own power—and pocketbook. The comic defeat, not to say humiliation, that Cleon is made to suffer onstage was intended simultaneously to deflate this wily demagogue and to educate the audience even while delighting it. Aristophanes thus availed himself of the talents that were peculiarly and spectacularly his own to damage Cleon, if not in the popular Assembly then in the venue that was most Aristophanes' own, the comic theater. And, as today's satirists may be able to attest, to bring others to laugh at a public figure is to begin to have them take that figure much less seriously. Laughter can be an acid that corrodes the pretentions, and the prerogatives, of the powerful.

As it happens, the earliest instance of the Greek term for "demagoguery" (*dēmagōgia*) appears here (*Knights* 191). This term could be used, and indeed was used, in a neutral or even positive way, for it means simply "leading the demos,"[6] the demos being the largest political class that is by definition the poorest and hence also the least educated. Yet "demagoguery" also soon came to have, as it has in Aristophanes, much the same negative connotation that it has for us: a "demagogue" can also be an unscrupulous master of often bombastic rhetoric who manipulates the crowd for his own ends, the needs of the common good be damned. As a character in the *Knights* puts it, "Demagoguery no longer belongs to a man

---

6. Consider, e.g., Isocrates, *To Nicocles* 16: "And you will nobly lead the demos [*dēmagōgēseis*]."

acquainted with the things of the Muses or to one whose ways are upright / But to one who is unlearned and loathsome" (191–92).

The problem with demagoguery as Aristophanes presents it here is twofold. First, of course, is the demagogue himself, who in the *Knights* is shown to be endlessly flattering of the demos, even as he thinks himself far above them: he despises the demos he nonetheless feels compelled to fawn over. He tells the Athenian demos—represented here as a single character named Demos—whatever he thinks they want to hear, and in particular he promises Demos endless material benefits and comforts, something not unknown to us: the promise of inexpensive healthcare for all, say, "free" college tuition, a nice bump in the old age pension, all of it with a lower tax bill to boot—or rather no bill at all. The successful demagogue, then, must constantly curry favor with the masses, even as he will enrich himself through bribe-taking and other shakedown operations. But he will also fiercely attack any and all who challenge his dominance by seeking high public office themselves. Here the tools of the trade include slander, lawsuits or the threat of them, and any trumped-up charges that are useful in damaging the good reputation of a fellow citizen. So it is that Cleon-Paphlagon is a master of calumny and the like, even as he shamelessly takes credit for the good deeds, including the military exploits, of others.

The second feature of demagoguery as Aristophanes presents it may hit a little too close to home, for the poet makes plain that the demagogue, the "leader of the demos," needs a demos ready and even eager to be led—or rather misled. There's one born every minute. Accordingly, Aristophanes does not spare the Athenian people, the very citizens making up the great bulk of his audience in the theater and laughing at the very jokes that sometimes also sting: he charges them with being amazingly gullible, "half-deaf," irascible, ignorant of what is being done in their name at home and abroad. In the *Knights*, Aristophanes hammers away at the thought that the Athenian people are particularly susceptible to being hoodwinked by those who claim to speak in the name of a god or gods, through oracular pronouncements of various sorts.[7] There is, to say it again, one born every minute.

It is Aristophanes' focus on the conduct of democratic politics, in matters foreign and domestic, that most obviously renders the *Acharnians* and *Knights* deserving of our attention today. Our own experience of demagoguery is in some ways different, to be sure, for we are less concerned (at present) with the conduct of a war than we are with such divisive questions as immigration and race relations, questions without a direct parallel in the Athenian case. But it is nonetheless true that democratic politics, then and now, remains open to the manipulations of demagogic actors. The *Acharnians* and *Knights* present raucous portraits of just such a demagogue in action, together with the pleasing spectacle of his just comeuppance.

. . .

The translations of the *Acharnians* and *Knights* offered here aim at giving readers more or less direct access to the texts of Aristophanes, based on the best available Greek editions,[8] and, to that end, they

7. Consider *Knights* 61, 109 and following, 997 and following.

8. I have used the Greek text of the *Acharnians* and *Knights* in *Aristophane*, ed. Victor Coulon and Hilaire van Daele, Budé ed. (Paris: Les Belles Lettres, 1995), vol. 1, although I have also consulted the Oxford Classical Text edition: Aristophanes, *Fabulae*, vol. 1, *Acharnenses Equites Nubes Vespae Pax Aves*, ed. N. Wilson (Oxford: Clarendon Press, 2007). In the case of the *Acharnians* I have

attempt to be as literal as sound English usage permits. This means that I have tried to render consistently all key terms—*justice, wisdom, courage, god, man, human being*—by what seemed to me their closest English equivalents, resorting to explanatory footnotes where such consistency proved impossible. Readers may therefore be confident that when *nature* appears in the translations, for example, it is reflecting the presence of the same word or family of words (*physis, phyō*) in the original. The translations also strive to reproduce the most striking details of Aristophanes' text—its wide variety of oaths, for example, and terms of address that are too often suppressed or altered by modern scholars. In one respect, however, the versions offered here depart from the letter, if not I hope the spirit, of Aristophanes. For the plays were recited or sung in poetic meter, whereas the present translations are in prose. For this translator, at least, even the attempt to render Aristophanes into English verse would not only fail to convey the dazzling brilliance of the original poetry but also likely sacrifice the clear meaning of the words or a sense of the playwright's intention.[9] I have chosen, then, to try to convey that intention in the medium of prose alone. Readers dissatisfied (or for that matter satisfied) with this

benefited from the masterful commentary of S. Douglas Olson: Aristophanes, *Acharnians* (Oxford: Oxford University Press, 2002). Very helpful too are the editions of both plays prepared by Alan H. Sommerstein: *The Comedies of Aristophanes,* vols. 1–2 (Warminster: Aris & Phillips, 1980–81). Material in square brackets does not appear in the Greek and is therefore the responsibility of the translator. Line numbers attempt to reflect as closely as possible those in the Greek text.

9. For a classic rendering of the plays into English verse, see the Loeb Classical Library edition of the plays of Aristophanes by B. B. Rogers (Cambridge, MA: Harvard University Press, 1924).

choice are of course encouraged to learn to read Aristophanes' marvelous poetry in the original language.

The texts are accompanied by explanatory notes intended to aid a first reading of the plays, with their many political and literary allusions, and by interpretive essays meant to foster further reflection.[10] The essays for the most part follow the plays as they unfold. They draw readers' attention to the most important plot points, explain the significance of various characters, foreign and homegrown, and shed light on the meaning of Aristophanes' often madcap, rapid-fire episodes. Above all, the essays strive to disentangle Aristophanes' serious teaching about democratic politics from his many jokes and pratfalls: he puts on display in both the *Acharnians* and the *Knights* the frailties peculiar to democracy. In general, then, the essays attempt to vindicate Aristophanes' claim to "teach the just things" while "making a comedy of the city."

It is my hope that this volume will foster the study of Aristophanes understood not only as a comic genius but also as an important political thinker, not least in times of democratic turmoil. In the medium of comedy, Aristophanes proves to be a tough critic of democracy as well as a prudent advisor to it. He sets forth with great power the dangers to which democracies, then and now, are prone: the threats posed by external warfare and by internal division. Above all, Aristophanes has a keen eye for the seductive allure of demagogues and the damage they can do to a more or less healthy democracy. He is particularly skilled at portraying the toxic mix of a ruthlessly ambitious man with a people at once ill-informed about the doings of their own democracy and too ready

---

10. An earlier version of the essay on the *Acharnians* first appeared in *Interpretation: A Journal of Political Philosophy* 45:3 (2019): 365–82.

to believe empty promises or idle flattery. The demagogue Cleon is Aristophanes' greatest opponent in both the *Acharnians* and the *Knights,* and his comedic skewering of the man still resonates. If not all jokes travel well, Aristophanes' singular blend of wisecracking wisdom certainly does.

The *Acharnians*

Dramatis Personae

DICAEOPOLIS ["JUST CITY"]

HERALD

AMPHITHEUS ["GOD ON BOTH SIDES"]

ATHENIAN AMBASSADORS

PSEUDARTABAS

THEORUS

CHORUS OF ACHARNIANS

DAUGHTER OF DICAEOPOLIS

SERVANT OF EURIPIDES

EURIPIDES

LAMACHUS

MEGARIAN

MAIDEN DAUGHTERS OF THE MEGARIAN

SYCOPHANT

THEBAN

NICARCHUS

MESSENGER(S)

FARMER

BEST MAN

The *Acharnians*

DICAEOPOLIS

By how many things has my own heart been stung!
And I've been pleased by few—very few—things: four.
But as for the things I've been pained by, gazillions!
Now let me see . . . what has pleased me that's deserving of . . .
    delectation?
I know what it was my heart took delight in—when I saw   5
The five talents[1] that Cleon[2] vomited up!
How I positively glowed at that, and I'm a friend to the Knights
On account of that deed, "for it is a thing worthy of Greece"![3]
But I felt a pain, in turn, connected with tragedy,
When I stood agape in expectation of Aeschylus,   10
But then the fellow announced, "Theognis, bring in the chorus!"[4]
Can you imagine how this shook my heart?!

---

1. A talent (of silver) was a measure of weight equivalent to six thousand drachmas.

2. Athenian politician and demagogue (d. 422 B.C.E.), active in the Peloponnesian War; Thucydides describes him as "the most violent man" in Athens (*Peloponnesian War* 3.36). There is no clear historical record of such a fine for Cleon, and it is quite possible that Dicaeopolis here refers to an event in a comedy, perhaps his own *Babylonians* of the previous year.

3. A quotation from Euripides' lost *Telephus*—the first of what are many such quotations or parodies of that tragedy here.

4. Not to be confused with the elegiac poet of the sixth century of the same name, this Theognis is an Athenian tragic poet and contemporary of Aristophanes; see 138–40 below as well as *Thesmophoriazusae* 170.

But I had another pleasure that time when, right after Moschus,
Dexitheus came on singing a Boeotian tune.[5]

15 But just this year I died, in fact I was tortured, when I saw
Chaeris poke his head out to do the Orthion [tune].[6]
But never once since the time I began to soap up
Have my brows been so stung by suds
As now, when the regular Assembly's to meet

20 At dawn—yet the Pnyx[7] here is empty,
While people chatter away in the marketplace and
Flee higgledy-piggledy the ochre-red cord.[8]
Not even the Prytaneis[9] have come, but come
They will—late—and when they do can you imagine

25 How they'll push and shove one another for the first row?
A torrent pouring in! But as for how there'll be peace,
They pay it no mind at all. O City, City!
But me, I'm always the very first in the Assembly

---

5. The identity of both Moschus and Dexitheus is uncertain; evidently
Dexitheus was a superior musician to Moschus (so Sommerstein, *Acharnians*;
Olson; and the Budé ad loc.). "Moschus" means "calf," and some have specu-
lated that the line points to Dexitheus coming on stage "dressed as a rustic"
and "mounted on a young bull or heifer"; C. E. Graves, *Aristophanes, Acharnians* (1905; Exeter: Bristol Classical Press, 1982) ad loc.

6. Chaeris was a notoriously bad musician; see 866 below as well as *Peace*
951 and *Birds* 858. See also Andrew Hartwig, "A Reconsideration of the Musician Chaeris," *Classical Quarterly* 59:2 (2009): 383–97. The Orthion was a
famous tune said to have been composed by Terpander.

7. The locale of the Assembly in Athens, just inside the city walls.

8. Officials tried to encourage attendance at the Assembly by (among other
things) "stretching out a long ochred cord . . . which was used as a sort of drag-
net, with anyone whose clothes were stained by it being subject to a fine"
(Olson ad loc.). Consider also *Assembly of Women* 379.

9. The officials presiding over the Assembly.

To hurry and take my seat. And then, since I'm alone,
I yawn, I gape, I stretch myself, I fart,   30
I'm perplexed, I write, pluck my hair, reckon up,
While looking off to the fields, loving peace,
Loathing town, longing for my own deme,[10]
That never yet said, "Buy charcoal!"
Or vinegar, or oil, and in fact it did not know "Buy!"[11]   35
Instead it itself used to bring forth all things, and the buyer
     wasn't there.
So now I've come, simply put, all ready
To cry out, to interrupt, to revile the orators
If somebody speaks of anything other than peace.
But the Prytaneis are here . . . it's noon!   40
Didn't I proclaim it? *This* is what I was talking about!
Every man's pushing and shoving for a front-row seat!

HERALD
Move forward!
Move along, so you're within the sanctified area!

AMPHITHEUS
[*To Dicaeopolis*] Has anybody already spoken?

HERALD
[*Addressing the Assembly*] Who wishes to address the Assembly?   45

AMPHITHEUS
I do!

---

10. Athens was organized into neighborhood districts or "demes."

11. "Buy" (*priō*) in this context may be either a nickname or even a proper name: "Mr. Buy" (so Wilson ad loc.).

HERALD

Who are you?

AMPHITHEUS

Amphitheus.

HERALD

Not a human being?

AMPHITHEUS

No,

But an immortal. For Amphitheus[12] was son of Demeter
And Triptolemus, and to him was born Celeus.
And Celeus married Phaenarete my grandmother,
50   From whom Lycinus came to be. And from him, me!
Immortal I am, and to me the gods entrusted
The making of a treaty with the Lacedaemonians,[13] to me alone!
But, since I'm an immortal, men, I don't have travel-money.
For the Prytaneis aren't giving me any.

HERALD

Police![14]

---

12. "This Amphitheus . . . is mentioned nowhere else in Eleusinian mythol-
ogy" (Olson ad loc.), and the whole genealogy seems garbled ("wildly confused": Sommerstein, *Acharnians* ad loc.). Lowell Edmunds suggests it is "a
genealogy in the Euripidean style" and hence a parody; Edmunds, "Aristophanes' *Acharnians*," in *Aristophanes: Essays in Interpretation*, ed. Jeffrey Henderson (Cambridge: Cambridge University Press, 1980), 4.

13. That is, the Spartans, here and throughout.

14. Literally, "Archers!" or "Bowmen!" These were Scythian slaves, not
Athenian citizens (see, e.g., *Thesmophoriasuzae* 1001 and following).

AMPHITHEUS

O Triptolemus and Celeus, will you overlook my [being treated   55
this way]?

DICAEOPOLIS

Men, Prytaneis, you're committing an injustice against the
Assembly
By leading away the man who was willing to make a treaty for us
and hang up the shields!

HERALD

Sit down! Keep quiet!

DICAEOPOLIS

No, by Apollo, I won't!
Not if you won't put peace on the agenda for me!   60

HERALD

[*To the Assembly*] The ambassadors back from the King
[of Persia]!

DICAEOPOLIS

"King" indeed! These ambassadors irk me, what with their
peacocks and their boasts!

HERALD

Quiet!

DICAEOPOLIS

Aye yi yi! O Ecbatana,¹⁵ what a getup!

---

15. The capital of Media and summer home of the King of Persia.

AMBASSADOR

65 You sent us to the Great King
Earning pay of two drachmas a day
In the archonship of Euthymenes.[16]

DICAEOPOLIS

Ugh, the drachmas!

AMBASSADOR

And we simply wore ourselves out as we roamed around
Over the Caystrian plains in our covered carriages,
70 Softly reclining on litters,
Just perishing . . .

DICAEOPOLIS

Then I must have really been safe,
Reclining on the wall's ramparts amid all the trash![17]

AMBASSADOR

And while being received as guests we were forced to drink,
From crystal and golden goblets,
Unmixed sweet wine.[18]

---

16. That is, in the year 437–436 B.C.E. and hence eleven years before the performance of the *Acharnians:* the Athenian ambassadors have been on the public payroll for a long time.

17. Part of Pericles' war strategy involved having the rural population of Athens abandon their homes to the enemy and come to live within the city's walls, which led to much crowding and hardship: "Many even made their homes in the towers of the city walls" (Thucydides 2.17).

18. Greeks typically diluted their wine with water. Hence the ambassadors were "forced" to drink good wine straight.

DICAEOPOLIS

O Cranaus's city!¹⁹

75

Do you perceive the ambassador mocking you?

AMBASSADOR

For the barbarians regard as real men
Only those capable of devouring and drinking the most.

DICAEOPOLIS

But with us it's cocksuckers²⁰ and buggers!

AMBASSADOR

In the fourth year we arrived at the palace

80

But he had taken the army and gone off to the outhouse,
And for eight months was crapping on the Golden Hills.

DICAEOPOLIS

At what time did he close up his butthole?
At the full moon?²¹

---

19. Cranaus was an early king of Athens.

20. The precise meaning of the noun (*laikastas*)—though not its obscene tone—occasioned some controversy, Henderson originally contending that the verb related to it is simply equivalent to *binein* (screw), others that it refers to fellatio, a view Henderson himself came to adopt; see A. E. Houseman, "Praefanda," *Hermes* 66 (1931): 402–12; H. D. Jocelyn, "A Greek Indecency and Its Students: *Laikazein*," *Proceedings of the Cambridge Philological Society*, n.s., 26 (1980): 12–66; and Olson, 96 (on *Acharnians* 79). Compare Henderson 153 with 249. See also *Knights* 167.

21. Some MSS give this line (without the question mark) to the Ambassador. "The expression is proverbial for 'never'" (Edmunds, "Aristophanes' *Acharnians*," 39).

AMBASSADOR

And then he went off toward home.
85 Then he received us as guests and set beside us
Whole oxen from a casserole dish.

DICAEOPOLIS

And who's ever seen
Ox casserole?! What boastful baloney![22]

AMBASSADOR

And, yes—by Zeus!—a bird three times the size of Cleonymus
He served up for us. Its name was "robin."[23]

DICAEOPOLIS

90 So you were robbing all this while getting your two drachmas
a day!

AMBASSADOR

And now we've come here, bringing along Pseudartabas,
The King's Eye![24]

DICAEOPOLIS

Let a crow peck it out, and yours too, the ambassador's!

---

22. Consider, however, Herodotus, *Histories* 1.133.1, where just such a menu item is mentioned.

23. The name is literally "cheat" (*phenax*), which resembles the name of the bird "phoenix." Thus "robin" and "robbin'" in English. Cleonymus is mocked by Aristophanes for his gluttony and girth; see also 844 as well as *Knights* 958.

24. A genuine office in the Persian court; consider Herodotus, *Histories* 1.114.2 as well as Xenophon, *The Education of Cyrus* 8.2.10 and 8.6.16. Naturally Aristophanes interprets the title as literally as possible.

HERALD

[*To the Assembly*] The King's Eye!

[*Enter Pseudartabas, dressed in elaborate Persian finery and sporting a single huge eye in the middle of his forehead*]

DICAEOPOLIS

Lord Heracles!
In the name of the gods—hey guy,[25] are you giving me a salty-   95
    nautical look?
Or are you looking for a ship's berth as you round a cape?
You've got a porthole, I suppose, down there below your eye?

AMBASSADOR

So come now, tell us whatever it is the King has sent you
To say to the Athenians, O Pseudartabas!

PSEUDARTABAS

Iarta name xarxana pisona satra.[26]   100

AMBASSADOR

Did you get what he's saying?

DICAEOPOLIS

By Apollo, no, I certainly didn't!

AMBASSADOR

He contends that the King will send you[27] gold!
[*To Pseudartabas*] Now you, speak at greater length, and clearly,
    about "gold."

---

25. Literally, "O human being."
26. Gibberish meant to imitate the sound of Persian to Greek ears.
27. The plural "you."

PSEUDARTABAS

Will no goldo get, butthole-gapey Ionio!

DICAEOPOLIS

105 Damn! *That* he says clearly!

AMBASSADOR

So *what's* he saying?!?

DICAEOPOLIS

What, you ask? He's saying that Ionians have gaping buttholes,
If they expect gold from barbarians.

AMBASSADOR

No—rather, this fellow here's saying great "gobs" of gold "in the
hold."

DICAEOPOLIS

What "gobs"?!? *You* are a big boaster!
110 Just get lost. And I'll put this guy to the test by myself.

[*Exit Ambassadors*]

[*To Pseudartabas*] So come on, tell it to me clearly, before *this!*
       [*raises a fist*],
So I won't dye you Sardian red![28]
The Great King, is he going to send us gold? [*Pseudartabas and
       attendants nod "no"*]
So then we're being completely duped by the ambassadors?
       [*Pseudartabas and attendants nod "yes"*]

---

28. Dicaeopolis alludes to Sardis, principal city of Lydia and part of the Persian Empire. Consider also *Peace* 1173–74.

These men here have a Greek way of nodding,[29]   115
And there's no way they aren't from right here!
And of these two eunuchs, this one here,
I know who he is, Cleisthenes son of Sibyrtius![30]
"O hot-tempered"[31] . . . shaver of butthole,
With *this* sort of a beard, you monkey,   120
You came to us fitted out as a eunuch?
But who is this guy here, surely not Straton?![32]

HERALD

Keep quiet! Sit down!
The Council invites the King's Eye
To the Prytaneum![33]

[*Exit the King's Eye and attendants*]

DICAEOPOLIS

Don't these things just make you choke?   125

---

29. Pseudartabus and perhaps the eunuch attendants "respond to the question by nodding their heads back in the gesture that for the Greeks meant (and means) 'No'" (Olson ad loc.).

30. Aristophanes repeatedly ridicules Cleisthenes because of his effeminacy and beardlessness, perhaps the latter's attempt to make himself more boyish and hence attractive to lovers. The identity of Sibyrtius is uncertain, as is therefore the joke.

31. According to the scholiast, the beginning of a line of Euripides.

32. Aristophanes mentions Cleisthenes and Straton together also at *Knights* 1373-74.

33. Housing the city's sacred hearth, the Prytaneum was used to host foreign dignitaries and returning Athenian ambassadors. Athenian citizens who had performed some signal service to the city were rewarded with free meals for life in the Prytaneum, an honor bestowed on Cleon; see also *Knights* 819.

And so then I'm to twiddle my thumbs here
While the door's never closed for [the Council] to entertain these
    guys?!
But I'll do a certain clever deed, and great.
But where's Amphitheus for me?

AMPHITHEUS

Right here!

DICAEOPOLIS

130   For me, take these eight drachmas here
To strike a treaty with the Lacedaemonians, for me alone
And my kids and my spouse.
[*To the audience*] But *you* keep sending off embassies, gaping all
    the while!

HERALD

Let Theorus approach, back from [the court of] Sitalkes!³⁴

[*Enter Theorus*]

THEORUS

Here I am.

DICAEOPOLIS

135   Here's another boaster announced!

THEORUS

We would not have been in Thrace for such a long time—

---

34. Theorus was an associate of Cleon; see also *Knights* 608. Sitalkes was king of the Odrysians, barbarians and sometime allies of Athens who were powerful in the Thracian Chersonese.

DICAEOPOLIS

[*Aside*] By Zeus, no, he wouldn't have, if he hadn't got paid a lot!

THEORUS

If the whole of Thrace had not been covered in snow
And the rivers frozen—

DICAEOPOLIS

[*Aside*] At the same time Theognis was competing here![35]   140

THEORUS

During this time I was drinking with Sitalkes
And in fact he was so extraordinarily pro-Athenian
And truly a lover of yours that
He even wrote on the walls, "Athenians are beautiful!"[36]
And his son, whom we made an Athenian citizen,[37]   145
Had a passionate desire to eat sausages from the Apatourian
      festival[38]
And kept beseeching his father to aid his [new] fatherland.
He swore as he poured a libation that he would come to its aid
Having an army so great that Athenians would say:
"How great a swarm of locusts draws near!"   150

---

35. The suggestion is that Theognis's poetry is as "frigid" as a Thracian winter; according to the scholiast, Theognis's nickname was "Snow." (On the term as applied to rhetoric, consider Aristotle, *Art of Rhetoric* 1405b–1406b.) See also 10–11 above.

36. The formula suggests the standard way lovers addressed their beloveds ("So-and-so is handsome!"); see Olson ad loc.

37. See Thucydides 2.29: to court Sitalkes, the Athenians granted his son, Sadokos, Athenian citizenship.

38. A three-day festival celebrating the entrance of new citizens and children into "phratries" or kinship groups.

DICAEOPOLIS

Might I perish in the worst way, if I'm persuaded by any of the things

He says here—except that part about the locusts.

THEORUS

And in fact he is now sending you the most warlike tribe in Thrace.

DICAEOPOLIS

That, at least, is already clear!

HERALD

155 Let the Thracians come forward, whom Theorus brought!

DICAEOPOLIS

What evil is this?!?

THEORUS

An army of Odomantians.³⁹

DICAEOPOLIS

Odomantians indeed! [*Looking them up and down*] Tell me, what's *that?!?*

Who pruned the Odomantians' dicks?⁴⁰

THEORUS

If somebody pays them two drachmas,

160 They'll pour peltasts⁴¹ over the whole of Boeotia.

---

39. A Thracian tribe; consider Thucydides 2.101 as well as 5.6.

40. Odomantians were apparently circumcised, as Greek men were not.

41. Lightly armed skirmishers.

DICAEOPOLIS

Two drachmas for these foreskin-less dicks?
Well, the mass of rowers would sure grumble,
Our city-saviors. [*The Odomantians turn on Dicaeopolis*] Hey,
    wretched me, I'm a goner,
My garlic's being plundered by the Odomantians!
Won't you put down my garlic!?!

THEORUS

You bloody fool,   165
Don't approach them when they're garlic-primed![42]

DICAEOPOLIS

Are you Prytaneis overlooking my suffering all this—
In the fatherland and at the hands of barbarian men to boot?
But I forbid going on with an Assembly
Concerning the Thracians' pay. And I say to you that   170
There's a sign from Zeus: in fact, a raindrop just fell on me!

HERALD

The Thracians are to leave and be present the day after tomorrow.
For the Prytaneis dissolve the Assembly.

[*All exit except Dicaeopolis*]

DICAEOPOLIS

Ah, wretched me, so much garlic pesto I've lost!
But here's Amphitheus back from Lacedaemon!   175
Good day, Amphitheus!

---

42. Cockfighters would feed their cocks garlic to incite them to fight; see,
e.g., Xenophon, *Symposium* 4.9.

AMPHITHEUS

Not yet it isn't, not till I stop running!
For I'm on the run and have to escape from Acharnians![43]

DICAEOPOLIS

What is it?!?

AMPHITHEUS

Bearing a treaty for you,
I was hastening here. But certain elders got a whiff of it,
180   Acharnians, tough old geezers, sturdy stuff,
Hard, Marathon-fighters, hearts of maple wood.
Then all cried out, "You bloodiest bastard,
You bring a treaty when our vines are cut up?!"
And they began to gather stones in their simple cloaks.
185   Me, I started to flee; they kept pursuing me and shouting.

DICAEOPOLIS

Well, let 'em shout. But are you carrying the treaty-libations?[44]

AMPHITHEUS

I am indeed, I say: here are three tastings.
This one is for five years. Take it and have a taste.

DICAEOPOLIS

Yuck!

---

43. Acharnians are Athenian citizens who hail from the deme or district of Acharnae, the largest of the demes and most remote from Athens proper; see Thucydides 2.19–23.

44. The next series of jokes depends on the ambiguity of the word for "treaty" (*spondai*), which means literally the libation (wine) poured to affirm the treaty signed and, by extension, the treaty itself.

AMPHITHEUS

What is it??

DICAEOPOLIS

I don't like it because
It smells of pitch and the outfitting of ships!⁴⁵   190

AMPHITHEUS

Well take this ten-year one and have a taste.

DICAEOPOLIS

This one smells of embassies to the cities [in the empire],
Very vinegary, like the wearing down of the allies.

AMPHITHEUS

But this here, you see, is your thirty-year one
Pertaining to both land and sea.

DICAEOPOLIS

O Dionysia!   195
This one smells of ambrosia and nectar
And not of having to keep an eye out for "three days' rations,"⁴⁶
And it says to my stomach, "Go wherever you like!"
This I accept and pour the libation and drink it down.
I bid fare-thee-well and so long to the Acharnians.   200
Me, I'm done with war and its evils.
I'll go and celebrate the Rural Dionysia.⁴⁷

---

45. Pitch, or resin, was used not only to seal the hulls of ships but also to line wine jars and even to flavor the wine itself, as in retsina today.

46. Soldiers called to battle would be asked to bring with them three days' worth of food; see, e.g., *Peace* 312.

47. "This festival (to be sharply distinguished from the springtime City Dionysia) was held in and by the individual local communities (demes) of

AMPHITHEUS

And I'll flee the Acharnians!

[Exit Dicaeopolis and Amphitheus]

CHORUS [OF ACHARNIANS]
This way, everybody, follow, pursue him, and put a question
    about the man
205 To every passerby! For to the city it's a worthwhile thing
To seize this man. [To the audience] But you all reveal to me,
If anybody knows where on earth the guy with the treaty has
    turned.

[CHORUS LEADER]
He's fled, he's gone clean away.
210 Oh, wretched me, these years of mine!
In the time of my youth, when
I carried a load of charcoal[48]
215 And used to follow Phayllus[49] at a run, this treaty-carrier here,
    pursued by me then,
Wouldn't have gotten away or trotted off so lightly!
But now, since my shin is stiff
220 And ancient Lacrateides' legs are heavy,

Attica. . . . Since the outbreak of the war Dicaeopolis has not been able to celebrate it in *his own* deme"; Sommerstein, *Acharnians* ad loc. (emphasis original).

48. As becomes clear from the action of the play, these Acharnians depended for their livelihood on the manufacture of charcoal.

49. The name of a famous athlete who also commanded a ship at the battle of Salamis in 480; see also *Wasps* 1206.

The guy got away. But we must pursue—lest he ever laugh in our
    faces
Or get away from Acharnians, old indeed though we are.
He it is—O Father Zeus and Gods!—
Who made a treaty with enemies,   225
With whom hate-filled war, as far as I'm concerned, will only
    increase, on account of my lands.
And I'll not let up until, like a shaft, I'm plunged in them in   230
    revenge
Sharp, painful, and up to the hilt, so that
Never again may they trample my vines!
But we must seek the man out and look toward Poundsville[50]
And pursue from one land to the next, till he is discovered at last.   235
As for me, I could never get my fill of pounding him with stones!

DICAEOPOLIS

Hush, please, speak words of good omen!

CHORUS

Everyone quiet! Did you hear, men, that "hush"?
This is the very guy we're seeking! But everybody
Out of the way here. For the man's coming over, as it seems, to   240
    perform a sacrifice.

[*Dicaeopolis enters with his Wife and Daughter, together with two
slaves holding a large phallus*][51]

---

50. Although the MSS differ here, Aristophanes evidently coins a word that
blends the name of a deme of Athens (Pallene) with a verb that can mean "to
strike or pound" (*ballō*): Ballene.

51. "Oversize models of an erect penis balanced on a pair of wooden carry-
ing-poles were a standard feature of Dionysiac processions" (Olson ad loc.).

DICAEOPOLIS

Hush, please, speak words of good omen!
Let her step forward a bit, the basket-carrier.
Let Xanthias stand the phallus up straight!
Put down the basket, daughter, so we may commence.

DAUGHTER

245   Mother, hand up the soup ladle
So I may pour broth over this flat cake here.

DICAEOPOLIS

And that's nobly propitious indeed. O Master Dionysus!
In a manner gratifying to You may this procession
And these sacrifices be performed with the members of my
     household,
250   And with good fortune may I conduct the Rural Dionysia,
Freed of army campaigning; and may the Thirty-Year Treaty turn
     out nobly for me.
Come, then, daughter, beautiful as you are you'll carry the
     basket beautifully, with a savory-sour look about you. How
     blessed
255   Is he who will marry you and beget . . . weasels[52]
No fewer than the farts you produce, when it's just before
     dawn.
Lead the way! And among the crowd of people be much on your
     guard

See also Walter Burkert, *Greek Religion* (Cambridge, MA: Harvard University
Press, 1985), 290 and context.

52. Weasels were welcomed in Greek households for their keen ability to
catch mice.

Lest anybody nibble your golden baubles, undetected by you.[53]
[*To the slaves*] Xanthias, you two must hold upright
The phallus behind the basket-bearer. 260
I'll follow along and sing the phallic song.
And you, wife, you look upon me from the roof. Lead the way!
O Penis, comrade of Bacchus,[54]
Fellow reveler, night roamer,
Adulterer,[55] boy-lover! 265
In the sixth year I greet you
As I gladly return to my deme,
Having made a treaty for myself,
Rid of troubles and battles
And Lamachuses.[56] 270
For it's much more pleasant, O Penis, Penis,
To catch a girl in her bloom stealing wood,
Strymodorus's Thratta[57] from the rocky ground,
Then taking her round the waist, lifting her up, tossing
Her down, plucking the flower. 275
Penis, Penis!

---

53. Henderson, *Acharnians* (ad loc.) detects in "golden baubles" (*ta chrysia*) an echo of the word for "vulva" (*kysos*).

54. That is, Dionysus, god of (among other things) wine.

55. Or, perhaps, "seducer" (*moiche*), "not just of another man's wife but of any free woman," as Olson (ad loc.) suggests. But its frequent sense of "adulterer" should not be ignored.

56. Lamachus was an Athenian general involved in the conduct of the Peloponnesian War who will soon appear in the play. Consider Thucydides 4.75; 5.19, 24; 6.8, 49–50, 101 (death of Lamachus), 103. The word for "Lamachuses" (*lamachōn*) contains the word for "battles" (*machōn*) that appears in the previous line.

57. Presumably a female slave; the name suggests a Thracian origin.

If you drink together with us, then after the boozing
From morning on you'll quaff down a cup of peace,
And the shield will be hung in the chimney!

CHORUS

280 There he is! That's him!
Strike, strike, strike, strike,
Beat, beat the bastard!
Won't you strike, won't you strike?!?

DICAEOPOLIS

Heracles, what's *this*?!? You're going to shatter my pot!

CHORUS

285 It's *you* we'll stone to death, you bloody bastard!

DICAEOPOLIS

On what charge, most reverend Acharnian elders?

CHORUS

You're asking this?!? You're utterly shameless and disgusting!
290 You traitor to the fatherland, you alone among us
Make a treaty, then can look me in the eye!?!

DICAEOPOLIS

But did you hear why I made the treaty? Just listen.

CHORUS

295 Are we to listen to *you*? Die! We'll crush you with stones.

DICAEOPOLIS

No no, at least not before you hear! Just hold on, good
fellows!

CHORUS

I will *not* hold on, and don't give me your speech.
I'm full of hatred for you even more than I hate Cleon, whom   300
I'll cut up into shoe leather for the Knights.[58]
And I won't listen to you giving long speeches,
You who signed a treaty with the Laconians![59] Instead, I'll get
    my revenge!

DICAEOPOLIS

Good fellows! As for the Laconians, put them aside   305
And listen to my treaty, as to whether I concluded it nobly.

CHORUS

How could you still say "nobly," once you've made peace
With those who abide by no altar or pledge or oath!

DICAEOPOLIS

I know that in fact the Laconians, whom we lay into too much,
Are not the cause of *all* our troubles!   310

CHORUS

Not *all,* you dirty crook?!? So you dare say these things
Right to our faces? And then I'm going to *spare* you?

DICAEOPOLIS

Not *all,* not *all* [our troubles]. But in speaking here and now
I could affirm that in many respects *they* are actually the ones
    being treated unjustly!

---

58. Though somewhat controversial among scholars, these lines may serve
as an advertisement of sorts for Aristophanes' next play, the *Knights;* see Olson
ad loc. and Henderson, *Acharnians,* 95 n. 42.

59. That is, the Spartans.

CHORUS

315 This really is a terrible utterance and disturbing to the core,
     If you'll dare to speak to us on behalf of the enemy!

DICAEOPOLIS

And if I don't say what's just, and don't do so in the opinion of the
     multitude,
I'll be willing to speak with my head on the chopping block.[60]

CHORUS

Tell me, why are we sparing the stones, fellow demesmen,
320 And not shredding this man till he's a crimson robe?

DICAEOPOLIS

How black, in turn, is the smoldering charcoal that's flamed up in
     you!
You won't listen, you really won't listen, sons of Acharneus?

CHORUS

That's right, we won't listen!

DICAEOPOLIS

Then I'm going to suffer terribly!

CHORUS

I'd perish, were I to listen!

DICAEOPOLIS

No, no, Acharnians!

---

60. An allusion to a fragment of Euripides' *Telephus:* "Not even if someone
holding an ax were about to drive it into my neck will I be silent when I have just
things to say in response" (so Olson ad loc.).

CHORUS

Know that you're going to die, right now!

DICAEOPOLIS

Then . . . I'll bite you!   325
For in return I'll kill your nearest and dearest,
Since I have hostages against you, whom I'll get and execute!

CHORUS

Tell me, how does this remark, fellow demesmen, threaten
Us Acharnians? Surely he doesn't hold someone's child,
One of ours here, locked up inside? Why's he so bold?   330

DICAEOPOLIS

Strike me, if you want to. For I'll destroy . . . *this!* [*holds up a basket
    of charcoal*].
I'll know soon who among you has any care at all for charcoal!

CHORUS

Oh! We're done for! The charcoal basket here is my demesman!
Don't do what you're about to do, not at all, oh! Not at all!

DICAEOPOLIS

Oh, I'll kill it all right. Shout [all you like]: I won't listen!   335

CHORUS

Then you'll destroy this, my charcoal-pal here, my age-mate?

DICAEOPOLIS

You didn't even listen to me as I was speaking just now.

CHORUS

But say *now* whatever seems best to you, and
In what way the Lacedaemonian is a friend to you.

340   Because this dear little charcoal basket here, I'll never
            betray it!

DICAEOPOLIS

First let the stones fall to the ground for me.

CHORUS

[*Emptying their pockets*] There they are on the ground for you, and
            you in turn lay down your sword.

DICAEOPOLIS

But see to it there're no stones lurking in your cloaks somewhere.

CHORUS

[*Dancing a frenetic, spinning jig*] They've been shaken out, on the
            ground. Don't you see it being shaken?
345   But don't give me any excuse, just lay down your shaft.
            For this here's getting shaken, as I turn about.

DICAEOPOLIS

So you all were bound to shake up [and down] your shouting,[61]
            And the Parnasian[62] charcoal nearly died,
            And on account of the strangeness of its fellow demesmen at
                that!
350   And through its fear, the coal basket
            Has splattered me with a load of dust, like a squid!

61. The reading of the MSS, although most modern editors read the emendation of Dobree that would give this translation: "So you all were bound to
cease your shouting."

62. Parnes is the mountain range north of Athens that supplied the wood
with which the Acharnians made their charcoal; the deme of Acharnae was
located in its foothills.

For it's a terrible thing that the spirited anger of men
Has grown so sour as to strike and shout
And be unwilling to listen to anything evenly balanced,
Though I'm willing to say, [with my head] on the chopping block,   355
Quite all that I may say in favor of the Lacedaemonians!
And yet I love my soul,[63] I do.

CHORUS

Why then don't you bring out a chopping block from inside
    and state
Whatever this big thing is, you rogue, that you've got?   360
For a great longing grips me as to whatever it is you're thinking!
But in just the way that you yourself prescribed your trial,
Set down the block here and undertake to speak.   365

[*Dicaeopolis goes inside and fetches a chopping block*]

DICAEOPOLIS

See? Look: here's the chopping block,
And here's the man who's going to speak, small as he is.
Rest assured, by Zeus, I won't just hide behind my shield,
But instead I'll say in behalf of the Lacedaemonians what seems
    to me so.
[*Aside, as soliloquy*] Yet I'm much afraid: I know the characters of   370
    the country folk,
Who take exceeding delight if somebody—a man who's a
    boaster—
Eulogizes them and the city, be it justly or unjustly.
And then, unawares, they get sold down the river.

---

63. Or simply "life" (*psychē*).

375 And of the elders, in turn, I know their souls—that
They look to nothing except biting with a ballot.
And as for me, I myself know what I suffered at the hands of
    Cleon
On account of my comedy last year.[64]
For dragging me into the courtroom,
380 He kept slandering me and slobbering his lies all over me
And matched the din of the Cycloborus [River] and drenched me,
    such that I very nearly
Perished, mixed up in his nasty business.
So now, permit me first, before speaking,
To outfit myself as piteously as possible.

CHORUS

385 Why are you twisting this way and scheming and making
    delays?
As far as I'm concerned, get from Hieronymus
390 Some shadowy-shaggy-thick-haired cap of Hades
And then reveal the devices of Sisyphus![65]
This contest will admit of no grounds for leniency!

[*Dicaeopolis walks off*]

DICAEOPOLIS

Now is the moment to take hold of a steadfast soul!
And I must proceed to Euripides.

---

64. A reference to Aristophanes' lost play *Babylonians*.

65. Hieronymus was a tragic and dithyrambic poet who, in addition to being hairy (consider *Clouds* 349), apparently used frightening masks in his plays. The cap of Hades made one invisible. Sisyphus, king of Ephyra (or Corinth), was renowned for his cleverness.

[*Arrives at the front door*]
Boy! Boy!

SERVANT

Who is it?

DICAEOPOLIS

Is Euripides at home?   395

SERVANT

He's not at home *and* he's at home, if you've got wit.

DICAEOPOLIS

How is he at home, then also *not* at home?

SERVANT

Correctly so, old man.
His mind, while gathering together little phraselets outside,
Is not at home, but he himself is at home, with his feet up,
Writing tragedy.

DICAEOPOLIS

O thrice-blessed Euripides!   400
Since this slave here interprets you wisely![66]
[*To the slave*] Call out to him.

SERVANT

But that's impossible.

DICAEOPOLIS

Just do it anyway.

---

66. Some MSS read: "Since this slave here answered so clearly."

For I won't leave. [*Servant slams the door*] But I'll knock at the door! Euripides, Euripidipides!

405 Lend an ear, if you've ever done so to any human being.

I, Dicaeopolis, am calling you, I from [the deme of] Cholleidae.[67]

EURIPIDES

[*From within*] But I'm not at leisure.

DICAEOPOLIS

Just have yourself wheeled about on stage.[68]

EURIPIDES

But that's impossible.

DICAEOPOLIS

Do it anyway.

EURIPIDES

Well, I'll have myself wheeled about. But I'm not at leisure to get up.[69]

[*Euripides is revealed to the audience*]

---

67. A genuine Athenian deme (see n. 10 above), but it seems to have been an urban one, whereas Dicaeopolis is from the country. Perhaps the name is meant to remind the audience of "lame" (*chōlos*), an allusion to Euripides' fondness for portraying cripples on stage; see also Olson ad loc.

68. The verb refers to a stage device, an eccyclema, a sort of platform that could be wheeled out or around to reveal a new setting onstage.

69. More literally, "to come down." Scholars divide over whether Euripides speaks from upstairs or whether he means simply that he cannot put his feet down from his reclining position.

DICAEOPOLIS

Euripides!

EURIPIDES

Why have you bellowed?

DICAEOPOLIS

You write with your feet up,   410
When it can be done with the feet on the ground. No wonder you
    write cripples!
Why do you have on the rags from tragedy,
Pitiable clothing? No wonder you write beggars!
But I beseech you, by your knees, Euripides,
Give me some little rag from an old play.   415
For I must give a long speech to the Chorus.
And it'll bring death, if I speak badly!

EURIPIDES

What sort of tattered garments? Surely not those in which Oeneus
    here,
That ill-starred old man, once competed?[70]

DICAEOPOLIS

No, not those of Oeneus, but of somebody more wretched still!   420

EURIPIDES

Those of blind Phoenix?[71]

---

70. Oeneus was king of Calydon and father of Meleager and Tydeus, and
was deposed from the throne. "Competed" suggests that Euripides is referring
to a play of his entered into competition.

71. Accounts of Phoenix differ somewhat. According to the scholiast, however, Euripides presented him as wrongly accused of making sexual advances

DICAEOPOLIS

Not of Phoenix, no,
But somebody else more wretched than Phoenix.

EURIPIDES

What sort of tattered robes is the man asking for—
Or . . . do you mean those of Philoctetes the beggar?[72]

DICAEOPOLIS

425   No, but of someone much more beggarly than he.

EURIPIDES

Well . . . do you want the squalid garments
That Bellerophon, that cripple, wore?[73]

DICAEOPOLIS

Not Bellerophon. But in fact the guy *was*
A cripple, beseeching, chattering, clever at speaking.

EURIPIDES

I know the man in question—Mysian Telephus![74]

---

on his father's concubine, was disbelieved by his father, and blinded as a result
(see Olson ad loc.).

72. Philoctetes, son of Poias, the king of Malia, was bitten by a snake on the
island of Tenedus and subsequently abandoned after his foul wound failed to
heal. He is of course the subject of Euripides' *Philoctetes*.

73. Bellerophon of Ephyre and grandson of Sisyphus. Euripides' play concerning him is no longer extant. It is said that he tried to fly to heaven on the
back of Pegasus in order to confront the gods over their poor providential care
of the world, but he was thrown from his horse, badly injured, and subsequently died.

74. Telephus was king of Mysia. When the Greeks invaded there, in the
mistaken impression they were at Troy, Telephus was wounded by Achilles.

DICAEOPOLIS

Yes, Telephus! 430

Give me his swaddling clothes, I implore you!

EURIPIDES

Boy! Give him the rags of Telephus.

They're stored above the rags of Thyestes[75]

Right by those of Ino.[76] [*To Dicaeopolis*] Here, take these.

DICAEOPOLIS

O Zeus, who sees through everything and looks down upon all, 435

Outfit me as pitiably as possible![77]

Euripides, since in fact you've gratified me in these things,

Give me also what accompanies the rags,

The little Mysian felt hat for my head.

According to an oracle, the one who wounded him would also heal him, and so Telephus proceeded, in disguise as a beggar, to Argos in search of Achilles. See Sommerstein, *Acharnians* ad loc., as well as E. W. Handley and John Rea, *The Telephus of Euripides* (London: Institute of Classical Studies, 1957).

75. Accounts of Thyestes vary, but according to a report of Euripides' *Cretan Women,* Atreus, king of Mycenae, discovered the affair between his wife, Aerope, and his brother Thyestes, whom he punished by having him unknowingly eat the flesh of his own children.

76. According to reports of Euripides' play concerning her, Ino, daughter of Cadmus and wife of King Athamas of Boeotia, disappeared on Mt. Parnassus. Athamas then married another woman but, on learning that Ino remained alive, brought her to his household in disguise. The new wife, Themisto, confessed to this stranger that she intended to kill Ino's two children. Ino contrived it, however, that Themisto killed her own two children instead, and she subsequently committed suicide. Athamas then went insane, killed one of his sons, and Ino leapt into the sea, being transformed into a goddess in the process.

77. This line is identical in the Greek to 384 and is for that reason excised by some editors.

440 For "I must seem to be a beggar today,
To be who in fact I am, but appear not to be."[78]
The spectators must know me as I am,
But those in the Chorus, by contrast, must stand there like
knuckleheads
So I may give them the finger with little phraselets.

EURIPIDES

445 I'll give it. For you with your shrewd mind contrive subtle
things.

DICAEOPOLIS

May you be happy! "But to Telephus, the things that I'm
thinking!"[79]
Well done! What phraselets I'm filled with already!
But I do need a beggar's walking stick.

EURIPIDES

Take this and "depart the stony abode."

DICAEOPOLIS

450 [Aside] O Heart—since you see that I'm thrust from the halls
Though many are the implements I need—now become
Importunate, beseeching, and unctuous. Euripides:
Give me a little wicker basket that's been burned through
by a lamp.

EURIPIDES

And what need, wretched you, have you of this woven thing?

---

78. The lines are thought to be from Euripides' *Telephus*.
79. Another parody of a line from Euripides' *Telephus*.

DICAEOPOLIS

On the one hand, no need; but, on the other, I want to have it   455
nonetheless.

EURIPIDES

Know that you are troublesome, and be gone from my halls!

[*Euripides hands over the basket*]

DICAEOPOLIS

Ah!

May you be happy, as your mother once was.

EURIPIDES

Withdraw from me now!

DICAEOPOLIS

No, but give me one last thing,
A little cup with its lip knocked off.

EURIPIDES

Take this and blast you! Know that you're irksome in these   460
halls!

DICAEOPOLIS

Don't you yet know, by Zeus, the sorts of bad things you yourself
produce?[80]

---

80. Both the proper reading of this line and its interpretation have
prompted debate. Olson (ad loc.) suggests that Dicaeopolis means, first, that
Euripides is producing trouble for Dicaeopolis, in denying him what he needs,
and "either that the tragedian's plays promote vicious behavior and do incalcu-
lable damage to the city . . . or (perhaps less likely) that his long-winded pro-
logues or constant reuse of the same things makes his work tiresome."

But, sweetest Euripides, just this alone:
Give me a little pot plugged up with a little sponge.

EURIPIDES

Human being! You'll strip me of [the art of] tragedy!
Take this here and be off!

DICAEOPOLIS

465 I'm leaving!
[*Aside*] Yet what am I to do? For there's one thing I needs must
          have, and if I don't get it
I'm a goner! [*To Euripides*] Listen, sweetest Euripides,
In getting this, I'm off and won't draw near again.
Give me withered herbs for my little basket.

EURIPIDES

470 You'll ruin me! Here, look. My plays are clean undone!

DICAEOPOLIS

Well, there's nothing more: I'm leaving! For in fact I *am* overly
Irksome, "not opining that the ruling chieftains loathe me!"[81]—
[*Pauses*] Oh boy, wretched me! How I'm done for! I forgot
The very thing on which all my affairs depend!
475 Little Euripides, sweetest and dearest,
Would that I perish in the worst way, should I ask you for anything
          further,
Except . . . just one thing more, this alone, this alone,
Give me some chervil that you got from your mother![82]

---

81. According to the scholiast, this is a line from Euripides' lost *Oeneus*.
82. Aristophanes frequently portrays Euripides' mother as a humble seller
of herbs, as she assuredly was not: *Thesmophoriazusae* 387, *Knights* 19, *Frogs*

EURIPIDES

The man is insolent! Shut the door to the halls!

DICAEOPOLIS

[*Aside*] O Heart! Without chervil you must make your way.   480
Don't you know how great is the contest you'll soon engage in,
Being about to speak in behalf of Lacedaemonian men?
Advance now, O Heart! There's the starting line.
You're standing still? Won't you go, having scarfed down . . .
    Euripides?[83]
[*Begins to walk*] I applaud you! Come now, O wretched Heart,   485
Go over yonder, and then your head
Offer up there, saying whatever seems best to you yourself.
Be bold, come now, proceed! I admire my heart!

CHORUS

What are you going to do? What will you assert? Now know   490
    well
That you're a man shameless and iron-hard,
Who, while offering up your neck to the city,
Is going to speak, one man, in opposition to each and to all!
The man doesn't tremble at the affair! So now proceed:
Since in fact you yourself choose to do so, speak!   495

DICAEOPOLIS [TO THE AUDIENCE]

Don't hold a grudge, spectator men,
If, being a beggar, I nonetheless, in the presence of Athenians,

---

840. The words translated as "that you got from your mother" echo Aeschylus,
Libation Bearers 750.

    83. A surprise substitution for "garlic" (see 166 above).

Am going to speak about the city, while making a comedy.[84]

500 For when it comes to what's just, comedy too knows it.

And I'll say things terribly clever, but just.

For now Cleon won't slander me on the grounds that,

When foreigners are present, I speak badly of the city.

For we are here by ourselves, and the contest is the Lenaean,[85]

505 And foreigners are not yet present. For neither has the tribute
   come

Nor have the allies from the cities.

But we ourselves now are here, stripped of the chaff,

For the resident aliens I say are the bran of the town.[86]

[*To the Acharnians as well as the audience*] In fact I hate the
   Lacedaemonians intensely,

510 And may Poseidon, god at Taenarus,

Shake them and bring their houses down on top of them all![87]

---

84. Here and in the next line Aristophanes uses his own comical term for comedy, "trygedy," the root of which is derived from the word (*trux*) for "raw wine" or "the dregs of wine," and so may remind one of Dionysus, god of wine and of the theater. See also 628 and 886.

85. An Athenian religious festival at which five comedies and two sets of tragedies (Olson ad loc.) were presented in competition. It was held in (the equivalent of) January, a time when travel by sea was difficult. Hence the audience is made up, largely though probably not entirely, of Athenians; see also Sommerstein, *Acharnians* ad loc.

86. Dicaeopolis suggests that the citizens are the barley grain, resident aliens the bran (*achura*)—good but less good than citizens proper—while foreigners are simply the chaff. The line is controversial, however ("a notorious crux": Olson ad loc.) because the meaning of *achura* is contested, and it is excised by Wilson.

87. Poseidon was said to be responsible for earthquakes, to which Sparta and its environs were prone; see, e.g., Thucydides 1.101 as well as *Lysistrate* 1142.

For I too have vines that have been cut.
But—since those present here for the speech are friends—
Why do we blame these things on the Laconians?
For it was some of our men—I don't say the city,   515
Remember this, that I'm not saying the city—
Half-men lowlifes, ill-struck,
Without honor, counterfeit and alien,
Who, sycophant style, began to denounce little Megarian[88]
    cloaks.

And if ever they should see anywhere a cucumber or bunny   520
Or piglet or garlic clove or rock salt,
These were "Megarian" and auctioned off the same day.

And these things, to be sure, were petty and local,
But as for Simaetha the whore, when some youths went to
    Megara,
Drunk from cottabus playing,[89] they stole her away!   525
And then the Megarians, rendered by their pains garlic-primed
    feisty,
Stole Aspasia's[90] two whores in response!
And thereupon the beginning of the war broke out
For all Greeks, from three suckers of cock!
At this, in his anger, Pericles the Olympian   530
Sent bolts of lightning, he thundered, Greece he utterly
    confounded,
Posited laws written like drinking songs,

_____

88. Neighboring Megara had been placed under a blockade by Pericles, an
act that contributed to the outbreak of the Peloponnesian War.

89. Cottabus was a game played at drinking parties and involved tossing a
bit of wine from one's cup at a target.

90. A concubine and Pericles' mistress.

To the effect that Megarians must not remain "either on land or in the marketplace,
   Either at sea or on the mainland."

535 At this the Megarians, growing gradually hungrier,
   Asked the Lacedaemonians that the decree
   Be reversed, the one traceable to the cocksuckers.
   But we were unwilling, though they often asked.
   And then came the crashing of shields.

540 Someone will say: "They ought not to have." But what *ought* they have done? Say it!
   Come now, if some Lacedaemonian, sailing out on a ship,
   Denounced and then sold off a puppy belonging to the Seriphians,[91]
   Would you have "remained seated in your halls"? Far from it!
   In fact you'd have immediately launched

545 Three hundred ships, and the city would be full
   Of the uproar of soldiers, shouting around the ships' captains,
   Pay being given, figureheads of Pallas [Athena] being gilded,
   A portico resounding, grains being measured,
   Wineskins, oar-thongs, buyers of jars,

550 Garlic, olives, onions in nets,
   Wreaths, anchovies, flute-girls, black eyes.
   And the dockyard, in turn [would be full of] oar spars being planed,
   Wooden pins resounding, [oars] being attached to the tholepins,
   Flutes, boatswains, whistles, pipe sounds.

555 These things, I know, you would have done. "But Telephus
   We suppose wouldn't have?"[92] In us there is no sense.

———————

91. Seriphus was a small island among the Cyclades and hence (a tiny) part of the Athenian Empire.

92. Either a quotation or paraphrase from Euripides' *Telephus*.

HALF-CHORUS A

Is that so, you bloody bastard who deserves to be crushed?!
These things you—a beggar!—dare say to *us?*
And you level reproaches, if someone [among us] was a
    sycophant?

HALF-CHORUS B

Yes, by Poseidon, and all that he says   560
Is just, and in none of it does he lie.

HALF-CHORUS A

Then even if just, is *this* the guy who ought to have said it?
But he'll get no delight in daring to say these things.

[*Half-Chorus A begins to pursue Dicaeopolis*]

HALF-CHORUS B

[*To the other half of the Chorus*] You there, where're you running
    to? Won't you stay put? If you strike
This man, you'll soon be snatched up.[93]   565

HALF-CHORUS A

Ah! Lamachus! You with the lightning-flash look!
Appear and aid us, O fierce Gorgon-crested one!
Ah! Lamachus! Friend, fellow tribesman,
Or if there's a taxiarch or general or
Wall-battling man, let him come to our aid   570
In a hurry! For I'm held by the waist!

---

93. That is, grabbed around the waist and, by implication, lifted up and
then thrown to the ground, as in wrestling (see also 571).

LAMACHUS

Whence comes the cry for a warrior I heard?
Where ought assistance to go? Where to inject Battle-Din?[94]
Who has awakened Gorgon from her case?[95]

DICAEOPOLIS

575 O Lamachus, hero of helmet-crests and ambushes![96]

HALF-CHORUS A

O Lamachus, isn't *this* the guy
Who for a long time now has been reviling our entire city?

LAMACHUS

[*Addressing Dicaeopolis*] You there! Do you dare, beggar that you
    are, to say these things?

DICAEOPOLIS

O Lamachus, hero! But have some sympathy,
If, being a beggar, I said something and prattled on.

LAMACHUS

What did you say regarding us? Won't you say?

DICAEOPOLIS

580 As yet I don't know.

---

94. Battle-Din (Kudoimos) appears as a character in *Peace* 254 and context, as assistant to Polemos (War).

95. Lamachus thus dubs his shield, normally kept in a case, Gorgon. The name designated one of three sisters—Stheno, Euryale, and Medusa—who had the power to turn to stone anyone who looked at them. Lamachus's shield is emblazoned with the frightening depiction of a Gorgon.

96. The word for "crests" (*lophōn*) is close to that for "ambushes" (*lochōn*).

For through fear of your armaments I'm dizzy!
But, I beseech you, [*pointing to Lamachus's shield*] take that
　　Mormo[97] away from me!

LAMACHUS
There, look.

DICAEOPOLIS
Now set it upside down alongside me.

LAMACHUS
There it lies.

DICAEOPOLIS
Now bring me a feather from your helmet.

LAMACHUS
[*Plucks a feather from the crest of his helmet*] Here's a plume for you.

DICAEOPOLIS
Now hold my head   585
So I can vomit—for helmet-crests turn my stomach!

LAMACHUS
You there, what are you doing?! You're going to vomit by using the
　　plume?
For it's a plume—

DICAEOPOLIS
Tell me,
Whatever bird is this from? A big-mouthed-boaster bird?

---

97. A terrifying she-monster invoked by nursemaids and mothers to
frighten children; see also *Knights* 693.

LAMACHUS

Ah, you're going to die!

DICAEOPOLIS

590 No no, Lamachus,
It's not a question of force. And if you *are* strong,
Why've you not peeled back my foreskin? You're certainly well
equipped!

LAMACHUS

You say these things to a general—you, a beggar!?!

DICAEOPOLIS

Am I a beggar?

LAMACHUS

Well, who are you then?

DICAEOPOLIS

595 Who, you ask? A decent citizen, not-serious-about-office-seeking,
But since the war began, a Son of a Gun,[98]
And you, since the war began, an officer-for-hire-and-pay.

LAMACHUS

Yes, they elected me . . .

DICAEOPOLIS

Three cuckoos did, that is!
So, being disgusted at these things, I struck up a truce,
600 Seeing gray-haired men in the lines of battle,

---

98. A comic patronymic suggesting that he is the offspring of a good soldier.

And the young such as you run away,
Some getting three drachmas pay in the region of Thrace—
Teisamenus-Phaenippus, Rogue-Hipparchides—
And others with Chares, some among the Chaonians—
Geres-Theodorus, Boaster-from-Diomeia—   605
Others in Camarina and Gela and Catagela.⁹⁹

LAMACHUS
Yes, they were elected!

DICAEOPOLIS
But what's the cause
Of you're always getting pay somehow or other
But these fellows here [*pointing to Half-Chorus A*] get nothing?
    Really, now, Marilades,
Have *you* ever served as ambassador, gray as you are?   610
He nods "no"—and yet he's prudent and hardworking.
And what about Anthracyllus or Euphorides or Prinides?¹⁰⁰
Who among you has seen Ecbatana or the Chaonians?
They deny it. But the son of Coisyras¹⁰¹ and Lamachus have;

---

99. None of the people mentioned and mocked here can be identified with
certainty. Chaonians were a barbarian and warlike people of Epirus in north-
west Greece; probably more important is the fact that their name suggests the
verb meaning "to gape" (*chaskein*). Camarina and Gela were Greek cities on
the island of Sicily. Catagela is a made-up word suggesting the word for "ridic-
ulous" (*katagelos*).

100. These proper names include the words for "charcoal," "good carrier,"
and "oak": i.e., salt of the earth types.

101. A woman connected to the family of Megacles and hence the bluest of
blue bloods: an aristocratic fellow is thus lumped together with Lamachus.
Consider also *Clouds* 48 and 800.

615 And just the other day, on account of their loans and their
     debts,
   Like those who pour out the evening's dirty wash water,
   Quite all their friends advised, "Keep your distance!"

LAMACHUS

O democracy! Are these things to be tolerated?

DICAEOPOLIS

No indeed—unless Lamachus gets his pay!

LAMACHUS

620 Well, anyway, I, against all the Peloponnesians,
   Will ever wage war and everywhere cause havoc,
   With both ships and infantry, with all my might!

DICAEOPOLIS

And I make a public proclamation to the Peloponnesians,
   To quite all of them, as well as to the Megarians and Boeotians,
625 To offer to sell in my marketplace—but not to Lamachus!

[*Exit Dicaeopolis and Lamachus*]

CHORUS

The man is victorious with his arguments and persuades the
     demos
   About the treaty. But let us strip and proceed to the anapests.[102]

---

102. The members of the Chorus now remove their cloaks, which in the
context means that they will become a chorus of actors and no longer be Acharnian elders. The prelude (626–27) and the chorus-leader's speech (628–64) are
in anapestic tetrameters.

From the time when our producer[103] took charge of the comic[104]
   choruses
Never yet has he come forward intending to say how clever
   he is.
But being slandered by enemies, among Athenians too-hasty-in-   630
   counsel,
On the grounds that he's making a comedy of our city and
   treating the demos with utter insolence,
He must now offer a response to Athenians given to changing
   their minds.
And he asserts that he's the cause of many good things for you,
   the poet does,
By keeping you from being overly deceived by the speeches of
   foreigners,
And from the pleasure you take in subtle flattery, and from being   635
   slack-jawed-gaping-citizens.
Before, the ambassadors from the [subject] cities quite deceived
   you,
First by calling you "violet-crowned."[105] And when someone
   should say this,
Immediately, on account of those "crowns," you sat on the tips of
   your little butt cheeks.
But if somebody, subtly flattering you, should call Athens
   "gleaming,"

---

103. Literally, "the teacher" (*didaskalos*), the usual term for the person
responsible for training and directing the actors. Aristophanes has himself in
mind.

104. More literally, "trygic," Aristophanes' comic term for comedy; see
also n. 84 above.

105. An epithet of Athens in Pindar. Consider also *Knights* 1323 and 1329.

He'd gain everything on account of those "gleamings," by
attaching an honor belonging to smelts!

640 So, having done these things, [the poet] has become the cause of
many good things for you,
And he's shown how the populaces in the [subject] cities are
"democratically" governed.[106]
So now, that's why those who bring the tribute to us from the
cities
Will bring it—because of their desire to see the poet who's best,

645 He who ran risks among Athenians in order to state the just things.
And in this way fame of his daring has already reached far and
wide,
Since even the King [of Persia], in testing the embassy from the
Lacedaemonians,[107]
Asked them, first, which of the two is stronger in ships,
And then about which of the two this poet lambastes more.

650 For [the King] said that these human beings have become much
better
And would greatly prevail in the war because they have him as
advisor.
For these reasons Lacedaemonians are proposing peace with you
And demanding the return of Aegina: as for that island,
They give it no thought, except so they can take this poet away![108]

---

106. Interpretations of this line differ, but Aristophanes may be suggesting
how undemocratically Athens has governed them in fact. The word for "populaces" here is *demoi*, the plural of *demos*.

107. Consider Thucydides 4.50.

108. At some point subsequent to defeat at the hands of Athens in 459,
Aegina was promised an autonomy that never materialized. Accordingly, prior
to the outbreak of the Peloponnesian War, Aegina complained to Sparta and

But now don't *you* ever let him go, since he'll make a comedy of   655
    the just things!
And he affirms that he'll teach[109] you many good things, so you'll
    be happy,
Not flattering, or setting out the prospect of pay, or fooling you
    through and through,
Nor acting nastily nor sprinkling with praise, but teaching the
    things that are best.
Given these things, let Cleon skillfully manage
And contrive everything against me.   660
For what's good and what's just, here with me,
Will be my ally, and there's no way I'll ever be caught
Being such as he is when it comes to the city:
A coward and a bugger supreme!

CHORUS [OF ACHARNIANS]
Come hither, flaming Muse   665
Possessed of the strength of fire,
Intense, Acharnian!
As from oaken charcoal
A spark leaps up, roused
By a fan's favorable breeze,
When the sprats   670
Are laid out

---

urged it to begin hostilities with Athens; see Thucydides 1.67 as well as 1.139. The line also suggests some connection between Aristophanes and Aegina— though no one is certain quite what.

    109. See n. 103 above: he will teach the audience by putting on his plays.

And some are mixing up a Thasian [*sauce*] "of gleaming
    fillet,"[110]
Others are kneading the dough—so come,
And a lively tune,
Vigorous, most apt for the country,
675   Bring to me, your demesman.
We who are old, ancient, we blame the city.
For we are not tended to by you in our old age,
In a manner worthy of the naval battles we fought, but instead
    suffer terribly.
Some throw old men into indictments
680   And by youthful orators let them be ridiculed,
[Old] men who are nothing, but mute and played out,
Whose walking stick is Poseidon Unstumbling.[111]
Mumbling in old age we stand alongside the stone,[112]
Seeing nothing of the legal suit except its shadow.
685   But the young fellow, eager to plead his own case,
Quickly strikes with rounded words as he joins the fray,
And then dragging [the old man] up he cross-examines him,
    setting up word-snares,

---

110. Pindar's epithet for the Muses in *Nemean* 7.15. According to the Budé, the oil in the sauce or marinade would cling to the fish and so form a gleaming band.

111. Said to be a standard epithet of Poseidon. "The joke is that the only security . . . the old men have any longer against stumbling . . . is their walking-sticks" (Olson ad loc.).

112. Perhaps the stone on which a defendant would be asked to stand in court, perhaps "the stone on which jurors' voting-pebbles were counted" (Olson ad loc., quoting Wilhelm Wachsmuth).

Taking to pieces and confounding and mixing him up, a man
 [as old as] Tithonus.[113]
But he, through old age, purses his lips and then leaves convicted
 and fined.
He then sobs and cries and says to his friends,   690
"That with which I ought to have bought my coffin, this I leave
 owing in fines!"
How are these things reasonable—to destroy
A gray old man 'round the water clock,[114]
One who's toiled much with you and wiped away hot
Manly sweat, and much of it indeed,   695
Being a good man at Marathon, for the city?
Then, when we were at Marathon, *we* were the ones to pursue,
But now by very base men we're *being* pursued[115]
And getting caught-and-convicted!   700
What Marpsias[116] will speak against these points?
How is it reasonable that a stooped man, of the age
 Thucydides is,[117]
Is utterly ruined, in coming to grips with the desolate wilderness
 of Scythia,

113. Tithonus was a son of King Laomedon of Troy, renowned for his
beauty. Dawn (Eos) fell in love with him and asked Zeus to grant Tithonus eternal life. Unfortunately, she did not ask also for Tithonus to enjoy eternal youth,
and he grew ever older.

114. A device used to time courtroom speeches; see, e.g., Plato, *Theaetetus*
172e1.

115. The same word for "pursue" can also mean "prosecute."

116. Unknown outside comedy, the name may be a nickname ("Snatcher,"
"Grabber").

117. Not the historian but the aristocratic politician, a contemporary of
Pericles and his opponent.

705 By that son of Cephisodemus, the chattering prosecutor?[118]
And so, I felt pity as a result and wiped away a tear when I saw
The elderly man rendered confused by a bowman[119]
Who, by Demeter, when he was *the* Thucydides [in his prime],
Would not have easily put up with Achaia herself[120]
710 But would have first wrestled down ten Euathluses[121]
And shouted down with a roar three thousand bowmen
And outshot the kin of [Euathlus's] father.
But since you don't permit the old men to get any sleep,
Vote that their indictments be separate, so that
715 The old man's prosecutor would be old and toothless,
The young men's would be the son of Cleinias, wide buttholed
and chattering.[122]

---

118. After being ostracized from Athens in the late 440s, Thucydides evidently was prosecuted on an unknown charge (either by Cephisodemus or his son; the text here is uncertain), and became tongue-tied in the course of his defense speech (see *Wasps* 946–48). The text also suggests that Cephisodemus (or his son) had a Scythian mother, whether she was actually from Scythia or, as the term also meant, was blonde and hence foreign; see Olson ad loc.

119. Scythians were known for fighting with bow and arrow.

120. An epithet of Demeter. Commentators are baffled by the line ("The puzzle of this line remains unsolved": Wilson ad loc.), and emendations have been suggested. Lowell Edmunds (following E. K. Borthwick) suggests reading Artachaiēn instead of Achaian of the MSS: Artachaees was a great nobleman said to be the tallest of all the Persians with the loudest voice in the world (Herodotus 7.117).

121. Identity uncertain. He may have been a demagogue (*Wasps* 592) responsible for the prosecution of the sophist Protagoras on a charge of impiety.

122. "The son of Cleinias" is Alcibiades, ward of Pericles, sometime student of Socrates who appears in four Platonic dialogues, and later an Athenian general who managed to ally himself with three sides in the course of the Peloponnesian War—Athens, Sparta, and Persia—before being recalled to Athens.

And in future—if somebody evades this, then fine him—old man
  should be banished by old man, young by young.

DICAEOPOLIS
These are the boundaries of my market.

Here all the Peloponnesians are permitted to trade,   720
Megarians as well as Boeotians too,
On condition that they sell to me but not to Lamachus.
As market-regulators of the place I appoint
These three who've been allotted leather whips from Flogville.   725
Let enter here neither sycophant
Nor any other Phasian¹²³ man.
And as for the stele,¹²⁴ bearing the terms of the treaty I signed,
I'll go get it, to set it up in the market plain as day.

[*Dicaeopolis goes into his house*]

MEGARIAN¹²⁵
Hello, Athenian market, dear to Megarians!
I was longing for you, by the God of Friendship,¹²⁶ as for a   730
  mother.
But, you pitiable little girls of a miserable father,
Come up here for the barley-cake, if you find some somewhere.

---

123. Phasia was "the easternmost city on the southern coast of the Black
Sea" (Olson ad loc.), but the name in this context is meant to recall the word for
"denunciation" (*phasis*).
124. An upright stone pillar on which public decrees were inscribed.
125. The Megarian speaks in a dialect throughout, impossible to convey in
translation. For Pericles' blockade of Megara, which imposed great hardships
on the city, see n. 88 above and Thucydides 1.67 and 1.139.
126. One of the epithets of Zeus.

So listen, turn to me the attention of your . . . stomach.
Do you want to be sold or badly to starve?

GIRLS

735   Sold! Sold!

MEGARIAN

I myself say so too. But who'd be so foolish
As to buy you, an obvious loss?
But . . . I have a certain Megarian trick!
For I'll assert that I'm bringing you decked out as pussy kittens![127]
740   Put on these pussies' paws
So that you seem to be from a good cat.
Because, by Hermes, if in fact you come home
Unsold, you'll undergo evil starvation.
But put on these whiskers, too,
745   And climb into the burlap sack here.
And see that you mewl and meow
And let loose the sound of pussies at the Mysteries![128]
I'll announce Dicaeopolis's name [and find out] where he is.
[*Calling out*] Dicaeopolis, do you want to buy some little pussies?

DICAEOPOLIS

What's this? A Megarian man?

127. Literally, "piglets," here and throughout the section, a term that is also
Greek slang for the female genitalia.

128. The Eleusinian Mysteries were important initiation rites connected to
the cult of Demeter and Persephone. The line alludes more specifically to
"events on the second day of the Greater Mysteries . . . when initiands took a
piglet down to the sea, washed it and themselves there, and most likely sacrificed it upon their return to the city" (Olson ad loc.).

MEGARIAN

We've come to trade in your market.   750

DICAEOPOLIS

How are you[129] doing?

MEGARIAN

We spend our time continually fasting by the fire.

DICAEOPOLIS

Well, that's pleasant, you know, by Zeus—continually
    feasting[130]—if there's a flute nearby!
But what else are the Megarians doing now?

MEGARIAN

Well, such as we do.
When I was making my way from there,
The Councilmen were doing this for the city: 755
Seeing how we might perish as quickly and badly as possible!

DICAEOPOLIS

Soon you'll be rid of your troubles.

MEGARIAN

Of course!

---

129. The plural "you."

130. The Megarian uses a word that appears nowhere else in Greek (*diapei-names*) and means roughly "continually starving," but, perhaps on account of the Megarian's accent, Dicaeopolis hears instead *diapinomen* (continually drinking). Thus "fasting/feasting," following the clever suggestion of Jeffrey Henderson (Henderson [Loeb] ad loc.).

DICAEOPOLIS

What else is up at Megara? What's the price of grain?

MEGARIAN

With us it's as expensive[131] as the gods!

DICAEOPOLIS

So then are you bringing salt [to sell]?

MEGARIAN

760 Don't you rule over it?[132]

DICAEOPOLIS

Not garlic either?

MEGARIAN

What garlic?!? You always,
Whenever you invade, like field mice,
Dig up the bulbs with pegs!

DICAEOPOLIS

So what *are* you bringing?

MEGARIAN

I've got pussycats used in the Mysteries!

DICAEOPOLIS

What you say is fine. Show them.

MEGARIAN

765 Well, they're beautiful.

---

131. The word for "expensive" can also mean "much honored" (*polytimatos*).

132. The word for "salt" can also mean the (briny) sea; Megarian thus alludes to the Athenian naval empire that is strangling Megara.

Reach out to touch, if you like. How plump and beautiful! [*The*
Megarian brings his daughters out of the sack]

DICAEOPOLIS

What's *that?!?!*

MEGARIAN

A pussy, by Zeus!

DICAEOPOLIS

What do you mean? Where'd this pussy come from?!?

MEGARIAN

It's Megarian!
Or isn't that a pussy?

DICAEOPOLIS

Doesn't appear to be to me, at least!

MEGARIAN

[*To the audience*] Isn't this terrible? See how distrusting he is!   770
He denies that this is a pussy! [*To Dicaeopolis*] But,
If you like, make a bet with me, for a wager of seasoned salt,
That this isn't a pussy, according to Greek custom.[133]

DICAEOPOLIS

But it's of a human being![134]

133. Or "law" (*nomos*). What cannot be proved according to nature can evidently be proved according to *nomos*.

134. The phrase is ambiguous; it could mean "born of a human being" or "belongs to a human being," and the Megarian of course takes it in the latter sense.

MEGARIAN

Yes, by Diocles,[135]

775 She's mine! Whose does she seem to you to be?

Do you want to hear her make some noise?

DICAEOPOLIS

Yes, by the gods,

I certainly do!

MEGARIAN

Quick, make some noise, little pussy! [*The girl remains silent*]

You don't want to? You're keeping quiet?!? Damn you in the worst

way!

I'll cart you off back home again, by Hermes!

GIRL

780 Meow! Meow!

MEGARIAN

So is that a pussy or what?

DICAEOPOLIS

For the moment, at least, she does seem to be a pussy . . .

But once grown up she'll be a snatch!

MEGARIAN

Within five years,

Know it well, she'll resemble her mother!

---

135. Legendary king of Eleusis who was driven from there to Megara,
where he subsequently died in battle defending his lover, for which act he was
subsequently honored.

DICAEOPOLIS

But this one here isn't fit for sacrifice.[136]

MEGARIAN

Of course she is!

In what way isn't she?

DICAEOPOLIS

She doesn't have a tail![137]   785

MEGARIAN

For she's young! But once grown to full pussyhood,

She'll take a big thick pink one!

But if you want to raise one, this pussy here is beautiful! [*Displays his other daughter*]

DICAEOPOLIS

How this one's snatch is akin to the other one's!

MEGARIAN

Yes, for they have the same mother and father.   790

And if she plumps up and becomes downy with hair,

She'll be a most beautiful pussy to sacrifice to Aphrodite!

DICAEOPOLIS

But a pussy isn't sacrificed to Aphrodite![138]

---

136. Pigs (though not cats) were among the animals used for religious sacrifice, including at the Mysteries (747).

137. The term is also slang for "penis."

138. Piglets (as the Greek is) were sacrificial animals, but evidently not to Aphrodite, goddess of erotic love. The scholiast suggests that because Aphrodite's lover, Adonis, was killed by a boar, the sacrifice of a pig would not be pleasing to her.

MEGARIAN

Not a pussy to Aphrodite?! To her alone of the divinities!

795 And the flesh of these pussies becomes
Most pleasant, when it's pierced with a skewer!

DICAEOPOLIS

And by now they'd eat without their mother?

MEGARIAN

Yes, by Poseidon! And without their father too!

DICAEOPOLIS

And what especially do they eat?

MEGARIAN

Anything you might give them.
But you yourself ask!

DICAEOPOLIS

Kitty kitty!

GIRL

800 Meow! Meow!

DICAEOPOLIS

Would you nibble on chickpeas?[139]

GIRL

Meow meow meow!

DICAEOPOLIS

What about this? Phibalean figs?

---

139. A "chickpea" is also a slang term for "penis"; see, e.g., *Frogs* 545.

GIRL

Meow! Meow!

DICAEOPOLIS

[*To the other daughter*] What about you? Would you yourself eat
them?¹⁴⁰

SECOND GIRL

Meow meow!

DICAEOPOLIS

How shrilly you clamor at the mention of "figs"!
Let someone bring out some figs from inside   805
For the little pussycats! Will they nibble them? [*Figs are tossed to
the girls*] Damn!
How they go to town on them, most honored Heracles!¹⁴¹
Where are these pussies from?!? From Nibblesville, as it
appears!¹⁴²

MEGARIAN

[*To the audience*] But they didn't scarf down *all* the figs.
For I nabbed *this* one from them!   810

140. This line and the next are uncertain and have prompted much commentary and emendation. Both the proper reading of the text and its attribution are at issue.

141. The word for "most honored" is the same as that translated as "expensive" above at 759; see n. 131. Aristophanes depicts Heracles as having a vora-
cious appetite; see, e.g., *Frogs* 549 and following, as well as *Birds* 1604.

142. From Tragasai, a city located in the Troad, but it suggests a link to the
verb *tragein* (to nibble).

DICAEOPOLIS

By Zeus, they are two charming creatures!
At what price may I buy these two little pussies? Just name it.

MEGARIAN

This one here for a bunch of garlic,
The other one, if you like, for just a measure of salt.

DICAEOPOLIS

I'll buy 'em from you! Wait here!

[*Dicaeopolis leaves*]

MEGARIAN

815   Okay . . .
Hermes [God of] Commerce![143] May I give up
At this price my wife and my own mother too!

SYCOPHANT

Hey guy,[144] where're you from?

MEGARIAN

Megarian pussy-seller.

SYCOPHANT

Well, I denounce these little pussies here
As belonging to the enemy—and you too!

---

143. One of the traditional epithets of Hermes; see, e.g., *Knights* 297 and
Wealth 1154. A bronze statue of Hermes stood in the Athenian agora or marketplace.
144. Literally, "human being."

MEGARIAN

Here we go again: back   820
To the beginning from which our troubles grew!

SYCOPHANT

You'll be weeping if you pull a Megarian! Let go of the sack!

MEGARIAN

Dicaeopolis! Dicaeopolis! I'm being denounced!

DICAEOPOLIS

[*Running out of his house*] By whom? Who's denouncing you?
Market-regulators,
Keep the sycophants away from the house!   825
What's put it into your head to bring things to light without a
   wick?[145]

SYCOPHANT

I'm not to denounce the enemies?!?

DICAEOPOLIS

You'll weep if you do,
Unless you run off and do your sycophantic stuff somewhere else!

[*Sycophant runs off*]

MEGARIAN

Such is the evil that's present in Athens!

---

145. The line depends on the ambiguity of the verb *phainesthai*, which
means "to bring to light or cause to appear" but also (in a legalistic context) "to
denounce." It may be that the Sycophant is not wearing the usual phallic
appendage characteristic of comedy and so lacks his "wick."

DICAEOPOLIS

830　Be of good cheer, Megarian. Take what you got for the little
　　　pussies,
　　　This garlic here and the salt,
　　　And fare-thee-well!

MEGARIAN

But *that's* not native to us!

DICAEOPOLIS

[Am I being] meddlesome now? Let it be on my head.[146]

MEGARIAN

O Little Pussies, try even without your father
835　To keep banging your flat cake with salt, if somebody gives
　　　you one.[147]

CHORUS

Happy is this human being!
Didn't you hear how
The matter of his plan is progressing?
For the man will reap fruits
As he sits in the marketplace

---

146. Imperial Athens was often charged with being "meddlesome," a busybody—but the precise meaning of the line is controversial ("difficult": Wilson ad loc.). Edmunds, "Aristophanes' *Acharnians*," 39, suggests reading *polycharmosunē* instead of *polypragmosunē* of the MSS and giving it (and the next word) to the Megarian: "But *that's* not native to us. There's much warmongering."

147. This somewhat cryptic line has prompted considerable commentary. Henderson suggests that the line also means "to bang your cunt against the phallus, in case someone should give you any" (*Maculate Muse,* 113).

And if some Ctesias[148] enters,
Or other sycophant,   840
That guy will wail when he sits down!
And no other human being,
By undercutting your prices, will bring you to ruin at all,
Nor will Prepis[149] wipe off
His wide buttholedness on you,
Nor will you collide with Cleonymus.[150]
But, wearing a shiny clean cloak, you'll go about   845
And Hyperbolus[151] won't encounter you,
Infecting you with lawsuits!
And Cratinus lighting upon the marketplace
Won't approach you as he walks,
He who is always shaved, adultery-style, with a single blade,[152]
An exceedingly nasty Artemon,[153]   850
Overly hasty with his Musical art,
His armpits smelling badly,

---

148. The name is common and suggests a connection to the verb "to acquire" (*ktaomai*).

149. Identity uncertain; perhaps a wealthy and politically prominent Athenian.

150. See 88-89 above: a glutton of impressive girth.

151. The leading demagogue in Athens after the death of Cleon. See also *Knights* 1304 and 1363.

152. Cratinus was a comic poet against whom Aristophanes competed; see also 1172. Either Cratinus is attempting what he thinks is a stylish cut, or his haircut resembles that of a punishment meted out to adulterers: having their head shaved.

153. A contemporary of the poet Anacreon, who ridiculed Artemon as "borne about in a litter" (*periphorētos*), which Aristophanes transforms into "exceedingly nasty" (*periponēros*).

Son of a father from Goatstown.[154]

Nor again, in turn, will you be mocked

By Pauson[155] that altogether nasty fellow,

And neither will Lysistratus, in the marketplace,

855 The reproach of Cholargus,[156]

Deeply dyed in evils,

Ever freezing and starving

For more than thirty days each month!

[*Enter a Theban man with his servant, Ismenias, both heavily laden with goods and accompanied by flute players*]

THEBAN[157]

860 May Heracles witness, my shoulder hurts badly!

Set down your mint gently, Ismenias, and you, all you flute
players from Thebes,

Blow on those bones, "The Dog's Butthole"! [*They begin
to play*]

DICAEOPOLIS

[*Coming out of his house*] Stop! To the crows with you! You wasps,
won't you get away from the doors!?!

---

154. *Tragesai:* the root of the name suggests *tragos,* a male goat. Hence Cratinus's armpits smell like goats.

155. A painter of comic or satirical works.

156. The identity of this impoverished Lysistratus is uncertain; he may have been an Athenian orator; see also *Knights* 1267. Cholargus was the name of one of the demes or districts of Athens.

157. The Theban speaks throughout in Boeotian dialect and with a heavy accent.

These buzzing bagpipers—be damned!—where'd they fly from   865
To my door, sons of Chaeris?![158]

THEBAN

By Iolaus,[159] you've done me a favor, stranger,
For they've been following behind me from Thebes, blowing away,
The mint blossoms they've shaken to the ground.
But if you're at all willing, buy what I'm carrying,   870
The chicks or the four-winged creatures.[160]

DICAEOPOLIS

Greetings, roll-eating little Boeotian!
What are you carrying?

THEBAN

All that's simply good in the eyes of Boeotians:
Marjoram, mint, reed mats, wicks,
Ducks, jackdaws, francolins, coot birds,   875
Plovers, dabchicks.

DICAEOPOLIS

Just like a fowl storm, then,
You've blown into the marketplace!

THEBAN

Indeed, and I'm carrying geese, hares, foxes,
Mole rats, hedgehogs, cats, badgers,
Martens, otters, Copaic eels![161]   880

---

158. See 15–16 above: a notoriously bad musician whom Dicaeopolis loathes.
159. Heracles' nephew and a fellow hero.
160. Probably locusts or cicadas.
161. As Dicaeopolis's reaction suggests, this last in the list was regarded as a delicacy. Lake Copais was in Boeotia.

DICAEOPOLIS

O You who bring the most delightful slice of fish for human
beings!
Allow me to say hello to the eels, if you're carrying them!

THEBAN

[*Addressing the eels*] Eldest of fifty Copaic maidens!¹⁶²
Come out here and grant your favors to the stranger!

DICAEOPOLIS

885 [*Addressing an eel*] O You who are dearest and longed for, for a
very long time now!
You've come, longed for by the comic¹⁶³ choruses
And dear to Morychus!¹⁶⁴ Servants, bring out
The brazier and the fan here for me.
Examine, children, the best eel,

890 Who's finally come after six years, though longed for [all the
while]!
Say hello to her, kids. And the charcoal I'll
Supply you, for the sake of this lady guest here!
But bring her out, for "not even when dead
Would I be apart from you,"¹⁶⁵ when you're wrapped up in
beet-greens!

---

162. According to the scholiast, this is a parody of a line from a lost play of
Aeschylus.

163. More literally, "trygic," Aristophanes' comic term for comedy; see nn.
84 and 104 above.

164. A notorious glutton: *Peace* 1008-9.

165. A parody of Euripides, *Alcestis* 367-68.

THEBAN

Where will my payment for these things come from?   895

DICAEOPOLIS

You'll give her to me, I suppose, as a market fee!

But if you're selling these other things here [*points to the many*
   goods the Theban has brought], say so!

THEBAN

I'm selling all these.

DICAEOPOLIS

Come then, how much do you say?

Or will you take back this other merchandise from here [in
   exchange]?

THEBAN

Whatever's in Athens but not found among the Boeotians!   900

DICAEOPOLIS

Sprats from Phaleron, then, you'll buy and take back,

Or pottery.

THEBAN

Sprats or pottery? But they're there [in Thebes].

Instead, what we don't have, but there's a lot of [here].

DICAEOPOLIS

I've got it! Take back a sycophant,

Once you've packed him up like pottery!

THEBAN

Yes, by the Twins![166]   905

---

166. Presumably Amphion and Zethus, mythical founders of Thebes.

I'd get a lot of profit, bringing him back,
Full of much mischief, like a monkey!

DICAEOPOLIS

And indeed there's Nicarchus, coming to denounce us!

THEBAN

The guy's short in stature!

DICAEOPOLIS

But bad head to toe!

NICARCHUS

Whose goods are these?

THEBAN

910   They're mine,
From Thebes, may Zeus witness!

NICARCHUS

I, here and now,
Denounce these things as belonging to the enemy!

THEBAN

What's the matter with you,
That you declare war on little winged birds and do battle?

NICARCHUS

And you *too* I denounce, in addition to these things!

THEBAN

What injustice have I committed?

NICARCHUS

I'll tell you "for the sake of those assembled."[167]   915
You're importing wicks from the enemies!

DICAEOPOLIS

So then you denounce him on account of a wick?

NICARCHUS

For it could set the shipyard ablaze!

DICAEOPOLIS

A shipyard by means of a wick!?!

NICARCHUS

I think so.

DICAEOPOLIS

In what way?

NICARCHUS

A Boeotian man, setting it on a cockroach   920
And lighting it, could send it into the shipyard
Through a drain hole, keeping a watch out for a big northerly
    wind.
If in fact the fire should touch the ships once,
They'd immediately be set alight![168]

DICAEOPOLIS

O perish in the worst way! [*Dicaeopolis starts to whale on Nicarchus*]
They'd be set alight by a cockroach and a wick?!?   925

167. A formula used by orators.
168. Consider Thucydides 4.100 for an example of Theban pyrotechnics in warfare.

NICARCHUS

I call witnesses!

DICAEOPOLIS

Arrest his mouth!

Give me some trash so that, in packaging him up, I can pass him
along,

Just like pottery, so he doesn't break while in transit!

CHORUS

Pack up, O Best Fellow,
930   The merchandise finely for the stranger
So that carrying him in this way he won't break him!

DICAEOPOLIS

I'll take care of these things, since
In fact he's making a certain chattering and
The sound of cracking in the kiln
And is otherwise hateful to gods!

CHORUS

935   What in the world will he use him for?

DICAEOPOLIS

He'll be an altogether useful vessel,
A mixing bowl of evils, mortar of lawsuits,
Lampstand to denounce audited officials and a cup
For stirring up troubles.

CHORUS

940   How might somebody have been persuaded
To use such a vessel

At home
When he's always sounding so much?

DICAEOPOLIS

He's strong, good fellow, so
He'd never break, even if
He should be hung upside down by his feet!   945

CHORUS

[*To the Theban*] Now it's all set for you beautifully!

THEBAN

I'm going to reap a harvest!

CHORUS

Well, best of strangers, reap away,
And take him and throw him wherever you want as you go,   950
[Useful] for everything—a sycophant is!

DICAEOPOLIS

Only with difficulty did I get him packaged up, the bastard!
Here, take your pottery, Boeotian!

THEBAN

Come and lower your shoulder, Ismenias.

DICAEOPOLIS

And see that you'll carry him off with due caution.   955
In any case you'll carry nothing healthy or sound, but
        still and all . . .
And if you profit by taking this cargo,
You'll be well-off,[169] as far as sycophants are concerned, at any rate!

---

169. Or "happy."

LAMACHUS'S MESSENGER

Dicaeopolis!

DICAEOPOLIS

Who[170] is it? Why are you calling out for me?

MESSENGER

Why?

960   Lamachus has ordered you, for this drachma here,
       To give him some of your thrushes for the Pitchers festival[171]
       And he's ordered you [to give him], for three drachmas, an eel
          from Copais.

DICAEOPOLIS

Which Lamachus is this—an *eel?!?*

MESSENGER

The terrible, the bull's-hide-shield-bearer,
965   Who brandishes the Gorgon
       While shaking "three o'ershadowing crests."[172]

DICAEOPOLIS

No, by Zeus, not even if he should give me his shield!
But let him shake his crests for salt-fish,
And if he puts up a fuss, I'll call the market-regulators!
But as for me, I'll take this merchandise for myself

---

170. Reading, with the principal MSS, "who" (*tis*) rather than "what" (*ti*) of the Budé.

171. Or Choes festival, celebrated on the second of the three days of the Anthesteria, at the sanctuary of Dionysus. The festival of the Pots (*Chytroi*) was celebrated on the final day.

172. From Aeschylus, *Seven Against Thebes* 384.

And I'll go in, accompanied by wings of thrushes and   970
  blackbirds.

CHORUS

You saw, O City Entire, the prudent man, super-wise,
And the sorts of imported goods he has to sell to others, because
  he concluded the treaty,
Some goods useful in the household, some, in turn, fit to gulp   975
  down straight from the fire.
All good things are spontaneously supplied him!
Never will I welcome War into my home,
Nor will he ever sing the Harmodius[173] [song], reclining
  alongside me,
Because the man's naturally a drunkard
Whose riotous revelry burst in on those possessed of everything   980
  good
And wrought everything bad, continually overturning and spilling
And fighting; and, in addition, when I repeatedly proposed that
  he
"Drink, lie down, take this cup of friendship,"
Still all the more did he torch with fire our vine props[174]
And violently did he spill the wine from our vines.   985

[*Dicaeopolis comes out of his house and discards the feathers from the
birds he is preparing*]

---

173. Harmodius and Aristogeiton were popularly credited with the assassination of Hipparchus, son of Peisistratus, and so with bringing the rule of tyranny in Athens to an end. The Chorus thus refers to a popular drinking song in honor of Harmodius.

174. The Peloponnesians made regular incursions into Athenian territory to destroy crops and vines.

He's all in a flutter over the dinner and at the same time is
　　thinking big thoughts indeed,
And as indication of his manner of life he's cast out from his
　　doors these feathers.

[*A young woman appears on stage, accompanied by female attendants*]

O You who were reared together with Cypris[175] the beautiful and
　　the Graces dear, O Reconciliation,

990　It escaped notice how beautiful is your face!
How might some Eros take hold of me and you and bring us
　　together,
Like the Eros depicted in the painting,[176] wearing a wreath of
　　flowers?
Or do you regard me as being very much a little old man,
　　perhaps?
But if I got hold of you, I think, at least, I'd still bang you three
　　times over!

995　First I'd plow a long row of young vine,
Then, alongside that, fresh shoots of fig-slips,
And, third, a row of grapevines, this old man here would!
And all around the entire field, olive trees
So that, from them, we'd anoint ourselves, you and I, for the New
　　Moon day! [177]

---

175. That is, Aphrodite.

176. According to the scholiast, this refers to a painting of Eros by Zeuxis,
located in a temple of Aphrodite in Athens.

177. That is, the first day of the month, which was a holiday and so associ-
ated with private and public rites, as well as being a market day; see *Knights*
43–44.

HERALD

Hear ye, People! In accord with the traditional ways,   1000
Begin drinking from the pitchers at the sound of the trumpet. And
    he who drinks it down
First out of everyone, he'll get the wineskin full of . . . Ctesiphon![178]

DICAEOPOLIS

O Boys![179] O Women! Didn't you hear?
What are you doing? Don't you hear the herald?
Braise, roast well, rotate, pull off   1005
The hares, quick! String the wreaths!
Bring the skewers, so I may put the thrushes on a spit!

CHORUS

I envy you your good counsel
And more your cheerful feasting,
My fellow,[180] here and now.   1010

DICAEOPOLIS

What then, when the thrushes
You see are roasting?

CHORUS

I think this too that you say is good!

DICAEOPOLIS

[*To a servant*] Stir up the fire!

---

178. Identity unknown. Some suggest he must have been a heavy drinker,
others that he was overweight and so had a belly resembling a full wineskin (for
the latter, consider *Clouds* 1237–38).

179. That is, "Slaves!"

180. Literally, "human being."

CHORUS

1015 Did you hear how gourmet-ily
How both refinedly and dine-tastically
He serves himself?

FARMER

Ah, wretched me!

DICAEOPOLIS

O Heracles! Who's *this?!?*

FARMER

An unhappy man!

DICAEOPOLIS

Well, keep your unhappiness to yourself.

FARMER

1020 Dearest fellow, since the treaty is yours alone,
Measure out some peace for me, even if only five years' worth!

DICAEOPOLIS

What's happened to you?

FARMER

I'm ruined because I lost my two oxen!

DICAEOPOLIS

From where?

FARMER

From Phyle[181] the Boeotians took them!

---

181. A remote Athenian deme "on the most direct road from Athens to Thebes" (Olson ad loc.) and hence liable to Boeotian raids.

DICAEOPOLIS

O thrice-ill-starred fellow—and you're wearing white?!?[182]

FARMER

And by Zeus these used to support me   1025
With all manner of manure!

DICAEOPOLIS

So what are you in need of right now?

FARMER

I've ruined my eyes crying for my two oxen!
But if you have any care for [me,] Dercetes of Phyle,
Anoint my eyes with peace, quick!

DICAEOPOLIS

But, you rascal, I don't happen to be a public servant!   1030

FARMER

Come now, I beseech you—if somehow I may get my two oxen
    back.

DICAEOPOLIS

There's no way, but go cry to Pittalus's people.[183]

FARMER

But, for me, just one drop of peace
Drip into this tube here!

---

182. The surprise comes from the fact that mourners should wear black.
183. Apparently a public doctor; thus here his students or associates. See also 1222 below.

DICAEOPOLIS

1035 Not even the least [little droplet], but go off somewhere, off
toward home.

FARMER

Oh, wretched me, my two little oxen from the farm!

CHORUS

The man has discovered
In the treaty something pleasant, and
It seems he'll share it with no one.

DICAEOPOLIS

1040 [*To his servants*] Baste the sausage with honey.
Grill the cuttlefish!

CHORUS

[*To the audience*] Did you hear his commanding tone?

DICAEOPOLIS

Broil the eels!

CHORUS

You're killing me and the neighbors with hunger,
1045 And with the smoky savor
And with your voice, ordering such things!

DICAEOPOLIS

Broil these here, and brown those ones beautifully!

BEST MAN

Dicaeopolis!

DICAEOPOLIS

Who is it? Who is it?

BEST MAN

A certain bridegroom sent this meat here to you
From the wedding feast.

DICAEOPOLIS

Nobly done, whoever it was.   1050

BEST MAN

And he bade you, for the meat—
So that he'd not go out on campaign, but could stay home and
    screw—
To pour out one ladleful of peace into the vial.

DICAEOPOLIS

Take it away, take away the meat and don't give it to me,
Because I wouldn't pour any for a thousand drachmas!   1055
But . . . who's this girl here?

BEST MAN

The bridesmaid
Needs to say something to you alone about the bride.

DICAEOPOLIS

Come now, what is it you're saying? [*She whispers in his ear*] How
    funny, O Gods,
Is the bride's request, which she asks me so intently—
That her groom's cock stay at home!   1060
[*To a servant*] Bring the treaty here, so I may give some to her alone,
Since a woman doesn't deserve[184] the war.

---

184. Following the suggestion of a modern scholar, the Budé reads "A
woman isn't the cause [*aitia*] of the war," but the principal MSS have instead
"deserve" (*axia*). See also Edmunds, "Aristophanes' *Acharnians*," 22 n. 69.

[*To the bridesmaid*] Hold the container under here this way, O
   woman.
Do you know how this is done? Explain this to the bride:

1065 Whenever they're enlisting soldiers, with this [*pointing to the
   contents of the vial*]
At night let the groom's cock be polished!

[*Best Man and Bridesmaid leave*]

[*To a servant*] Take away the treaty, bring the wine decanter
So I may get the wine and pour it into the pitchers.

CHORUS

And now this fellow here, whoever he is, with knitted brows
1070 Is making haste, resembling somebody with a terrible
   announcement.

HERALD

O toils and battles and Lamachuses![185]

LAMACHUS

Who is crashing about my bronzed-bedecked halls?

HERALD

The generals command you to go today
Quickly, taking your ambushes and crests,[186]
1075 And then to watch over the points of entry as it snows.

---

185. The word for "Lamachuses" (*lamachōn*) contains the word for "battles" (*machōn*); see also n. 56 above.
   186. The word for "crests" (*lophōn*) is close to that for "ambushes" (*lochōn*);
see also n. 96 above.

For someone has reported to them that, during their Pitchers and
    Pots festivals,[187]
Boeotian bandits will invade!

DICAEOPOLIS

Ah, generals—more numerous than good.

LAMACHUS

Isn't it terrible that I'm not permitted even to celebrate the
    festival?

DICAEOPOLIS

Ah, the war-battling-Lamachian campaign!   1080

LAMACHUS

Ah, wretched me! Now you're ridiculing me!

DICAEOPOLIS

Do you want to do battle with the four-winged Geryon?[188]

LAMACHUS

Alas,
Such news the herald has brought me!

DICAEOPOLIS

Alas, what news from this messenger running toward *me,* in turn?

MESSENGER

Dicaeopolis!

---

187. That is, the festivals of the Pitchers and Pots celebrated as part of the
Anthesteria, in honor of Dionysus and Hermes.

188. Geryon was a triple-bodied monster killed by Heracles—though commentators puzzle over the mention here of "four-winged."

DICAEOPOLIS

What is it?

MESSENGER

1085　To dinner
Go quickly, bringing the basket and pitcher.
For the priest of Dionysus sends for you.
Just be quick: you've been holding up dinner for a long while
　　now!
All else is provided for:
1090　Couches, tables, head pillows, blankets,
Wreaths, perfume, delicacies—whores alongside—
Pastries, flat cakes, sesame snacks, crackers,
Dancing girls, "the things dearest to Harmodius."[189]
Just hurry along as quickly as possible!

[*Exit Messenger*]

LAMACHUS

Unhappy me!

DICAEOPOLIS

1095　For in fact you drew the Gorgon large [on your shield].
[*To a servant*] Lock up and have someone pack my dinner.

LAMACHUS

Boy, boy, bring my rucksack out here!

DICAEOPOLIS

Boy, boy, bring my basket out here!

---

189. From the popular drinking song mentioned above; see. n. 173.

LAMACHUS

Bring the seasoned salt, boy, and onion!

DICAEOPOLIS

To me the sliced fish—for I loathe onions!   1100

LAMACHUS

Bring me here, boy, a fig-leaf wrapped 'round stale pickled fish!

DICAEOPOLIS

And to me, boy, a fig-leaf: I'll cook [the fish] there.

LAMACHUS

Bring the two plumes from my helmet there.

DICAEOPOLIS

And to me bring the doves and the thrushes!

LAMACHUS

Beautiful and white is the ostrich's plume!   1105

DICAEOPOLIS

Beautiful and browned is the flesh of the dove!

LAMACHUS

Human being, stop ridiculing my armaments!

DICAEOPOLIS

Human being, do you mind ceasing to look at my thrushes?!?

LAMACHUS

Bring out the crest case with the triple crests!

DICAEOPOLIS

And bring me the dish with the rabbit meat!   1110

LAMACHUS

Ah! Have moths eaten my crests?!?

DICAEOPOLIS

Ah! Will I eat up the rabbit stew before dinner?!?

LAMACHUS

Human being, do you mind not addressing me?

DICAEOPOLIS

No, [I'm not,] but for a long time the slave and I've been
    wrangling.

1115   [*To the slave*] Do you want to make a wager and leave it to
    Lamachus to judge

Which is more pleasant, locusts or thrushes?

LAMACHUS

Ah! How insolent you are!

DICAEOPOLIS

He judges locusts to be very much more so!

LAMACHUS

Boy, boy! Come and bring the spear to me here!

DICAEOPOLIS

Boy, boy! Pull off the sausage and bring it here!

LAMACHUS

1120   Come, let me pull off the case from the spear.

Here, hang on to it, boy!

DICAEOPOLIS

And you, boy, hold on to *this* [*hands him one end of the skewer*].

LAMACHUS

Bring me the stand, boy, for my shield!

DICAEOPOLIS

And for my [stomach], bring out the loaves of bread![190]

LAMACHUS

Bring here my shield, Gorgon-embossed and round.

DICAEOPOLIS

And to me give a flat cake cheesy and round!   1125

LAMACHUS

[To the audience] Isn't this flat-out ridicule in the eyes of human
    beings?

DICAEOPOLIS

Isn't this flat cake sweet in the eyes of human beings?

LAMACHUS

Pour on the polishing oil, boy. In this bronze [of my shield]
I espy an old man going to be prosecuted for cowardice!

DICAEOPOLIS

You, pour on the honey! Here too an old man's plain to see   1130
Ordering Lamachus son of Gorgasus[191] to weep!

LAMACHUS

Bring here, boy, my warrior's corselet.

---

190. The word for "loaves of bread" (*kribanitas*) is somewhat similar to
that for "stand(s)" (*killibantas*) in the previous line.

191. Presumably a play on "Gorgon"; Lamachus's father was named
Xenophanes.

DICAEOPOLIS

Fetch, boy, *my* corselet—that is, my pitcher!

LAMACHUS

With this here I gird myself against my enemies!

DICAEOPOLIS

1135 With *this* I gird myself against my fellow drinkers!

LAMACHUS

My bedding, boy, tie to the shield.

DICAEOPOLIS

My dinner, boy, tie to the basket.

LAMACHUS

And I myself will go and bring my rucksack.

DICAEOPOLIS

And I'll go get my cloak and be off!

LAMACHUS

1140 Pick up the shield and proceed with it, boy.
It's snowing! Curses! Wintry affairs[192] . . .

DICAEOPOLIS

Pick up the dinner! Boozing-it-up affairs!

[*Exit Dicaeopolis and Lamachus*]

CHORUS

Go and fare well on campaign!
How dissimilar the paths you two are taking!

192. The word for "affairs" (*pragmata*) often means "troubles."

Drinking for the one, bedecked with a wreath,   1145
But for you, freezing and standing on guard!
For him, going to bed
With a young maiden in her bloom
Getting his you-know-what rubbed!
Antimachus, son of Psacadus,[193] the writer, poet of tunes,   1150
To state it with a simple account: would that Zeus utterly
    destroy him!
He it was who, as chorus-leader at the Lenaea, dismissed   1155
    wretched me without dinner![194]
Would that I might see him still in need of squid,
And may it be grilled
And sizzling beside the sea, lying out on a table,
There beached. And then just as he's going to grab it
A dog would snatch it up and run away with it!   1160
So this is one evil for him, and then another would come at
    night.
For while shivering as he walks home after a ride,   1165
Some drunk would then crack him on the head, some lunatic
    Orestes,[195]

---

193. Since Antimachus is a common name, the identity of the fellow in question is unknown. His patronymic, as the scholiast suggests, means "sprayer" and perhaps refers to Antimachus's habit of spraying saliva when he talked. Consider also *Clouds* 1022.

194. The "chorus-leader" was a wealthy citizen whose duties included paying for the production of a play and apparently also a celebratory dinner afterward. The Chorus here is clearly not speaking as Acharnians but (once again) as a troupe of actors.

195. After killing his mother (Clytemnestra) to avenge her murder of his father (Agamemnon), Orestes wandered back to Athens, out of his mind. Here, a proverbial madman.

And he, wanting to get a stone in the darkness, would get
1170 In his hand a freshly crapped turd instead
And holding that marble he'd rush at him
And then—missing!—he'd hit Cratinus![196]

MESSENGER
O servants who are in the home of Lamachus![197]
1175 Water, heat water in a little pot!
Get ready bandages and salve,
Oiled wool, a dressing for his ankle!
The man's been wounded by a stick as he leapt across a ditch
And, falling backwards, he sprained his ankle!
1180 And his head he banged on a stone as he fell,
And Gorgon he waked from his shield!
And as a great feather from a big-mouthed-boaster bird fell
On the rocks, he uttered a terrible lament:
"O Famed Eye, seeing you now for the very last time
1185 I am leaving this light; I am . . . no more!"
Having said this much and falling into the irrigation ditch,
He rose up and, encountering [his own] men in flight,
"He expelled and drove the bandits on by the spear."
But here he is, the fellow himself! Just open the door!

[*Enter Lamachus, bandaged and limping*]

---

196. An Athenian comic poet against whom the young Aristophanes competed; see also 848 and following above.

197. A mockery of the language often used by messengers in tragedies.

LAMACHUS

Aaaaaah! Aaaaaaah!198   1190
Hateful are these chilly sufferings! Wretched me!
I am perishing, struck by an enemy's spear!
But that would be lamentable for me—   1195
If Dicaeopolis should see me wounded
And then scoff at my misfortunes!

[*Enter Dicaeopolis, fresh from the contest, supported by two dancing-girls*]

DICAEOPOLIS

Aaaaaah! Aaaaaaah!
Ah, the titties, how firm and quince-like!
Kiss me softly, my Two Golden Ones,   1200
Open-mouthed and amply tongued!
For I am the first to have downed the pitcher!

LAMACHUS

O you wretched confluence of my evils!
Ah, ah, how painful my wounds!   1205

DICAEOPOLIS

Ha ha, Lamachippius, hello!

LAMACHUS

I suffer hatefully!

DICAEOPOLIS

[*To the girls*] Why are you kissing me?

---

198. The Budé suggests a spoof on the laments characteristic of tragedy and of Euripides, *Hippolytus* 1347 and following in particular.

LAMACHUS

I am distressed!

DICAEOPOLIS

[*To the girls*] Why are you nibbling me?

LAMACHUS

1210   Wretched me, how grievous the encounter!

DICAEOPOLIS

Was somebody taking up contributions[199] at the Pitchers
    festival?!?

LAMACHUS

Oh oh! Paean Paean![200]

DICAEOPOLIS

But the Paean festival isn't today!

LAMACHUS

Take hold of me, hold my leg. Owww!
1215   Take hold of it, friends!

DICAEOPOLIS

You two take hold of my dick, right in the middle,
Take hold of it, lady friends!

---

199. The word for "contributions" (*xumbolas*) (to a common meal) is the
same as that for "encounter" in the previous line. Evidently guests were to
bring their own meal (as Dicaeopolis did), but the host would supply the enter-
tainment, and to solicit contributions to pay for it would be inappropriate. Most
MSS add the phrase "in battle" at 1210, but modern editors reject it as an
unmetrical and intrusive gloss.

200. Epithet of Apollo, a god responsible for healing. Lamachus thus in
effect calls on the god to heal him.

LAMACHUS

I grow dizzy, struck by a stone upon the head,
And succumb to the dark . . .

DICAEOPOLIS

And I want to go to bed, with a raging hard-on,   1220
And screw in the dark![201]

LAMACHUS

Carry me off to the doors of Pittalus,
With paeanean-healing hands!

DICAEOPOLIS

Take me to the judges! Where's the king?[202]
Give me the wine sack I'm owed!   1225

LAMACHUS

[*As he is carried off stage*] Some spear has pierced through my
    bones painfully!

DICAEOPOLIS

[*Holding up his pitcher*] Look! This is empty! Hurray for the noble
    victor!

CHORUS

So hurray—since you invite us to do so, old man—noble victor!

---

201. The word Aristophanes coins for "screw in the dark" (*skotobiniō*) is
modeled on the word translated just above as "succumb to the dark" (i.e., black
out): *skotodiniō*.

202. The king, that is, of the Lenaean festival (*archon basileus*). Aristophanes-Dicaeopolis would seem to have in mind not only the wineskin but also
the comedy prize.

DICAEOPOLIS

And I poured it neat and chugged it right down!

CHORUS

1230   Hurray now, noble fellow! Take the wineskin and be on your way!

DICAEOPOLIS

Now you follow along and sing: "Hurray O Noble Victor!"

CHORUS

Well we'll follow along for your sake,
Singing "Hurray Noble Victor!"
For you and the wineskin!

On the *Acharnians*

The *Acharnians* is the earliest extant play of Aristophanes, only the names and a few fragments of his two previous works being known to us.[1] Aristophanes presented our play early in 425 B.C.E. at the Athenian religious-dramatic festival called the Lenaea, as distinguished from the principal other such festival, the City Dionysia—a fact to which Aristophanes draws our attention in the course of the play itself (498–506 and 513). As for the date of the play's performance, by 425 the Peloponnesian War was in its sixth year, as is noted by the lead character of the *Acharnians,* Dicaeopolis (890). And this fact is related to what we may call the obvious message of the play: Athens and Sparta should negotiate an end to the war now. Not only was the war started over what amount to trivialities, even allowing for comedic exaggeration or invention (513–39); but the war has also become a heavy burden on a great many Athenians and especially on those salt of the earth rural folk who have had to give up so much in the name of Pericles' war policy. For Pericles had decreed that the rural population should leave their homes and ancestral lands and come to live in the urban center of Athens,

1. The two earlier plays are *Banqueters* and *Babylonians.* A catalogue of Aristophanes' plays (in alphabetical order) was found in a fourteenth-century manuscript and published by F. Novati in "Index fabularum Aristophanis ex codice Abrosiano L 39," *Hermes* 14:3 (1879): 461–65; see also Victor Coulon, "Introduction," in the Budé, v. For the extant fragments, see Aristophanes, *Fragments,* ed. Jeffrey Henderson, Loeb Classical Library (Cambridge, MA: Harvard University Press, 2008).

safely behind its all-important defensive walls. The farmers would thus abandon their crops to the depredations of the Spartans, but for so long as Athens controlled the seas with its dominant navy, the city could use the greater world as its supply house. Let the Spartans exhaust themselves by destroying the Athenians' fields; they will gain no military advantage thereby. Yet, as Thucydides indicates so powerfully, Pericles' strategic policy brought great personal hardships to the rural Athenians.[2] The obvious message of the *Acharnians,* to say it again, is that peace is to be much preferred to war. War destroys life and with it all the very great goods, the delights, that life makes possible (consider 357)—a contention that Dicaeopolis demonstrates throughout with all the empirical evidence one could possibly wish for.

Now if it was Aristophanes' intention to encourage peace or even to bring peace about, by enticing his audience with a display of peacetime joys, it has to be said that he failed to realize that intention; the war was to grind on for twenty-one more years. And this despite the fact that the play, awarded first prize among the comedies in competition, must be judged to have been a smashing success. What is a comic poet, who is also an advocate of peace, to do? Dicaeopolis, for his part, is disgusted by the war and hurt by it, for he is an old man (398, 1129–30, 1228) from the country and as such knows firsthand the hardships of Pericles' policy (71–72). As the play opens, he is alone in the Athenian democratic Assembly, waiting more or less idly for the presiding officers and his fellow citizens to arrive, late again as they always are. When his attempt to debate the case for peace by proper democratic means fails miserably, Dicaeopolis resorts to a most remarkable stratagem—a fan-

---

2. Thucydides, *War of the Peloponnesians and Athenians* 2.13–14, 16–17.

tastical or miraculous and hence comedic one: he enlists a certain immortal, Amphitheus by name, to negotiate a private peace with Sparta for his sake, as well as for his spouse and children (132). Dicaeopolis's quest for a private peace issues in success as swiftly as his attempt to bring about a political peace had issued in failure. The household of Dicaeopolis, then, and only it, is soon at peace with Sparta and its allies; it is a little pocket of calm in the greater maelstrom of the war.

There is a name for a lone citizen in wartime who brings about such a private peace with the enemy: traitor. We cannot be surprised, then, that Dicaeopolis is labeled just that early on in the play, by the Chorus as it happens: "traitor to the fatherland" (290). The title of the play identifies the members of that chorus. They are men who hail from the rural Athenian deme or district of Acharnae, which is at once the largest of the demes[3] and the most remote from the urban center of Athens. But the Acharnians constituting the Chorus are also very elderly ("ancient": 676) veterans of the Persian Wars; they are the storied and justly honored men who fought at Marathon (181 and context, 696-97). These citizens, among the "greatest generation" of Athenians, are deeply conservative, patriotic, and—their age be damned—fiery still, if more in spirit, alas, than the flesh.[4] So great is their anger at Dicaeopolis, once they identify him as the traitor they seek, that they come very close indeed to stoning him. Such violence being impossible in comedy, it must be averted. It is averted in the event because Dicaeopolis proves to be a remarkably able speaker who brings all his skill to bear on his predicament.

---

3. Thucydides 2.19.

4. Consider, e.g., 180-84 and 321; compare 210-22 and 990-99.

Now Dicaeopolis's attainment of his peace is much less impressive than is his defense of it—the peace is a done deal by line 178—for, to repeat, he parries the Acharnians' charge of treason, which would seem to have much going for it. We must ask, then, how Dicaeopolis manages that feat and so proves to the satisfaction of the entire Chorus that he is no traitor (1–718). Further, we will have to consider what use Dicaeopolis then makes of his peace, in what constitutes the second half of the play (719–end). And what, finally, would Aristophanes in his wisdom[5] have us learn from the play—apart, of course, from developing a still greater appreciation for the pleasures afforded by peace?

The two latter questions, of Dicaeopolis's use of his peace and of Aristophanes' intention, are more closely related than they might seem. For early on our hero says this:

And as for me, I myself know what I suffered at the hands of
    Cleon
On account of my comedy last year.
For dragging me into the courtroom,
He kept slandering me and slobbering his lies all over me
And matched the din of the Cycloborus [River] and drenched me,
    such that I very nearly
Perished, mixed up in his nasty business. (377–82)

To say the least, we are surprised to learn that the young and urbane comic poet Aristophanes has thus donned the persona of "Dicaeopolis," an old farmer from rural Athens. Accordingly, in watching and listening to Dicaeopolis as he defends and then uses

---

5. Consider, e.g., *Clouds* 522–26.

his private peace, we are attending also to the deeds and words of Aristophanes himself. This strange fact also permits us to understand better the somewhat strange opening of the play, to which we may now turn.

Like all the plays of Aristophanes, the *Acharnians* begins with a complaint or lament or moan. Dicaeopolis's very core, he tells us, has been stung by numberless pains and been delighted by so few pleasures that he can count them on one hand: four. In fact, such are Dicaeopolis's pains that they prove to crowd out the enumeration of his pleasures, since we learn of only two of them: the fine that the Athenian demagogue Cleon was made to pay to the knights, which probably occurred not in the real world but in Aristophanes' own comedy of the year before;[6] and the performance of a certain Dexitheus singing a Boeotian tune (14). In keeping with the fact that Dicaeopolis's stated pleasures are peculiarly connected with the things of the Muses—as are the first two of his stated pains (9–12 and 15–16)—we note that the tune from which Dicaeopolis gained so much pleasure hails from what is enemy territory, as the play frequently reminds us,[7] but this fact in no way prevented him from enjoying it. To this point it is altogether unclear why Dicaeopolis is in the Assembly at all, let alone with such unrivaled eagerness; only now (26) do we learn that his principal concern at the moment is not in fact musical but political: "So now I've come, simply put, all ready / To cry out, to interrupt, to revile the orators / If somebody speaks of anything other than peace"

---

6. Regarding Cleon's fine, Alan H. Sommerstein considers the possibility "that this reference, like those in [lines] 9–16, is to a recent theatrical event, perhaps an incident in Ar.'s *Babylonians*" (*Acharnians* ad loc.). So also Leo Strauss, *Socrates and Aristophanes* (Chicago: University of Chicago Press, 1966), 58.

7. Consider 624, 721, 872 and context, 1020–23, and 1077.

(37–39). Inasmuch as Dicaeopolis the war-weary farmer is also Aristophanes the poet in disguise, we can expect that the political concerns of the one are somehow bound up with the "musical" concerns of the other. Aristophanes certainly gives the impression on occasion that being a bad musician or hack poet is as deplorable as being a corrupt politician or warmongering general.[8]

Five rapid-fire scenes follow. The central one features the return from Sparta of Amphitheus the god, private treaty in hand, the travel expenses for his astonishingly quick trip having been paid for by Dicaeopolis himself. This central scene is immediately preceded by the arrival of Athenian ambassadors from Persia, who are returning after many years on the public payroll and are accompanied by "the King's Eye"; it is immediately succeeded by the appearance of the Athenian Theorus, Cleon's crony,[9] back from King Sitalkes of the Odrysians and accompanied by Odomantian mercenary soldiers. Dicaeopolis clearly deplores Athens' dalliance with these barbarians in its foolhardy hope to gain their favor and therewith manpower and money or materiel. In fact, as Thucydides' narrative confirms, neither the Persian satraps nor barbarian mercenaries would help Athens much in the course of the war.[10]

---

8. In addition to the opening scene, consider 836–58, where the Chorus mocks in equal measure a leading demagogue, a sycophant, a comic poet, and a satirical painter.

9. See *Clouds* 399–400; *Wasps* 42 and context, 418–19, 599–600, and 1236–42.

10. Later in the war, for example, Athens' use of Thracian mercenaries resulted in what Thucydides regarded as a most lamentable episode of the war, the mercenaries' senseless slaughter of the entire town of Mycalessus, including a boys' school there (7.29–30).

When Amphitheus first appears, the herald of the Assembly asks him whether he is a human being, to which he replies: "No, / But an immortal" (47-48). The nonchalance of this exchange is striking. Athenians seem to take for granted the everyday presence of immortals walking among them. This goes together with the astonishing lack of respect accorded this peace-seeking emissary of the (other) gods (51-52): he is unceremoniously ejected from the Assembly. One could well receive the impression here that Athens is altogether impious, the stated wish of the gods for peace being no impediment whatever to the Athenians' continued pursuit of the war because it is not of the slightest interest to them. But this impression, while not without some warrant, must be balanced against what we witness in the last of these five scenes. There a vote for the pay of the Thracian (Odomantian) mercenary soldiers is at issue, a prospect that disgusts Dicaeopolis. Accordingly, in order to prevent the Assembly from approving it, Dicaeopolis must put a stop to the proceedings altogether. He does so by claiming that "a raindrop just fell on me," for this he interprets as "a sign from Zeus" (171). And with that the Herald immediately announces the dissolution of the Assembly. Our first impression that the Athenians are doubtful at best of the gods and hence of such things as oracles and divine signs, is thus belied. It is not only the obviously pious Spartans, but the "sophisticated" Athenians, too, who are deeply pious and so are given to seeking out the guidance of divine auguries and the like—at least when doing so accords with their perceived interest or felt need.[11]

---

11. Consider, among the many examples that might be given, Thucydides 2.21.3 and 8.1.1. See also the Clouds' beautiful description, as they float over the city, of the whole of Athens at worship (*Clouds* 298-313), as well as *Knights* 61 and the use of oracles or prophecies in that play in order to persuade Demos, i.e., the Athenian people (997-1099).

Enter now the Acharnians (204), hopping mad but slowed by age. Speaking in the name of "the city" (205) and calling upon "Father Zeus and Gods" (224), the Acharnians proclaim that the war will only increase for the damned traitor, as far as in them lies, "on account of my lands" that have been plundered and "my vines" that have been trampled (225-32). The concerns of the Acharnians are thus a mix of the patriotic (290) and the private. The Acharnians overhear and eventually interrupt Dicaeopolis as he is celebrating the Rural Dionysia,[12] together with his wife and daughter. And so we too witness the first of the uses to which our hero puts his private peace: he conducts a religious service in honor of Dionysus. Whatever arguments Dicaeopolis will use to sway the Acharnians, we can say this much already in his defense: he tried the democratic or political path to achieve peace for everyone, but was brusquely rebuffed; the gods, here represented by Amphitheus, clearly support peace in general[13] and Dicaeopolis's peace in particular; he is seeking peace, not just for himself, but for his whole family; and, to repeat, the first thing he does with it is conduct a religious ceremony. Dicaeopolis comes to sight here less as a model citizen, it is true, than as a pious family man, but this is to say that he is by no means narrowly selfish. We glimpse here the cluster of concerns that may pull us in different directions: the concern for the good of one's city, of one's family, and of oneself. And floating somewhere above these, so to speak, is the concern for the gods, who seem sometimes to support the city above all, but sometimes the family instead. In the play thus far the gods favor a political peace, but, failing that, they also support a private peace "for me

---

12. On this festival, see n. 47 to the translation of the *Acharnians*.
13. Consider also *Peace* 211-12.

alone / And my kids and my spouse" (130–32), as Dicaeopolis explains it to Amphitheus. ("For me alone" must here mean "for my family alone.") Still, even in the course of the Rural Dionysia, conducted in the bosom of the family, our hero gives pride of place in his joyful song to his male member, which he apostrophizes as a "comrade of Bacchus, / Fellow reveler, night roamer, / Adulterer, boy-lover" (263–65). As especially the last two epithets make plain, that august being is at least as likely to look beyond the bounds of conjugal bliss—to frolicking with an errant servant girl, to give a third example (271–75)—as it is to remain happily within them. This is an early clue that even "dutiful family man" (let alone "model citizen") may not quite capture the essence of Dicaeopolis. And Dicaeopolis's particular concern for Dionysus points us already or again in the direction of Aristophanes (consider *Clouds* 518–19).

Since it is impossible to convince by arguments those who refuse on principle even to listen to them, Dicaeopolis's first task in defending himself is to open the ears of the Acharnians. He gets off to what would seem to be a poor start by contending that the Acharnians ought to set aside the Spartans altogether and simply hear of the treaty itself. But how can the nobility (306–7) of a treaty be judged without recourse to the character of its signatories, who, in the case of the Spartans, "abide by no altar or pledge or oath" according to the Acharnians? Dicaeopolis is thus compelled to contend that in fact the Spartans are not the cause of *all* the Athenians' troubles—which only provokes the Acharnians further—and even that the Spartans are in some respects being treated unjustly. (Dicaeopolis does not go quite so far as to add what is nonetheless only too obvious: "by the Athenians.") In response to the Acharnians' still-firm refusal to listen and its accompanying threat of violence, Dicaeopolis resorts to a drastic measure; he threatens to kill the hostage he suddenly declares that he has taken, to the dismay of the Acharnians: a basket full of Acharnian-made charcoal! For the Acharnians we meet make a living from the production and sale of charcoal. The effect of Dicaeopolis's stratagem on the Acharnians is remarkable:

> But say *now* whatever seems best to you, and
> In what way the Lacedaemonian is a friend to you.
> Because this dear little charcoal basket here, I'll never betray it!
> (338–40)

The mix of patriotic and private motives we saw before in the Acharnians proves to be weighted rather more in favor of their private, and even private economic, interests. Their vaunted patriotism, then, is not all it is cracked up to be. In properly comic fashion, they proceed to disarm. Hence there will be no summary execution. This much, at least, Dicaeopolis has accomplished.

The Acharnians still demand a "trial" (364), however, and they eagerly accept or insist on Dicaeopolis's proffered submission to them in the form of speaking with his head on a chopping block. The fear that Dicaeopolis here admits to is based on his knowledge of two things: "the characters of the country folk" (370), on the one hand, who can be duped by some boaster's speech in praise of them and the city, justified or not; and "the souls" of the elderly (375), on the other, cantankerous and biting. (Dicaeopolis's opponents in this case are *both* rural *and* old.) It is here that Dicaeopolis reveals himself to be Aristophanes, and, with that revelation, he makes known his hard-won knowledge of how vulnerable his comedic takedowns of Cleon have made him: the old farmer is not the only one in hot water. In other words, the threat the Acharnians pose to Dicaeopolis in the world of the comedy is akin to the threat Cleon poses to Aristophanes in the real world. Yet the riskiness of speaking out as Aristophanes does cannot be traced entirely to Cleon and perhaps not even, in the present case at least, to Cleon at all. For we learn later that Cleon cannot now charge Aristophanes with slandering the city in front of foreigners, as he had done last year, since there are no (or at any rate few) foreigners at the Lenaea as distinguished from the City Dionysia (recall 498–506 and 513). Instead, as that same later statement contends, Aristophanes is "slandered by enemies, among Athenians too-hasty-in-counsel": Aristophanes has multiple enemies "among Athenians." Moreover, the slander at work against him is based on the thought that he is "making a comedy of our city and treating the demos with utter insolence [*kathubridzei*]" (630–31). Among Aristophanes' fellow citizens, then, there are those who contend that he lacks proper respect for both the city and the demos.[14] A demagogue like Cleon is dangerous only because there is a demos ready to be led or misled by him.

So great is the riskiness of his venture still that Aristophanes-Dicaeopolis must resort to fostering in his audience an antidote to anger. If Aristophanes, generally speaking, makes use of laughter as just such an antidote to anger, or rather as a prophylactic against it, here Dicaeopolis feels compelled to make use of pity instead, which

---

14. According to Xenophon (or "the Old Oligarch"), it is possible in democratic Athens to mock individuals in the city—the rich, well-born, or powerful, or even some busybodies among the poor—but it is intolerable to make a comedy of the demos as such (*Regime of the Athenians* 2.18).

we may define as "a certain pain at what is manifestly bad . . . [befalling] someone who does not deserve it, which one might expect to suffer oneself . . . and this when it appears close at hand."[15] The fostering of pity falls outside the purview of comedy because comedy cannot portray true suffering, let alone unjust suffering. As a result, Dicaeopolis is compelled to take over from Euripides the trappings of that great man's tragic art and so win from his still-hostile audience a modicum of pity. It hardly needs to be said that this very gesture in the direction of pity proves to be laughable: we hear of pity rather than come to feel it ourselves. Dicaeopolis the old farmer has a taste for Aeschylus (10); Dicaeopolis the young comic poet evidently prefers Euripides.[16] The whole of this scene spoofs a good many verses of Euripides, as is only to be expected, and it mocks the tragedian by having him suggest that his entire art (463–64) amounts to cheap or hackneyed devices—his usual cast of beggars and cripples, appropriately decked out—meant to jerk tears of pity from his audience. Yet Aristophanes also pays homage to Euripides here, as one poet-craftsman to another. For Euripides expresses no surprise at the news that Aristophanes-Dicaeopolis must address "the Chorus" at length (an event that takes place only onstage) or that he will be put to death if he speaks badly; Euripides asks only about which used stage costumes his visitor needs (consider 415–19). Euripides for his part affirms that Aristophanes-Dicaeopolis, with his "shrewd mind," "contrive[s] subtle things"

---

15. Aristotle, *Art of Rhetoric* 1384b13–16.

16. On the complex question of the relation of Aeschylus to Euripides, or the significance of the choice between them, consider the *Frogs* as a whole together with *Clouds* 1366 and following.

(445)—which is to say that Aristophanes has Euripides compliment . . . Aristophanes. Even more striking is Aristophanes-Dicaeopolis's contention here, evidently based on lines from Euripides' lost *Telephus*, that "'I must seem to be a beggar today, / To be who in fact I am, but appear not to be'" (440-41). Certainly Aristophanes-Dicaeopolis is the kind of person who may pretend to be a beggar, or for that matter an old farmer, and so donning a false appearance is in its way also revealing of the man; he slips in and out of misleading disguises, even as he comically draws attention to the fact. Aristophanes-Dicaeopolis applies the quoted remark to the division he now draws between the spectators and the Chorus: "The spectators must know me as I am, / But those in the Chorus, by contrast, must stand there like knuckleheads / So I may give them the finger with little phraselets" (442-44). The spectators—we are among them—know that Aristophanes-Dicaeopolis is putting on a disguise and a show, whereas the Chorus (of Acharnian elders) is to think of him as a pitiable beggar. The spectators, then, being in the know, are for that reason in a position to laugh at what is intended to soften the Chorus: Dicaeopolis dressed in rags. But then again, the Chorus of Acharnians has already seen and conversed with Dicaeopolis the farmer and knows that he is no beggar (238-40 and 280-392). More than that, just as Dicaeopolis is really Aristophanes, is not the Chorus really a collection of Athenian actors, as distinguished from elderly Acharnians, who know full well that "Dicaeopolis" is neither a beggar nor even a farmer but (a stand-in for) the poet? We are reminded of the complicated nature of the Chorus at the beginning of the parabasis, where it "strip[s]," refers to its own "anapests," and sings the praises of "our producer" (Aristophanes) who "took charge of the comic choruses": the Chorus emphatically identifies itself there as a chorus of actors (626–58; also 1150–72).[17] Who, then, is really in the know? Is it the great many in the audience who are "the spectators," or is it the few in the Chorus? Aristophanes may call directly on "the spectators," in this and in other plays, but the group so designated always proves to be a composite made up of disparate parts, the "clever" and the dull, the "wise" and the nonwise, or the "prudent" and the imprudent.[18] In the course of the *Acharnians*, the Chorus, addressing itself to the "city entire," will call Dicaeopolis a "prudent man, super-wise" (971).

In any event, once equipped with almost all the accoutrements he seeks from Euripides, Dicaeopolis steels his spirit and his heart (480, 483, 485) for the challenge ahead, and, true to the division he has just spoken of, Dicaeopolis addresses himself first to the spectators (496–508), then to the Chorus (509–56). To the former he has recourse to his new disguise, by calling himself a beggar, which suggests that that disguise is indeed not intended solely for the Chorus. And beggar though he may be, he will nonetheless speak to the Athenian audience about Athens in the course of making or writing his "trygedy"—the Aristophanic coinage for "comedy." This course of action Aristophanes-Dicaeopolis defends on the

---

17. Keith Sidwell raises the possibility that the "I" of the Chorus at 299–302 is referring, not, for example, to Aristophanes himself or to his next play, the *Knights,* but rather to "its past self as a chorus of Cratinus or Eupolis," that is, to itself qua chorus of actors; Sidwell, "Review of S. Douglas Olson, *Acharnians,*" *Classical Review* 54:1 (2004): 42.

18. Compare, for example, the distinction between "O spectators" and "the wise," on the one hand, with "O wisest spectators," on the other: *Clouds* 518–26 and 575; *Knights* 228 ("whoever is clever among the spectators") and 233 ("the audience is clever"); and *Assembly of Women* 1155–56 ("the wise" in the audience as distinguished from "the laughers").

grounds of justice: "For when it comes to what's just, comedy [trygedy] too knows it. / And I'll say things terribly clever, but just. / For now Cleon won't slander me . . . " (500–502). We might say, then, that Aristophanes the "trygedian" is as little a beggar as he is Dicaeopolis the farmer, but he most certainly is a teacher, and defender, of justice or the just cause. Now as Euripides knows well, some in the audience may be moved above all by the sight of "beggars" or by those who, not so very dissimilar to themselves, suffer unjustly and hence pitiably. But others may be rather more moved by the defense of justice or by the depiction of a kind of moral uprightness, especially if that defense is presented as coming at some real cost to the defender himself (377–82). Such moral uprightness is both pleasing to behold "in the opinion of the multitude" (consider 317) and compatible, as pity is not, with the pleasures specific to comedy: comedic cleverness and the defense of justice can go together not least in the merciless mockery of injustice. But this does not go far enough. For in the parabasis the Chorus will include among its high praises of Aristophanes the claim that he will "make a comedy of the just things" (655). Aristophanes mocks not only injustice or the unjust case, then, but justice or the just cause too; it is in part for this reason that Aristophanes' comedy has been called "the total comedy."[19] Not only do Cleon and Theorus come in for comedic skewering, then, but so do such democratically elected luminaries as Lamachus and Pericles—to say nothing of our hero and Aristophanes' doppelgänger: Dicaeopolis is a laughing and laugh-provoking hero. Above all, Aristophanes

19. Leo Strauss, "The Problem of Socrates," in *The Rebirth of Classical Political Rationalism,* ed. Thomas L. Pangle (Chicago: University of Chicago Press, 1989), 109–11 and 117, as well as Strauss, *Socrates and Aristophanes,* 312.

ridicules the unjust war, of course, but the just peace of Dicaeopolis proves to be more laughable still. We are entitled to wonder, then, whether even Aristophanes' portrait of himself as a teacher of justice is something of a disguise or whether the core of Aristophanes transcends even his concern for justice. Certainly he takes the greatest pride in the fact (of which he must inform many in his audience) that the play on which he labored most is distinguished by its superlative wisdom (*Clouds* 518–26). This much is clear: Aristophanes is a surprisingly elusive character, playing peekaboo behind the mask of an old farmer, and a beggar, and a teacher of justice who teaches us by lampooning everyone and everything— even justice.

Dicaeopolis turns next to address the Chorus as a chorus of elderly Acharnians once again. (It hardly needs to be said that the audience too hears Dicaeopolis's remarks.) His lengthy argument unfolds in stages. He first "identifies" with the Acharnians: "I hate the Lacedaemonians intensely" (509).[20] May Poseidon bring down upon them a devastating earthquake![21] Long gone now is his appeal to their being the victims of (Athenian) injustice. Moreover, Dicaeopolis's hatred stems from the fact that, just like the Acharnians, he too has had his vines cut or trampled by the marauding Spartans (compare 512 with 232). In short, Dicaeopolis feels the Acharnians' pain. (Being possessed of "vines" and hence land, Dicaeopolis can be no beggar.) Only now does he dare return to the question of the culpability for the war, and he proceeds to give an

---

20. For a comparable rhetorical move, consider *Thesmophoriazusae* 466–70 and context.

21. See Thucydides 1.101 for mention of a devastating earthquake that befell Sparta and its environs.

account of the origin of it that stresses the responsibility of "some"—but only some—of "our" men: "I don't say the city, / Remember this, that I'm not saying the city" (515-16). Athens, then, is simply beyond reproach in the matter, as distinguished from a handful of rogues within it. This is less unpalatable to the Acharnians than was Dicaeopolis's earlier treatment of the question inasmuch as the Acharnians have to this point understood themselves to be speaking in the name of precisely "the city" (205, 492) or "the fatherland" (290); to criticize some within the city for the sake of the city is simply a patriotic duty. As for Dicaeopolis's account of the war's cause, it contains at its noncomic core the contention that Pericles' blockade of neighboring Megara, at once unnecessary and cruel, is largely responsible for the conflict (consider also *Peace* 603-15). The seriousness of that cause is confirmed later on, according to the logic of the comedian, by the long and wildly obscene episode involving a starving Megarian father attempting to sell his two starving daughters disguised as "piglets."[22] The outrageousness of the scene goes together with, in fact it permits, what amounts to a very tough criticism of the Megarian decree and hence of Pericles, *the* revered leader of the demos.[23] In refusing to pay any heed to the Lacedaemonians' repeated requests to reverse that blockade, Dicaeopolis points out, "we" (538) made inevitable "the crashing of shields": the Lacedaemonians only came to the assistance of a harassed ally. Dicaeopolis thus implies, if he does not quite say, that the city of Athens is largely culpable for the war. After all, what would "we" Athenians have done if some Spartan had confiscated

---

22. *Acharnians* 729-835; see nn. 88 and 125 to the translation of the *Acharnians*.

23. Thucydides 1.139 and 2.65.

so much as a puppy belonging to one of *our* subject cities, however small? Aristophanes' answer is clear in his vivid and in its way beautiful description of the city exploding into activity in preparation for naval warfare (544–56).

The core of Dicaeopolis's criticism of the war is, to repeat, a criticism of Pericles. And this brings to light a crucial division within the heretofore united Chorus. For it turns out that "the Acharnians" include in their ranks members of the demos, the poor, who as such are much devoted to Pericles, as well as the upper class or classes, who as such are not devoted to Pericles.[24] In fact these latter now declare, in opposition to their fellow demesmen, that "all that he [Dicaeopolis] says / Is just, and in none of it does he lie" (560–61). So deep now is the previously latent division within the Chorus that they begin to wrestle one another, which prompts what we may call the democratic half of the Chorus to cry out for the assistance of Lamachus, a democratically elected (597) general. They do so in part on the grounds that Dicaeopolis, in criticizing a few within the city—some sycophants among the demos in addition to "Olympian" Pericles[25]—"for a long time now has been reviling our entire city" (577): in speaking up for Pericles and the demos, the half-Chorus thinks it is speaking up for Athens entire. Soon, it is true, the Chorus, speaking once again as a united chorus because it has been won over to Dicaeopolis's side, will *blame* precisely "the city" (676). But by that point the Chorus has been taught that it has interests separate from and even in some tension

---

24. Consider in this regard the Chorus's later defense (702–17) of the elderly Thucydides, the aristocratic opponent of Pericles, which defense is probably made possible by the fact that the members of the now-united Chorus remember less their political division than their shared decrepitude.

25. Consider 519 and context, 540–42, and 559.

with those of "the city," or it has been taught that "the city" is in fact a conglomeration of disparate factions, among them rich and poor and, of great import to the Chorus, old and young (for the latter, see 676–717).

But before any of that can happen, Dicaeopolis must bring over to his side the still-hostile part of the Chorus. This he does by lampooning at length the very man on whom the democratic or at any rate pro-Periclean half-Chorus depends, Lamachus. Soon shedding his persona of a beggar (compare 577–79 with 593), Dicaeopolis contends that he is simply a decent citizen, "not-serious-about-office-seeking," an ordinary foot soldier, in sharp contrast to Lamachus himself, "an officer-for-pay-and-hire" (*mistharchides:* 597). Dicaeopolis thus appeals to the distinction in the army between ordinary grunts, on the one hand, and "the brass," on the other.[26] Moreover, it is the old men of modest means who grind it out in the trenches and on the front lines while the younger and fancified rich, men like Lamachus, earn their pay far from the fighting or on cushy ambassadorial postings in exotic locales like Ecbatana.[27] Not so the more modest among the Acharnians! Hence Dicaeopolis brings home to them that they are fighting less for "the fatherland" and more for, or in the place of, the brass, the higher-ups, back home. This argument, together with the withering ridicule to which Lamachus is here subjected, proves sufficient to bring the demotic or democratic half-chorus around to Dicaeopolis: "The man is victorious with his arguments and persuades the demos / About the treaty" (626–27).

---

26. On the division within the Chorus (and the army) and Dicaeopolis's strategy to exploit it, see Strauss, *Socrates and Aristophanes,* 66–67.

27. Line 613 and context; recall the mention of Ecbatana at 64.

As his last words before the parabasis make clear, Dicaeopolis plans to use his new peace to set up a marketplace of his own, one open to quite all the Peloponnesians, Megarians, and Boeotians—Athenian enemies every one—but not to Lamachus (623–25). This use is surprising given Dicaeopolis's early statements of his loathing for the town, with its cries to buy charcoal, vinegar, or oil, and given his longing for the country, which used to bring forth all things bounteously without such busy commerce (32–36). Perhaps Dicaeopolis's forced stay in the city has opened his eyes to new opportunities; at any rate, he in effect brings the city's marketplace with him to the countryside. But this is as much as to say that Dicaeopolis will soon turn to the business of profiting from his peace—and hence from everyone else's war. Here we note that Dicaeopolis's initial case for peace, stated in soliloquy, failed to mention the injustice of making the elderly fight on the front lines or the unfair burden some are made to bear in the war's conduct: those arguments, to repeat, served the purpose of bringing over the rest of the Chorus to Dicaeopolis's side (compare 32–39 with 595–614, especially 599). The core of Dicaeopolis's opposition to the war, like the peace he now enjoys, seems altogether private-spirited.

In the first two marketplace transactions, at the beginning of the play's second part, Dicaeopolis certainly gets the better of the deals, not to say that he takes his sellers to the cleaners. The impoverished Megarian father sells his daughters for seasoned salt and some garlic (813–14), which were abundant in Megara before the war (759–63); and a Theban merchant gets for his rich array of goods (Copaic eels!) an irksome but useful Athenian sycophant, whom Dicaeopolis is only too glad to be rid of in any case (860–958). The appearances of a Megarian and then a Boeotian (Theban) lead us to expect that a Peloponnesian, perhaps even a Spartan, will appear next (recall 623-24). But evidently to portray Dicaeopolis's profitable dealings with *the* enemy would have been a step too far even for Aristophanes—if not for the Chorus, which is now entirely anti-war (977-85), then for the audience in the theater. There are instead brief appearances by Lamachus's messenger and a herald, the latter come to announce the festival of the Pitchers. These characters serve to set up both the climactic battle, so to speak, between Lamachus and Dicaeopolis (1069-1142) and Dicaeopolis's victory celebration in the wake of the festival, which is at the same time Lamachus's sorry decline or defeat (1174-end). That defeat includes not (as Lamachus pompously claims) wounds suffered at the hands of the enemy, which would cast him in too heroic a light, but a sprained ankle and other minor indignities incurred while crossing an irrigation ditch (compare 1174-80 with 1190-94 and 1226).[28]

A pathetic Athenian farmer now appears (1018-36). The farmer has lost his only pair of oxen to marauding Boeotians—Dicaeopolis's just-completed happy transaction with a Boeotian seems all the more questionable—and having ruined his eyes from crying over them, he seeks not to trade with his fellow farmer but to have him share a single drop of the peace-libation. This Dicaeopolis flatly refuses: he is no public servant! Dicaeopolis's distance from the city or his indifference to his fellow citizens could hardly be greater, and

---

28. Because Lamachus is said to receive his marching orders from "the generals" in Athens (1073-78), Sommerstein (*Acharnians* ad loc.) raises the possibility that Lamachus's initial claim to be one of them (593) may be in anticipation of his election to that office that has not yet occurred, even if it soon will. If this is so—and Thucydides does not mention Lamachus until the summer of 425 (4.75) and hence after the Lenaea—it would add considerably to Lamachus's boastfulness.

the comment of the Chorus here is surely not to be taken as praise: "The man has discovered / In the treaty something pleasant, and / It seems he'll share it with no one" (1037–39). Or, as the Chorus had just noted, Dicaeopolis "serves *himself*" a fine meal (1015–16, emphasis added; consider also 969): even the Chorus gets none of the delicacies he is so zestfully preparing. Hence Antimachus ("Against Battle") is not the only writer-poet who denies the Chorus a dinner at the Lenaea (1150–72). The selfishness of Dicaeopolis that is becoming ever more apparent as the play proceeds must be qualified somewhat, it is true, by the immediate sequel. For there Dicaeopolis does share with a newlywed bride one ladleful of the peace-libation. This he agrees to do, not in exchange for the proffered meat from the wedding feast nor even for one thousand drachmas, but so that the bride might linger in the matrimonial bed with her groom, who would, with the proper application of the peace-libation, be at peace and hence relieved of all military duty that would take him from his bride's side. Dicaeopolis has a certain empathy or compassion, then, but it is elicited by the altogether private or erotic sufferings of young lovers.

Lamachus's earlier request to purchase thrushes from Dicaeopolis "for the Pitchers festival," together with an eel, makes plain that the great general thought that he, too, would be celebrating (959–68). He and we now learn of his assignment "to watch over the points of entry as it snows," for it has been reported that "bandits"—from Boeotia—"will invade" (1073–77). Aristophanes then juxtaposes Lamachus, as he somberly prepares for battle, with Dicaeopolis as he joyously prepares for his feast and drinking competition. Each readies himself for his respective contest, the one the preserve of war and the warrior, the other of peace and the individual at peace. Could the burdens of the one and the delights of the other be made more manifest than this? The Chorus sums up the matter well:

> How dissimilar the paths you two are taking!
> Drinking for the one, bedecked with a wreath,
> But for you, freezing and standing on guard!
> For him, going to bed
> With a young maiden in her bloom
> Getting his you-know-what rubbed! (1144–49)

Here we might note that Dicaeopolis becomes not only more selfish, or self-sufficient, as the play proceeds, but also less and less a married man; the fact of his married status is quietly forgotten by the play's end (1198 and following). As the curtain descends, so to speak, the sound of the Chorus's final song rings out: "Hurray Noble Victor!"

. . .

We may now return to what we called the obvious message of the *Acharnians:* the Athenians should negotiate an end to the Peloponnesian War because peace is much preferable to war. That message may have appeared to be less obvious or anodyne or even insipid to Aristophanes' audience than it may seem to us, for the simple reason that one was much more likely then than now to hear praise of war and of the qualities of body and soul needed to be a great warrior—an Achilles. Still, we have to concede that the obvious message of the play, so stated, is hardly arresting. And if we look for concrete advice from the play, we see at most that Aristophanes counsels rescinding the Megarian decree, apart of course from the general advice to be rid of demagogues like Cleon.[29] Yet, as Aristophanes himself shows, some Athenians are profiting from that blockade and so would be at least reluctant to give it up (515–22). In any case, now that the conflagration is roaring, will extinguishing the match that lit it do much good? Aristophanes also indicates that many Athenians in positions of power are profiting from the war in other ways, generals, demagogues, and ambassadors among them. What may be more, Aristophanes reports the King of Persia as thinking that Athens with its superior navy (and world-class comic poet) is in fact likely to win the war (647–52). Even if peace is to be preferred to war in general, spurning the war at a time when it seems to promise victory would be foolish.[30] To put all of this in the terms of the play, Dicaeopolis's solution to the problem that is the war belongs in a comedy: it is manifestly impossible. The war goes on.

The puzzle of the import of the play is surely bound up with Dicaeopolis's "clever deed, and great," as he calls it (128 and context). What really is the purpose of his private peace? First impressions aside, Dicaeopolis does not in fact simply retire to the country, there to enjoy family life and the worship of Dionysus. In fact he opens a market and so profits from his peace. As we have noted, Dicaeopolis becomes more and more selfish, or less and less a family man, never mind a citizen, as the play proceeds; the two young

29. The *Acharnians* "offers very little in the way of concrete policy proposals" (Olson, xlix).

30. Consider Strauss, *Socrates and Aristophanes*, 69. Olson (xlix) notes "what appears to be a suggestion in the parabasis that a recent Spartan offer . . . to make peace if the Athenians would restore the Aiginetans . . . be rejected (652–5)."

women who accompany him at the play's end do not include his wife. He prepares an elaborate meal and eats it himself; he chugs down wine at a peerless pace; our last image of him is as he leaves the stage, off to enjoy matrimonial pleasures without benefit of matrimony. Are we to think, then, that Aristophanes means to praise the largely (though not entirely) solitary pleasures, the hedonism, of Dicaeopolis? Are we to think that according to Aristophanes the proper response to public upheaval is a withdrawal into an entirely private revelry?

That there are reminders here of the pleasures that peace makes possible is beyond dispute. But Aristophanes has something more in mind than making the case for a self-seeking hedonism. We have seen repeatedly that Dicaeopolis the farmer is also Aristophanes in costume, but we have so far ignored the still more obvious fact, which has been staring us in the face all along, that the name Dicaeopolis means "Just City."[31] Dicaeopolis also is or imitates a just city. Is it not the obligation of all cities and especially of just cities to be concerned with the common good, the good of all citizens, including the citizens' bodily security in the face of external threats; the provision of the necessities of mere life; and, beyond these, their material comfort or prosperity? Is it not the obligation of all cities but especially of just cities to be concerned with securing to the extent possible the good life for each and for all within their respective borders? Moreover, what is disconcerting or shocking in

---

31. So also, e.g., Lowell Edmunds, "Aristophanes' *Acharnians*," in *Aristophanes: Essays in Interpretation*, ed. Jeffrey Henderson (Cambridge: Cambridge University Press, 1980), 1 and n. 2; Henderson, *Acharnians*, 11; and Paul Ludwig, "A Portrait of the Artist in Politics: Justice and Self-Interest in Aristophanes' *Acharnians*," *American Political Science Review* 101:3 (2007): 479.

the actions of a lone individual becomes much less so in the case of an entire city or—making allowances for comic exaggeration—it becomes entirely respectable. The just city seeks stable peace when it can, for the benefit of its own citizens above all; it must make available, through markets and the force needed to secure them (consider 724–25 and 824–25), not only the necessities but also such delicacies as may bring a measure of delight to life. The just city makes a place for and helps protect the family—husband and wife and children (132, 889–91)—together with the worship of the gods. In other words, Dicaeopolis the remarkably selfish individual can also be understood as acting in the way that all individual cities, even or precisely all just cities, ought to act.

It is because Athens and Sparta wish to be just cities and understand themselves to be just that they have gone to war in the first place. Whatever else they may seek in and through the war, they seek to right a perceived wrong, an injustice (consider 230–32 and 514–56). And Dicaeopolis's actions, amusing as they are, do not render us hopeful that war will ever cease, even if all particular wars end eventually. For the clash of competing understandings of what justice demands, and the pursuit of "national interests" in a world of relatively scarce goods, together make conflict inevitable.

One might well object here that, however much "Dicaeopolis" points us in a political direction, Aristophanes nonetheless also chose to present himself as a zanily pleasure-loving old farmer who is not an exemplary citizen or husband (or father). When we first glimpse the man, we remember, he is alone; when we last see him, he is no longer alone, but neither is he returning to hearth and home. How are we finally to understand this guise?

Aristophanes' initial claim to fame in the *Acharnians* is that his comedies say things both terrifically clever and just (497–501). In particular, Aristophanes to a distinguished degree can speak of— that is, criticize—"the city" while making a comedy of it or because he makes a comedy of it (499). Aristophanes ventures to do the very thing, then, that his Dicaeopolis had at one point denied doing: castigating, not some faction within the city, but the city as such, "our city" (recall 515-16 in the light of 498-99 and 631). When in the parabasis the Acharnians return to Aristophanes' "making a comedy of our city," they do not stress the just things he teaches, for it is here the Chorus tells us that he will "make a comedy" of precisely "the just things"; the Chorus stresses instead the good or advantageous things he brings about for the city. We could say, then, with Aristophanes, that he has both the just and the good on his side as allies (660-62). But his greater concern may be the good. For example, Aristophanes has helped inoculate the city against being "overly deceived by the speeches of foreigners," with their attempts at subtle flattery that Aristophanes renders laughable (634). So great a poet is he, in fact, that the cities of the empire are positively eager to come to Athens to pay their compulsory tax—so as "to see the poet who's best" (644)! We already had occasion to note the King of Persia's great admiration for Aristophanes; the King is also of the view that whichever city the poet lambastes more will be much better off for it. Aristophanes' comedy improves even as it stings. "He affirms that he'll teach you many good things, so you'll be happy, . . . / teaching the things that are best" (656 and 658). Aristophanes does what he can, then, to improve his city with the means singularly at his disposal.

Still, it is difficult to deny that, in donning the disguise of Dicaeopolis, Aristophanes would seem to endorse the way of life, and the pleasures, of his remarkable farmer. We are forced to grant the point: Aristophanes does extol the goodness and even the supremacy of a certain pleasure-filled private life. But in comparison to at least some of Dicaeopolis's pleasures, Aristophanes' own are more social or public and even public-spirited. For those pleasures surely include thinking up "the most novel conceits" (*Wasps* 1044) and the "subtle things" (445) in his plays and then displaying them, to public acclaim and even thunderous applause. A great play is not fully what it is without being performed, which means that its potential is realized before a large and diverse crowd, as diverse, perhaps, as democracy itself. To write and all the more to stage a play, at least when the playwright is as prominent as an Aristophanes, is a public act. Aristophanes takes countless liberties, of course, but he also takes seriously his public responsibilities as he understands them. Some lines he will not cross. There is a limited but nonetheless genuine common good between the intense private pleasures of Aristophanes, in the writing of his comedies and the display of the wisdom they contain, and the well-being of Athens; this is true even if Aristophanes obviously exaggerates the good he does or can do his city. He tries, at least, to make Athens better—less foolish in matters foreign and domestic, more immune to demagogic flattery and the manipulations of oracle mongers, less vindictive or "waspish." If only very modest political improvement can be expected from the laughter he provokes, if Aristophanes cannot by himself bring an end to the war, we cannot fault him for trying or indeed for failing, just as Dicaeopolis had tried at the beginning of the play, with admittedly sorry results, to effect political improvement. Peace, then, is indeed to be preferred to war, but ultimately because it makes possible the enjoyment of essentially private pleasures. The pleasures enjoyed or anticipated by Dicaeopolis at the end of the play are a comic representation and hence in large part a distortion of Aristophanes' genuine pleasures. In the case of Aristophanes, those pleasures go together with a benevolent and even beneficent concern for Athens and a genuine respect for its needs as a city, without which, of course, the poet would be without the audience he needs.

The *Knights*

Dramatis Personae

DEMOSTHENES, A SERVANT[1]

NICIAS, A SERVANT

PAPHLAGON [= CLEON][2]

AGORACRITUS, A SAUSAGE-SELLER

CHORUS OF KNIGHTS[3]

DEMOS[4]

---

1. Against the text of the Budé, but with the OCT and Sommerstein, *Knights,* I follow the principal MSS in reading here the names of Demosthenes and Nicias, rather than Servant A and Servant B. Dindorf contends that the proper names were written, not by the poet, but by later scribes and inferred from the text; Wilhelm Dindorf, *Aristophanis Comoediae* (Oxford: Oxford University Press, 1837), 291. At all events, the identity of the "servants" is not controversial.

2. The principal MSS here identify Paphlagon as Cleon, although he is almost always referred to as Paphlagon, not Cleon, in the text of the play (the exception is 976). Cleon, whom Aristophanes presents as a dangerous demagogue, was active in Athenian democratic politics from about 429 to 422 B.C.E., when he was killed while fighting to recapture Amphipolis from Spartan control.

3. The Athenian Knights or cavalry, here said to be one thousand strong (225), were drawn from the wealthy upper middle class, since they were responsible for the cost of supplying and outfitting their horses.

4. Here personified as a single householder ("Mr. Demos"), *demos* refers to a political class in Athens, that of the great majority of citizens who as such were poor and hence largely uneducated. "Democracy" is of course the rule of the demos, of the poor majority.

The *Knights*

[Outside the house of Demos on the Pnyx, in Athens]

DEMOSTHENES[1]
[Running out of the house]
Yyy-ouououououououououch! What evils! Yyy-ouououououch!
If only the gods would evilly destroy that evil, newly purchased
    Paphlagon,[2]
Him and his schemes!
For from the time he entered the household
He's been inflicting blows on the servants nonstop!   5

NICIAS[3]
Very evilly indeed, that guy, first among Paphlagonians,
Him and his slanders!

DEMOSTHENES
[To Nicias] Wretched fellow, how're you doing?

---

1. Demosthenes (d. 413 B.C.E.) was among Athens' most distinguished generals, notable for his ingenuity, ability to learn from mistakes, and military tactics. He died in the course of Athens' attempt to conquer the island of Sicily.

2. The name seems to be chosen, not to suggest a connection to the people of Paphlagonia, on the Black Sea coast of north-central Anatolia, but rather to bring to mind the verb *paphladzō,* "to boil, bluster, splutter." Consider 919-20 below as well as *Peace* 313-14, where the word is used to describe Cleon.

3. Nicias (ca. 470-413 B.C.E.) was an outstanding Athenian general, older and more cautious than his contemporary Demosthenes. Both generals died in battle on the island of Sicily.

NICIAS

Badly, just like you!

DEMOSTHENES

Well, come over here then, so
We may wail a song of Olympus[4] in concert.

DEMOSTHENES AND NICIAS

10 "Mumu mumu mumu mumu mumu mumu!"

DEMOSTHENES

Why are we uttering this plaintive lament? Shouldn't we seek out some
Salvation for the two of us, rather than keep on crying?

NICIAS

So what might it be?

DEMOSTHENES

You say.

NICIAS

Now *you* tell *me,*
So I don't have to fight.

DEMOSTHENES

By Apollo, not I!
15 But be bold and say it, then I'll tell you.

---

4. Reputed to have been the founder of Greek flute (*aulos*) music, to whom many famous tunes were attributed.

NICIAS

"Would that you might say for me, what it is I ought to say."[5]
But there's no boldness in me. However might
I say it, then, in a subtle-Euripidean way?

DEMOSTHENES

Don't do that to me, not to me, don't chervil[6] me over!
Just discover some slinky-sly dance to get away from the   20
    master!

NICIAS

So say "lettuce . . . height . . . ale . . .," putting it together
    like this.

DEMOSTHENES

Okay: I say "lettuce-height-ale."

NICIAS

Now after that, say "auto hear."

DEMOSTHENES

"Auto hear!"

NICIAS

Beautifully done!
Now, just as if you're wanking, say it gently at first:
"Lettuce-height-ale," then "auto hear," and then bring it on   25
    faster.

---

5. Euripides, *Hippolytus* 345. Some editors move this two lines down, so as
to exemplify the "subtle-Euripidean way."

6. Aristophanes likes to imply that Euripides' mother was a humble seller
of herbs, which she surely was not; see *Acharnians* 457 and 478.

DEMOSTHENES

[*Speaking ever more quickly*] "Lettuce-height-ale-auto-hear,
     lettuce-height-ale . . . let us hightail it outta here!"[7]

NICIAS

Wasn't that sweet?!

DEMOSTHENES

Yes, by Zeus! Except, that is, when it comes to my skin—
I'm afraid about this omen.

NICIAS

Why so?

DEMOSTHENES

Because the skin of wankers comes off![8]

NICIAS

30   Well then, the most excellent thing, given what's available to us
          two,
     Is to go and prostrate ourselves before images of the gods.

DEMOSTHENES

What "images"?!? Come on now, do you really believe in gods?

NICIAS

I do indeed!

DEMOSTHENES

Using what sort of evidence?

---

7. That is, "let's desert," presumably from Athens to Sparta.

8. Demosthenes in effect expresses concern for being flayed as punishment for being a runaway slave.

NICIAS

That I'm hated by the gods! Isn't that likely enough?

DEMOSTHENES

You're doing a good job of convincing me! But let's examine it by   35
looking in another direction.
Do you want me to explain the matter to the audience?

NICIAS

Not a bad idea. But let's ask them for one thing:
To make it plain to us by their facial expressions
If they're delighting in our words and affairs.[9]

DEMOSTHENES

So now I'd like to speak. The master of the two of us   40
Is a rustic by temperament, a bean-chewer, quick to anger—
Demos of the Pnyx,[10] a disagreeable little geezer,
Half-deaf. On the previous New Moon day[11] he
Bought a slave, a leatherworker, Paphlagon,
Someone exceedingly crooked and slanderous.   45
This fellow, the leather-Paphlagonian, recognizing the old man's
ways,
Fawned over the master,
And started wheedling, toadying, flattering, utterly deceiving
him
With the odd leather scraps, saying such things as these:
"O Demos, have your bath, once you've first tried a single case.   50

---

9. Or "troubles" (*pragmata*).
10. The location of the Athenian Assembly.
11. That is, market day (see also *Acharnians* 999).

Open up, swallow it down, have dessert, take three obols.[12]
Do you want me to serve your evening meal?" And then
   snatching up
Whatever one of us is preparing for the master,
Paphlagon gladly gives it to him. And the other day, I
55 Was kneading a Laconian barley-cake at Pylos,[13]
How very much like the dirtiest crook did he run around me and
   snatch it up,
And he himself served the cake *I'd* kneaded!
Us he drives away and doesn't allow anyone else
To tend to the master, but holding a leather flyswatter,
60 While [Demos] is eating, he stands by and scares off . . . the
   orators.
And he chants oracles: the old man longs for Sibyls![14]
And because he sees how stupid [the old man] is,
He's come up with a technical art: those within [the household]
He falsely slanders outright. And then we're flogged!
65 But Paphlagon, running around after the servants,
Makes his demands, stirs up trouble, takes bribes, saying these
   things:
"Do you see Hylas being flogged on my say-so?
If you won't obey me, you'll die this very day!"
And we pay up. If we don't, then while being beaten

---

12. Cleon had raised from two obols to three the pay for serving on the
juries, according to the scholium on *Wasps* 88; see also 255 below.

13. Demosthenes here alludes to his capture of Spartan soldiers on the
island of Sphacteria, just off the coast of Pylos. Cleon managed to claim credit
for the military feat, although Thucydides makes clear that the operation was
Demosthenes' own.

14. Ecstatic prophetesses.

By the old man we crap out eight times as much! 70
So now let's think this through and be quick about it, good fellow,
As to what sort of path we two ought to turn to, and to whom.

NICIAS

The most excellent thing would be that "let's hightail it," good
fellow.

DEMOSTHENES

But it's impossible for anything to escape Paphlagon's notice,
Since he himself watches over everything. For he has one leg 75
In Pylos, the other in the Assembly.
So wide is the step he's taken
That his butthole is right in Gapesville,[15]
Both hands are in Shakedown-town, and his mind is among the
Kleptos![16]

NICIAS

Then the most excellent thing for us both would be to die!

DEMOSTHENES

Just consider 80
How we might die most courageously.

NICIAS

How indeed, how might it come to pass most courageously?

_____

15. Literally, "among the Chaonians," the first syllable of the name suggesting also "gaping" (_chaos_).

16. The name of the first (_Aitōlois_, "among the Aetolians") suggests the
verb _aitein_, which can mean "to demand something from someone"; and the
name of the second (_Klōpidōn_), "a small Attic hamlet" (Sommerstein, _Knights_
ad loc.), puns on _klōps_, meaning "thief."

Best for us is to drink bull's blood.[17]

For Themistocles' death is preferable.[18]

DEMOSTHENES

85   No, by Zeus, but [let's drink] unmixed wine of the Good
     Divinity![19]

For we might perhaps deliberate about something useful!

NICIAS

"Unmixed wine," come on! With you it's always about drinking!

How could a man deliberate about something useful when he's
     drunk?!?

DEMOSTHENES

Is that right?! You're a babbling-fountain-of-nonsense!

90   You dare reproach wine when it comes to thinking?

Could you discover something more practically useful than
     wine?

You see, whenever human beings drink, then

They are wealthy, get things done, win lawsuits,

---

17. A near quotation of a fragment of Sophocles. It was believed that drinking bull's blood brought about quick death; consider Herodotus, *Histories* 3.15.

18. In other words, death by suicide. Themistocles was the principal architect of Athenian naval supremacy and an extraordinarily capable leader of Athens. He was exiled, however, and eventually made his way to a place of prominence in the Persian court. There, Thucydides reports, Themistocles died a natural death—but it was popularly believed that he committed suicide by drinking a potion or poison (Thucydides, *Peloponnesian War* 1.138).

19. Or "good daemon." "The first libation at wine-drinking in general and in the Dionysos sanctuary in particular" was made in honor of the "Good Divinity" or daemon (*agathou daimonos*); Walter Burkert, *Greek Religion* (Cambridge, MA: Harvard University Press, 1985), 180.

Are happy, benefit friends.
But, quick, bring out a pitcher of wine for me,   95
So I may water my mind and say something clever!

NICIAS

Ah, what will you with your drinking do to us?

DEMOSTHENES

Good fellow, just bring it. And I'll put my feet up. [*Exit Nicias*]
For if I get drunk, I'm going to besprinkle all these things
    here
With deliberations and little judgments and insights!   100

[*Nicias returns*]

NICIAS

How lucky I didn't get caught inside,
Stealing the wine!

DEMOSTHENES

Tell me, what's Paphlagon doing?

NICIAS

The malicious sorcerer's been licking up cake-and-sauce that's
    been publicly confiscated
And he's snoring away, drunk and snoozing among his leather
    hides.

DEMOSTHENES

Come now, pour a large portion of unmixed libation for me!   105

NICIAS

So take it and make offering to the Good Divinity.

DEMOSTHENES

Quaff, quaff down the wine of the Pramnian[20] divinity!
  [*Demosthenes chugs down the wine*]
O Good Divinity, it's your plan, not mine!

NICIAS

Say—I beseech you!—what is it?

DEMOSTHENES

Quickly steal the oracles
110 Belonging to Paphlagon and bring them here from inside,
While he sleeps.

NICIAS

So be it. But of the divinity
I'm afraid, lest I become wretchedly unhappy![21] [*Nicias goes back
  into the house*]

DEMOSTHENES

Well now, let me get the pitcher for myself
So that I may water my mind and say something clever.

[*Nicias returns*]

NICIAS

115 How loudly Paphlagon farts and snores!
As a result, he didn't notice when I got the sacred oracle
That he was guarding especially closely.

---

20. Pramnian wine was noted for its excellence.

21. The word translated as "wretchedly unhappy" (*kakodaimonos*) means
more literally, "having a bad daemon"; Nicias is afraid that, by stealing oracles,
he will offend the Good Divinity (see n. 19 above) and so be made unhappy, i.e.,
be possessed of a bad daemon.

DEMOSTHENES

O Wisest One!
Bring it here, so I can read it. But hurry up and
Pour me a drink! Come, let me see, what's in it? [*Reads the oracle*]
O Prophecies! [*Points to the cup*] Give it to me, give me the little   120
  cup quick!

NICIAS

There. Now what does the oracle assert?

DEMOSTHENES

Pour me another.

NICIAS

"Pour me another" is in the prophecies?!?

DEMOSTHENES

O Bacis![22]

NICIAS

What is it?

DEMOSTHENES

Give me the little cup, quick!

NICIAS

Bacis sure used the little cup a lot!

DEMOSTHENES

Bloody Paphlagon! You've been guarding these things for a long   125
  time,
Because you dread the oracle pertaining to yourself!

---

22. The name of a prophet in Eleon, in Boeotian territory. His prophecies
seem to have been popular in the course of the Peloponnesian War.

NICIAS

Why?!?

DEMOSTHENES

In here it says that he himself is destroyed!

NICIAS

And how?

DEMOSTHENES

How, you ask? The oracle expressly says
That first there comes to be a dealer of oakum,
130   Who will first take hold of the city's affairs.²³

NICIAS

That's one seller.²⁴ What's next? Say it!

DEMOSTHENES

After him, in turn, is, second, a sheep dealer.²⁵

NICIAS

That's two sellers. And what must happen to *him?*

DEMOSTHENES

He must hold power, until another man, more loathsome
135   Than he is, arises. After this, he's destroyed.

---

23. This is taken to be a reference to Eucrates, a little-known Athenian politician; see also 254 below.

24. Sellers, or men engaged in commerce generally, were looked down on as low-class, at least by aristocrats.

25. The scholiast reports the view that this is Lysicles, who is mentioned explicitly below at 765. He is said to have lived with Pericles' mistress, Aspasia, after Pericles' death.

For Paphlagon the leather-seller succeeds him,
A robber, shrieker, with the voice of the Cycloborus [River].[26]

NICIAS

So the sheep dealer had to be destroyed
At the hands of a leather-seller?

DEMOSTHENES

Yes, by Zeus!

NICIAS

Ah, wretched me!
So from where, then, might one more seller come into being?   140

DEMOSTHENES

There is still one more, possessed of an extraordinary art!

NICIAS

Say—I beseech you!—who is it?!?

DEMOSTHENES

Am I to say?

NICIAS

Yes, by Zeus!

DEMOSTHENES

He who utterly destroys [Paphlagon] is . . . a sausage-seller!

NICIAS

A sausage-seller?!? O Poseidon, what an art!
Come, where will we find this man?   145

26. A raging river known for the sound produced by its torrent; see also
Acharnians 381.

DEMOSTHENES

Let's seek him out.

NICIAS[27]

But here's one coming over
Into the marketplace, as if divinely!

DEMOSTHENES

O Blessed
Sausage-Seller, here, here, dearest fellow,
Walk over, you're a savior made manifest, to the city and to the
two of us!

SAUSAGE-SELLER

What is it? Why are you calling me?

DEMOSTHENES

150 Come here, so you may learn
How fortunate you are and happy in a big way!

NICIAS

[*To Demosthenes*] Just take this table from him and
Inform him of what the god's oracle contains.
I'll go and keep a watchful eye on the Paphlagonian.

[*Nicias leaves*]

DEMOSTHENES

155 So now: first put your equipment on the ground.
Then make obeisance to the earth and the gods.

---

27. Some editions, including the Budé, give these lines to Demosthenes,
against the evidence of the majority of the MSS.

SAUSAGE-SELLER

There. What is it?

DEMOSTHENES

O blessed fellow, O wealthy,
O you who are nobody now, but super-big tomorrow!
O commander of the happy Athenians!

SAUSAGE-SELLER

Why, good fellow, don't you let me wash my tripe   160
And sell my sausages, rather than ridicule me?

DEMOSTHENES

You moron, "tripe" indeed! [*Pointing to the audience*] Look over
    here:
Do you see the rows of the people there?

SAUSAGE-SELLER

I see them.

DEMOSTHENES

You yourself will be the leader of *all* of them,
And of the marketplace and the harbors and the Pnyx.   165
You'll trample on the Council²⁸ and dress down generals!
You'll chain people up and lock 'em down, and in the Prytaneum
    you'll . . . get blow jobs!²⁹

---

28. The Athenian Council (*boulē* or *bouleutērion*) was a much smaller
elected body than the Assembly (*ekklēsia*) and charged with (among other
things) determining the matters that would be taken up by the Assembly.

29. A surprise substitution for "dine"; Athenians citizens who performed
some signal service to the city were given free meals for life in the Prytaneum.
Following the suggestion of Lowell Edmunds, I read the future middle form of

SAUSAGE-SELLER

Me?

DEMOSTHENES

Yes, you! And you don't even see everything yet!
Just get up here on this table
170 And look down on *all* the islands around!

SAUSAGE-SELLER

I see them down there.

DEMOSTHENES

What else? The ports and the merchantmen?

SAUSAGE-SELLER

I do indeed.

DEMOSTHENES

How then are you not happy in a big way?
And now cast your one eye toward Caria,
The right one, and the other one toward Carthage.[30]

SAUSAGE-SELLER

175 I'll be happy, if I twist myself cross-eyed?

DEMOSTHENES

No, but it's on account of you that all these things are for sale.

---

the verb (*laikasei*) found in one MS, as distinguished from the active form
found in most MSS; Edmunds, *Cleon, "Knights," and Aristophanes' Politics* (Lan-
ham, MD: University Press of America, 1987), 68. On the meaning and tone of
the word, see the translation of the *Acharnians*, n. 20.

30. Caria was in western Anatolia, well to the east of Athens; Carthage was
in North Africa.

For you're becoming—as this here oracle says—
A real man[31] of the very greatest sort!

SAUSAGE-SELLER
Tell me—how am I,
A sausage-seller, going to become a real man?

DEMOSTHENES
It's through this very thing, in fact, that you're becoming great—   180
Because you are low-class and of the marketplace and bold!

SAUSAGE-SELLER
I don't judge myself to deserve greatness!

DEMOSTHENES
Uh oh . . . Why in the world are you denying that you yourself are
    deserving?
You seem to me to be aware of having something noble about
    yourself . . .
Surely you're not descended from noble and good gentlemen, *are*
    you?!?

SAUSAGE-SELLER
By the gods no!   185
I'm from nothing except what's low-class!

DEMOSTHENES
[*With great relief*] O Blessed Luck!
So great is the good you've got, with a view to [political] affairs!

---

31. An *anēr,* a "real man," as distinguished from a mere "human being"
(*anthrōpos*).

SAUSAGE-SELLER

But, good fellow, I don't have any knowledge of the things of the
Muses,
Except for letters—and even this is really pretty bad.

DEMOSTHENES

190   This is the only thing that's hurt you—that it's even "really
pretty bad."
For demagoguery[32] no longer belongs to a man acquainted with
the things of the Muses or to one whose ways are upright,
But to one who is unlearned and loathsome. But don't
Cast aside the things the gods are giving you in the prophecies!

SAUSAGE-SELLER

How then does the oracle speak?

DEMOSTHENES

195   It speaks well, by the gods,
Posing riddles in a way that's somehow complex and wise!
"But when a crooked-clawed leather-eagle grasps
With its jaws a boneheaded blood-drinking serpent,
Then indeed the garlic-sauce of the Paphlagonians is destroyed,
200   But to tripe-sellers god grants great glory,
Unless they choose to sell sausages instead."

SAUSAGE-SELLER

So how do these things relate to me? Teach me.

DEMOSTHENES

This Paphlagon here is a "leather-eagle."

_____

32. That is, "the leading of the demos" (*dēmagōgia*); this is "the earliest
known use" of the term (Sommerstein, *Knights* ad loc.).

SAUSAGE-SELLER

But what's "crooked-clawed"?

DEMOSTHENES

Pretty much what it says:
That with crooked hands he snatches and takes away.   205

SAUSAGE-SELLER

And the "serpent" relates to what?

DEMOSTHENES

This is completely obvious!
For the serpent is long, and the sausage, in turn, is long.
Then "blood-drinking" is both the sausage and the serpent.
It contends, then, that the serpent will overpower the leather-eagle,
Unless he is softened by words.   210

SAUSAGE-SELLER

The prophecies flatter me. But I wonder how
I can govern the demos.

DEMOSTHENES

A very paltry task! Just do the things you do!
Stir up *all* the [political] affairs and turn them together into sausage,
And always win the demos over   215
By sweetening things with gourmet phraselets!
And the rest that's yours is demagogic too:
Brutal voice, bad lineage, marketplace made.
You have *everything* needed for political governance!
Oracles as well as the Pythia[33] concur!   220

33. That is, Apollo's priestess at Delphi.

But wreathe yourself and pour a libation to . . . Bonehead[34]
And see that you ward off[35] the man!

SAUSAGE-SELLER
And what ally
Will I have?
For the wealthy
Are afraid of him, and the crowd of the poor is petrified!

DEMOSTHENES
225 But there are knights—one thousand good men
Who hate him—they'll come to your aid,
And the noble and good gentlemen among the citizenry
And whoever is clever among the spectators.
And I, together with them, as well as the god, will assist!
230 And don't be afraid, for he isn't represented [onstage by a
      portrait-mask]:
Out of fear of him, no mask-maker was willing
To make a likeness of him! At all events
He'll be recognized, for the audience is clever.

NICIAS
[From within] Ah wretched me, Paphlagon is coming out!

PAPHLAGON
235 [Shouting loudly] No, by the Twelve Gods,[36] you two won't be
      rejoicing
'Cause for a long time now you've been conspiring against the
      demos!

---

34. A made-up divinity; see also 198, where the same word appears.
35. Or "defend yourself against."
36. That is, the twelve Olympian gods.

[*Notices Demosthenes' cup*] What's that Chalcidian wine-cup doing
here?!?

There's no way you two aren't inciting the Chalcidians to
revolt![37]

Perish! Die! Both you bloodiest bastards!

DEMOSTHENES

[*To the Sausage-Seller*] You there, why're you fleeing? Won't you   240
stay?!? O Well-Born

Sausage-Seller, don't forsake the affairs!

[*Turns to call offstage*] Men, Knights, draw near! Now is the crucial
moment! O Simon,

O Panaetius,[38] won't you drive toward the right side?

[*To the Sausage-Seller*] The men are near; just defend yourself—
pivot and charge!

The dust cloud is visible as they press hard together.   245

Just defend yourself and pursue him and put him to rout!

CHORUS OF KNIGHTS

Strike, strike the dirty crook and disturber-of-the-cavalry-corps

And tax farmer, and chasm and Charybdis[39] of thievery!

And a crook and a crook! I'll say that about him many times,

---

37. Chalcis was a city on the island of Euboea, under Athenian control
(consider *Clouds* 211–12) and important to Athens for its agriculture. To the dis-
pleasure of Athens, Sparta had recently founded a new colony, Heraclea, in
Trachis, which could facilitate invasion of the island and foment rebellion
against Athens; see Thucydides 3.92–93.

38. According to the scholiast, these are the names of two actual hipparchs
or cavalry commanders. A man named Simon wrote a treatise on horsemanship (see Xenophon, *On Horsemanship* 1.1).

39. Name of a deadly whirlpool in Homer.

250 Since he's been a dirty crook many times a day!
Just strike and pursue and stir and mix him up
And loathe him—for we do!—and, with a shout, attack!
But be careful lest he escape you, for he knows the routes
By which Eucrates[40] fled straight to the bran shops!

PAPHLAGON

255 O Elders of the Juries! Brethren of Three Obols[41]
Whom I feed by crying out both justly and unjustly!
Come to my aid: I'm being beaten up by conspiratorial men!

CHORUS

Justly so, since you gobble up the public funds before the lot has
given you [an office],
And, as if picking figs, you squeeze officials undergoing audit,
examining
260 Whoever among them is green or ripe or unripe.[42]
And if you know of anyone among them who refrains from
meddlesome-busyness and is all agape,
You lead him down from the Chersonese[43] and trip him up with
slander,
Then, twisting his shoulder around, you stomp on his gut!
And you examine who among the citizens is a sheep-like simpleton,

---

40. Eucrates was an Athenian politician who apparently dealt in oakum
and bran; see 129 above.

41. That is, the Athenian demos; on the three obols paid to jurors, see 51
above.

42. The Budé moves 264–65 so that they follow at this point in the text. I
follow the reading of the principal MSS.

43. This probably refers to Athenian merchants settled in what is today the
Gallipoli peninsula.

Wealthy and not crooked and quaking at the prospect of troubles.[44] 265

PAPHLAGON

Do *you* join in on the attack?!? And I, men, am being beaten up on
    your account,
Because I was about to say that it is just
To erect a memorial in the city in gratitude for your courage!

CHORUS

What a boaster! Smooth-as-leather! You see the sorts of things he
    does to insinuate himself!
Just as if we were old men, he dupes with stupid tricks! 270

SAUSAGE-SELLER [OR PERHAPS CHORUS][45]
But if he's victorious in this way, he'll be pummeled in that way,[46]
And if he ducks out, he'll butt against my leg right here!

PAPHLAGON

O City and Demos! I'm punched in the gut by wild animals!

DEMOSTHENES

And you shout, just as you're always turning the city upside down.

---

44. "Troubles" (*pragmata*) could also refer to (public) "affairs."

45. The order and attribution of these lines are contested, although the
order followed here is supported by important MSS. The Budé gives the lines
to the Chorus, perhaps rightly.

46. Commentators divide over the proper reading and meaning of this
line. Some object to "victorious," although it is in the MSS; and it is unclear
whether the Sausage-Seller (if indeed the line is his; see previous note) is pointing to, say, his fist, or whether the Chorus (if the line is theirs) is pointing to the
Sausage-Seller. See in general J.C.B. Lowe, "The Manuscript Evidence for
Changes of Speaker in Aristophanes," *Bulletin of the Institute of Classical Studies*
9:1 (1962): 35-39.

SAUSAGE-SELLER[47]

275   Well, with this shouting I'll rout you first!

CHORUS

[*To Paphlagon*] If you're victorious with your shouting, hurray for
   you.
But if he [*pointing to the Sausage-Seller*] outstrips you in
   shamelessness, then the victory cake is ours!

PAPHLAGON

[*Pointing to the Sausage-Seller*] This man here I denounce, and I
   assert that
He's exporting, for the Peloponnesian triremes, . . . stew![48]

SAUSAGE-SELLER

280   And I for my part denounce *him*, yes, by Zeus, because with an
   empty gut
He runs into the Prytaneum, then runs out again with a full one!

DEMOSTHENES

Yes, by Zeus, and for bringing out forbidden goods, cake and
   meat
And sliced fish, which *Pericles* was never deemed to deserve!

PAPHLAGON

You two will die right quick!

---

47. The MSS give this line to the Sausage-Seller, although the Budé and the
OCT give it to Paphlagon.

48. The word for "stew" (*zōmeumata*) probably puns on *hupozōma*, "rope
or timber used to strengthen the hull of a trireme." This suggestion is "as old as
the scholia, but does not help" according to Neil (ad loc.).

SAUSAGE-SELLER

I'll shout three times louder than you!   285

PAPHLAGON

I'll bellow and outbellow you!

SAUSAGE-SELLER

And I'll shout and outshout you!

PAPHLAGON

I'll slander you, if you're elected general!

SAUSAGE-SELLER

I'll beat your back like a dog's!

PAPHLAGON

I'll harass you with boasts!   290

SAUSAGE-SELLER

I'll cut off your [escape] routes!

PAPHLAGON

Look at me without blinking!

SAUSAGE-SELLER

I too was raised in the marketplace.

PAPHLAGON

I'll tear you to pieces, if you'll so much as grumble!

SAUSAGE-SELLER

I'll cart you off like dung, if you'll chatter your nonsense!   295

PAPHLAGON

I admit that I steal. But you don't.

SAUSAGE-SELLER

Yes I *do* admit it, by Hermes of the Marketplace![49]

PAPHLAGON

And I deny it with an oath, even when people are looking![50]

SAUSAGE-SELLER

Well then, you use sophistic tricks that aren't your own![51]

PAPHLAGON

300　And I'll denounce you to the Prytaneis
　　For having sacred tripe belonging to the gods,
　　For which the tithe's not been paid!

CHORUS

305　O foul and loathsome shout-downer! With your boldness
　　The whole earth is full, the whole Assembly too,
　　So too fees and indictments and courtrooms, O
　　Mud-Disturber—the entire city of ours you've stirred up.
310　You've deafened our Athens with shouting,
　　As you watch from the rocks above for tuna-fish-shoals of
　　　　tribute![52]

PAPHLAGON

I know where this affair was long ago stitched together!

---

49. Hermes was the god of trading, among other things (see *Acharnians* 816). A bronze statue of Hermes stood in the Athenian agora or marketplace.

50. The attribution of lines in this section is uncertain.

51. Or "that belong to others" (*allotria*); lying under oath is hardly a clever innovation.

52. Tuna fishermen would station someone on the rocks above the sea to watch for schools of tuna.

SAUSAGE-SELLER

And if you don't know stitching together, then I don't know   315
    sausage meats either!
You used to cut away the hide of lousy cattle and sell it,
Like a dirty crook, to rustic types, so it'd appear thick,
And after they wore it for less than a day, it'd be two
    handbreadths bigger!

DEMOSTHENES

Yes, by Zeus, he did this very same thing to me, and so I prompted
Much ridicule from my demesmen and friends!   320
For before I got to Pergase,[53] I was swimming in my shoes!

CHORUS

So didn't you from the beginning make Shamelessness apparent,
Which alone, in fact, stands sentry for orators?   325
Trusting in it, you milk the fruit-bearing foreigners,
You're first in that, while Hippodamus's son[54] pines away as he
    looks on.
Another man has appeared, much
More of a reprobate than you, and as a result I'm delighted!
He'll put a stop to you and outdo you, that's clear, on the spot, 330
In crookedness and boldness and duping-with-stupid-tricks!

---

53. The name of two demes or neighborhood districts (Upper and Lower
Pergase) in Athens.

54. Hippodamus of Miletus was a noted town planner responsible for lay-
ing out Athens' port, the Piraeus (see, in general, Aristotle, *Politics* 2.8). His son,
Archeptolemus, was apparently made an Athenian citizen; he may have somehow championed the cause of foreigners in Athens. In 411 he became active in
the short-lived oligarchy in Athens and was subsequently executed. Archeptolemus is mentioned by name below, at 794.

[*To the Sausage-Seller*] But you who've been raised where men are such as they are,
Demonstrate now that being raised in a moderate way means nothing!

SAUSAGE-SELLER

335 Just listen to what sort of citizen this guy is!

PAPHLAGON

You aren't going to let *me* [speak]?

SAUSAGE-SELLER

No, by Zeus, since I too am low-class!

DEMOSTHENES

And if he doesn't yield in this, say that you're also from low-class stock!

PAPHLAGON

You aren't going to let me?

SAUSAGE-SELLER

No, by Zeus!

PAPHLAGON

Yes, by Zeus!

SAUSAGE-SELLER

No, by Poseidon,
But I'll first do battle over this very thing—about who's the first to speak!

PAPHLAGON

Aah! I'm going to burst!!

SAUSAGE-SELLER

And yet I won't let you.   340

DEMOSTHENES

Let him, let him—in the name of the gods!—let him burst himself!

PAPHLAGON

And what's persuaded you that you deserve to speak against me?

SAUSAGE-SELLER

That I can both speak and stir up something nice!⁵⁵

PAPHLAGON

Look at that: "speaking"! You'd do beautifully if a matter fell into
    your lap,
Raw and torn to pieces, you'd carry it out right fine!   345
But do you know what's happened to you, it seems to me? Just
    what happens to the multitude:
If somewhere you argued a little case well, pertaining to a
    resident alien foreigner,⁵⁶
Then babbling and chattering away to yourself all night in the
    streets
And drinking [only] water and putting on a display and annoying
    your friends,
You began to suppose you're a capable speaker! You moron! What   350
    foolishness!

---

55. Literally, "make a *karukē* sauce," evidently composed of blood and
spices (*karukopoiein*). Some suggest this means in context "cause agitation or
confusion," others that it refers to flowery rhetoric.

56. Resident aliens (metics) were of course without rights of full
citizenship.

SAUSAGE-SELLER[57]

And what do *you* drink so that you've now made the city
Silent, tongue-tied[58] by you and you alone?

PAPHLAGON

What human being do you compare me to? I'm one who,
Scarfing down hot tuna right away and then downing a pitcher of
unmixed

355   Wine, I screw over the generals at Pylos!

SAUSAGE-SELLER

And I, gulping down cow's stomach and pig's tripe,
And then slurping up the gravy, with unwashed hands
I throttle the orators and stir up Nicias!

CHORUS[59]

The rest that you say I found pleasing, but one thing doesn't agree
with me:

360   That you alone will drink down the gravy from the [political]
affairs.

PAPHLAGON

But *you* won't eat up Milesian bass and then agitate-and-harass
them![60]

---

57. Some editors give these lines to Demosthenes, against the principal
MSS.

58. The word most commonly means "kissed with the tongue."

59. The MSS give these lines to the Chorus, but most editors give them
instead to Demosthenes.

60. The precise meaning of this line is controversial. Miletus was a wealthy
ally of Athens. Perhaps Cleon took a large bribe from Miletus but failed to
deliver on his promise to it.

SAUSAGE-SELLER

Having eaten ribs of beef, I'll buy [silver] mines!

PAPHLAGON

And having pounced on the Council, I'll stir it up violently!

SAUSAGE-SELLER

And I'll screw your butthole like a sausage casing!

PAPHLAGON

And I'll drag you outside by the butt, upside down!   365

DEMOSTHENES[61]

By Poseidon, then drag me out, too, if you do it to him!

PAPHLAGON

How I'll put you in stocks!

SAUSAGE-SELLER

I'll prosecute you for cowardice!

PAPHLAGON

Your hide will be stretched on a tanner's board!

SAUSAGE-SELLER

I'll skin you [and make] a thief's purse!   370

PAPHLAGON

I'll peg your hide to the ground!

SAUSAGE-SELLER

I'll make mincemeat of you!

---

61. Most MSS give this line to Demosthenes, but some assign it to the Chorus.

PAPHLAGON

Your eyelashes I'll pluck out!

SAUSAGE-SELLER

Your gullet I'll cut out!

DEMOSTHENES

375 And, by Zeus, we'll shove
A peg into his mouth, gourmet-style,
And then pulling out
His tongue from inside,
We'll examine him well and manfully,
380 Him and his gaping . . . butthole,
[To see] if he's diseased![62]

CHORUS

So there *was* something hotter than fire and
385 More shameless in the city than the speeches of the shameless!
And the matter at issue's no paltry thing,
Just attack and twist him, and do nothing small scale.
For now he's been seized round the middle!
If now you soften him up in the assault,
390 You'll discover him a coward—for I know his ways.

SAUSAGE-SELLER[63]

But despite being the sort of person he's been his whole life,
He was nonetheless held to be a real man, for reaping the
summer harvest of another.

---

62. Animals prepared for sacrifice had to be inspected for signs of disease or parasites.

63. Most MSS give these lines to the Sausage-Seller, but some editions (e.g., the Budé and the OCT) attribute them to Demosthenes.

And now those ears of corn that he brought back from there,
He's locked up in stocks and is drying out, and he wants to sell
    them.[64]

PAPHLAGON

I'm not afraid of you lot, while the Council is alive   395
And Demos sits there with a stupid look on his face.[65]

CHORUS

How shamelessly he acts before everyone and does not
Change his usual color!
If I don't hate you, would that I become a sheepskin blanket in   400
    Cratinus's house[66]
And be taught to sing in a tragedy by Morsimus![67]
O you who are concerned with everything, bearing on all
    affairs,
You alight on bribery-blooms.
Would that you spit out your mouthful as easily as you found it.
Only then would I sing,   405
"Drink, drink to the good times!"[68]
I suppose that the son of Oulius, too, the old man wheat-ogler,

---

64. An allusion to the Spartan prisoners captured by Demosthenes on the
island of Sphacteria.

65. Or, perhaps, "And the demos sits there with a stupid look on its face."

66. A comic poet and Aristophanes' sometime competitor. "From habits of
intemperance, the fleeces of the comic poet Cratinus, it appears, were not of
the most delicate description" (Mitchell ad loc.).

67. A tragic poet also mocked in *Frogs* 151 and *Peace* 803 and following.

68. From a victory ode of the poet Simonides.

Delighting in the paean [to Apollo], would sing the Bacche-
bacchus![69]

PAPHLAGON

You won't outdo me in shamelessness, by Poseidon,
410 Or may I never be present for the sacrificial meats of Zeus of the
Marketplace!

SAUSAGE-SELLER

For my part—[I swear] by the knuckles that, many times for many
reasons,
I endured from childhood on, and the blows of little knives!—
I think I'll outdo you in these things, or otherwise it was for
nothing
That I've grown this big, eating scraps.

PAPHLAGON

415 Scraps, like a dog? O you thoroughly depraved fellow, how
then
Will you fight with a dogheaded baboon[70] while eating dog
food?

SAUSAGE-SELLER

And by Zeus I've other tricks from when I was a boy,

---

69. Nothing certain is known of the man, and the reading of the MSS is
questioned; perhaps Oulius (and not his son) is here referred to, who "was a
son of the statesman Cimon and twin brother of the better-known Lacedaemo-
nius" (Sommerstein, *Knights* ad loc.). The gods alluded to are Apollo and Dionysus.

70. The word for "baboon" in Greek is literally "doghead" (see, e.g., Plato,
Theaetetus 161c5), "regarded as the fiercest of the simians" (Sommerstein,
Knights ad loc.).

For I used to deceive the cooks by saying things like this:
"Examine it, boys, don't you see? Spring's here . . . there's a
    swallow!"
And they used to look, and in that much time I'd steal some meat!   420

CHORUS[71]

O Most Clever Flesh! Wisely did you foresee!
You stole, just like eating nettles before the swallows come.[72]

SAUSAGE-SELLER

And got away with doing these things! But if one of them should
    see,
Then concealing it in my butt cheeks, I'd deny it on oath to the
    gods!
As a result, a man among the orators, seeing me do this, said: 425
"There's no way this boy won't govern the demos!"

CHORUS[73]

He reckoned that well! But it's clear what made him conclude that:
Because you swore a false oath after stealing, and had meat up
    your butthole!

PAPHLAGON

I'll put a stop to your boldness—of the both of you, I think!
For I'll go out and then swoop down on you like a keen and   430
    mighty wind,
Mixing up land and sea together pell-mell.

---

71. Some editions give these lines to Demosthenes, against the reading of
the principal MSS.

72. Nettles were eaten in the spring, when they were still tender.

73. Some editions give these lines to Demosthenes, against the reading of
the principal MSS.

SAUSAGE-SELLER

I'll shorten sail with my sausages and then let myself drift
On the waves with a favorable wind, telling you to lament big-time!

CHORUS[74]

And as for me, if there's any leak, I'll guard the ship's hold!

PAPHLAGON

By Demeter, you won't get off, since you stole
435   Many talents[75] [of silver] from the Athenians!

CHORUS[76]

Look sharp, slacken the sheet!
This one's blowing a nor'easter and a sycophant-wind!

SAUSAGE-SELLER

I know well that you've got ten talents from Potidaea![77]

PAPHLAGON

What of it? Want to take one of those talents and keep mum?

---

74. Some editions give this line to Demosthenes, against the reading of the
principal MSS.

75. A talent was a measure of weight and came to represent the worth
of that amount of silver or gold; see also *Acharnians* 6 and the accompanying
note.

76. Some editions give these lines to Demosthenes, against the reading of
the principal MSS.

77. In 430–429 B.C.E. Athens managed to recapture this rebel city, but
only after a lengthy and hence costly siege. How Cleon might have benefited
from Potidaea is unclear. Sommerstein speculates that Cleon might have
"denounced the [Athenian] generals as having taken bribes *before* the capitula-
tion, alleging that this was why they had not demanded unconditional surrender" (*Knights* ad loc.).

CHORUS[78]

The man would gladly take them! Slacken the ropes.   440
The wind is dying down.

PAPHLAGON

You'll be a defendant in four cases, at a hundred talents a piece.

SAUSAGE-SELLER

And *you'll* face a charge of dodging military service, for twenty,
And one of theft, for more than a thousand.

PAPHLAGON

I contend that you're descended   445
From those who've offended the goddess![79]

SAUSAGE-SELLER

I contend that your grandfather
Was among the bodyguards—

PAPHLAGON

What "bodyguards"?!?! Explain!

---

78. Some editions give these lines to Demosthenes, against the reading of
the principal MSS.

79. An allusion to the charge that Sparta brought, in the run-up to the Peloponnesian War, according to which Athens must drive out those connected
with the religious crime of killing supporters of a would-be tyrant (Cylon) who
had sought refuge in a temple; those who had killed the suppliants were thus
said to be cursed, and they included members of Pericles' family. The charge
of religious pollution from long ago was dredged up to discredit Pericles, the
leader of the war party in Athens. For the details, see Thucydides 1.126 and context.

SAUSAGE-SELLER

Those of Hippias's wife, Leatherina![80]

PAPHLAGON

You're a stupid trickster!

SAUSAGE-SELLER

450   You're a dirty crook!

CHORUS[81]

Strike him courageously!

PAPHLAGON

Ow ow!

The conspirators are beating me!

CHORUS[82]

Strike him most courageously and
Punch him in the gut, and with your entrails
455   And intestines,
See to it that you punish[83] the man!
O Most Noble Flesh and Best in Soul of All!
Both for the city and for us citizens, you're a savior made manifest!
How well and with such complexity you trapped[84] him in speeches.

---

80. Hippias was the last tyrant of Athens, and so the charge is that Paphlagon is descended from someone supportive of tyranny. "Leatherina" is of course a made-up name meant to call to mind Paphlagon's ignoble profession; the name of Hippias's wife was actually Myrrine (see Thucydides 6.55).

81. Some editions give this line to Demosthenes.

82. Some editions give the first four lines here to Demosthenes.

83. The word for "punish" (*kolai*) echoes the word for "intestines" (*kolois*) in the previous line.

84. Instead of "trapped" (*hupēlthes*) some MSS read "attacked" (*epēlthes*).

How might we praise you commensurate with our pleasure?   460

PAPHLAGON

I was not unaware, by Demeter, that these affairs
Had been fabricated—instead I knew
They all were being nailed and glued together.

SAUSAGE-SELLER

Well, I'm not unaware of the sorts of things you're carrying out in   465
Argos.[85]
The pretext is that he's making Argives our friends,
But in private he's getting together there with the
Lacedaemonians!

CHORUS[86]

Alas! Do you say nothing after the fashion of the wheelwright?[87]

SAUSAGE-SELLER

And the reasons these things have been welded together,
I know: they're being forged on account of the prisoners![88]

CHORUS[89]

Well done, well done! "Forging" in return for "gluing"!   470

---

85. Argos was an important rival to Sparta for power, and its thirty-year treaty with Sparta was to expire in 421 (see Thucydides 5.14). Athenian politicians, including Cleon and Alcibiades, were eager to court Argos.

86. Some editions give this line to Demosthenes.

87. This line, which is omitted in one MS, follows 463 in the MSS, but all modern editors place it between 467 and 468, as in the translation above.

88. Another allusion to the Spartan prisoners captured on the island of Sphacteria.

89. Some editions give this line to Demosthenes.

SAUSAGE-SELLER

And there are men from there,[90] in turn, hammering out
    [the deal]!

[*To Paphlagon*] And you won't persuade me, either by giving me
    silver or gold
Or by sending your friends for a visit,
Not to tell these things to the Athenians!

PAPHLAGON

475   Then I'll go immediately to the Council
And tell them of the conspiracies of you all!
And the nighttime gatherings in the city,
And all the deals you've made with the Medes and the King,[91]
And those cheesed-up affairs involving Boeotians![92]

SAUSAGE-SELLER

480   So what's cheese selling for among Boeotians?

PAPHLAGON

By Heracles, I'll lay your hide flat out!

[*Exit Cleon*]

CHORUS[93]

Come now, what thought do you have or what judgment?

---

90. That is, from Sparta.

91. That is, with the Persians and the King of Persia.

92. "The rich pastoral country of Boeotia was famous for its cheese" (Neil ad loc.). Around the time of the *Knights'* performance, Demosthenes was engaged in talks with the democratic faction among the Boeotians (Thucydides 4.76).

93. Some editions give these lines to Demosthenes, against the MSS.

You'll please inform us right now, if in fact you concealed
The meat in your butt cheeks, as you yourself say.
Run like a dart to the Council chamber,   485
Because he'll burst in there and slander
Us one and all and unleash his cries!

SAUSAGE-SELLER

I'm off! But first, on the spot, the tripe
And the cleavers I'll set down right here.

CHORUS[94]

Hold on now, anoint your neck with this,   490
So you can slip out of the slanders.[95]

SAUSAGE-SELLER

What you say's good, and that's just like a [wrestling] trainer!

CHORUS[96]

Hold on: take this and eat it up!

SAUSAGE-SELLER

Why?

CHORUS[97]

So you may fight better, my lad, being garlic-primed![98]
Now quick, make haste!

---

94. Some editions give these lines to Demosthenes, against the MSS. The
line attributions in this section are uncertain.

95. Wrestlers would anoint themselves with oil before a match.

96. Some editions give this line to Demosthenes, against the MSS.

97. Some editions give these lines to Demosthenes, against the MSS.

98. Cockfighters would feed garlic to their cocks to render them feisty for
battle; see, e.g., Xenophon, *Symposium* 4.9 as well as *Acharnians* 166.

SAUSAGE-SELLER

I'll do it!

CHORUS[99]

495 Now remember
To bite, to slander, to devour his cock's comb,
And see to it you'll come back having eaten his wattles!
Now be off and fare well, and would that you act
As I'd like,[100] and may you be guarded
500 By Zeus of the Marketplace. And once victorious
May you come back here again to us
Bedecked with wreaths!
[*To the audience*] But you, you apply your mind
To our anapests,
505 O you who are by yourselves already experienced
In all manner of Muse.
If some man, a comic producer, among the old-fashioned types
Compelled us [knights] to come before the audience to say lines,
He would not have easily attained it. But now the poet is
deserving of it,
510 Because he hates the same people we do and dares to say the just
things,
And in a well-born manner advances against the typhoon and the
hurricane.
As for those things he says that many of you who've approached
him wonder about

---

99. Some editions give the first three lines here to Demosthenes, against
the MSS.

100. Literally, "according to my mind" (*kata noun*). These lines (498–99)
are said to come from Sophocles.

And closely question him concerning—how it is that long ago he
    didn't ask for a chorus of his own—
He bade us explain this to you.[101] For the man asserts
That it was not through foolishness that he was so disposed as to   515
    delay, but rather his belief
That being a comic producer is the most difficult task of them all.
For though many indeed have attempted to woo Her, She has
    gratified few.[102]
And he recognized long ago that you are by nature given to
    frequent change,
And that you abandoned the previous poets as they aged.
He knows what happened to Magnes[103] as his gray hair   520
    descended,
He who had erected the most victory trophies over rival choruses:
Letting loose all kinds of sounds for you—plucking and flapping
And Lydianizing[104] and insect-buzzing and dyeing himself
    frog-green—
He didn't satisfy you, but in the end, in his old age (but not in his
    youth)
He was driven off stage as an elder, found wanting in the making   525
    of jokes.

---

101. For a consideration of the early career of Aristophanes, before he
wrote and produced plays under his own name, consider Stephen Halliwell,
"Aristophanes' Apprenticeship," *Classical Quarterly* 30:1 (1980): 33–45.

102. "She" here is presumably the Comic Muse.

103. Magnes was one of the two earliest comic poets in Athens. He is said
to have won eleven victories at the City Dionysia, a record never surpassed (so
far as we know).

104. Magnes produced a play called *The Lydians*.

Then [the poet] calls to mind Cratinus,[105] who once coursed
   along with much praise
And flowed over the smooth plains, and, sweeping away oaks and
   plane trees and enemies,
He used to carry them from their place, roots and all.
At a drinking party it wasn't possible to sing anything but
   "Goddess Bribery, Figwood-Sandaled"[106]
530   And "Craftsmen of Ingenious Hymns."[107] Thus was he in his
   bloom!
But now[108] you see him talking nonsense and you feel no pity for
   him,
His tuning pegs fallen out and his tone no longer there,
His joints[109] all agape. But being an old man, he flows around,
Just like Connas,[110] wearing a dried-out wreath, perishing from
   thirst,
535   He who, on account of his prior victories, ought to be drinking
   [for free] in the Prytaneum,
Not chattering drivel but looking on [in the theater] alongside
   Dionysus, and lauded.

---

105. Together with Aristophanes and Eupolis, Cratinus was held to be
among the greatest comic poets of Athens, winning six first-place victories at
the City Dionysia.

106. Apparently the beginning of one of his choral odes. The first syllable
of the word for "figwood-sandaled" (*sukopedile*) suggests "sycophant."

107. According to the scholiast, this ode was found in Cratinus's *Euneidae*.

108. Cratinus was competing against Aristophanes in the same festival in
424; his *Satyrs* would win second place, behind the *Knights*.

109. The same word (*harmoniōn*) can mean (musical) "harmony." It seems
that Cratinus is being compared to a worn-out lyre.

110. A flute (*aulos*) player apparently reduced to poverty after enjoying
much success.

And Crates[111] used to endure such a temper and abuse from you,
He who, from little expense, used to send you off with a meal,
Kneading together most urbane thoughts from his most clarion-
like mouth.
And yet he on his own persisted, sometimes stumbling,   540
sometimes not.
Dreading these things, [the poet] was always delaying; and in
addition to these considerations he claimed
That he ought to become a rower first before taking the rudder in
hand,
And from there exercise command at the bow and closely
examine the winds,
And *then* pilot for himself. For all these reasons, then,
Because he leapt in sensibly and not thoughtlessly, spouting   545
nonsense,
Raise a great round of applause for him, and send him forth with
an eleven-oar salute,[112]
A fine, Lenaean clamor
So the poet may go off gratified,
Having acted agreeably,[113]
Beaming with a glistening . . . forehead.[114]   550

---

111. An Athenian comic poet said to have won three victories at the City
Dionysia.

112. "The eleven figure has not been explained. Is there any chance that
this numeral had a special significance?" (Wilson ad loc.). Consider Marcel
Lysgaard Lech, "The Knights' Eleven Oars: In Praise of Phormio? Aristophanes' *Knights* 546-7," *Classical Journal* 105:1 (2009): 19-26.

113. More literally, "according to [our] mind" (*kata noun*); see also n. 104
above.

114. Aristophanes was bald at a young age.

Lord of Horses, Poseidon, pleased by

The din of brazen-hooved horses

And their neighing

And by triremes glossy-dark-hulled, swift,

555 Payload-bearing,[115]

And by contests of youths distinguishing themselves in chariots

Or brought low by unhappy fortune:

Come here to the chorus, You of the golden trident,

560 O guardian of dolphins, worshipped at Sounion,

You who are honored at Geraestus,[116] son of Cronus,

To Phormio[117] and to the Athenians at present,

Dearest above the other gods!

565 We want to speak in praise of our fathers, because

They were men worthy of this land and the Robe,[118]

Men who, in infantry battles and on naval campaign,

Were always victorious everywhere and so adorned this city.

For no one among them, on seeing their opponents,

570 Ever counted them up—rather his spirit was immediately at the
   ready.

But if somewhere they should fall on their shoulder in some
   battle,

---

115. "These are the triremes that brought the annual tribute from the Athenian allies, which became the pay of the rowers and juries," that is, of the poor; Edmunds, *Cleon, "Knights," and Aristophanes' Politics*, 39.

116. Sounion was located in southern Attica, Geraestus in the southern part of Euboea, and Poseidon was worshipped at both.

117. An outstanding commander in the Athenian navy early on in the Peloponnesian War.

118. The ceremonial robe (*peplos*) presented to Athena in the course of the Panathenaea festival.

This they'd wipe off, deny they had fallen,
And get back to the wrestling match once again. And not even
   one general
Of previous times would have begged and asked Cleaenetus[119]
   for public sustenance.
But as things stand now, if they don't have front-row seats and   575
   [free] meals,
They assert they won't fight! But we deem it right that we nobly
   defend
The city and the native gods, as a gift given without recompense.
We ask for nothing more save this much alone—
If ever there is peace and we cease our toils,
Don't begrudge us our long hair or our personal grooming   580
   devices![120]
O Pallas,[121] city defender,
Guardian of the most sacred land of quite all,
Surpassing in
War and poets and power: 585
Come, draw near, bringing our fellow worker
In campaigns and battles,
Nike, who, companion of choruses,
Stands together with us in opposition to the enemies.   590
Now come, here appear. For
On these men you ought to bestow victory
By every art,

---

119. Father of Cleon.

120. Long hair was a mark, among young men especially, of aristocratic
airs; see also *Wasps* 1317.

121. That is, Athena.

Now if ever before!

595 We want to praise our horses on points we can testify to.[122]

And they deserve to be spoken well of, for many troubles

They've borne with us to the end—incursions and battles.

But we do not admire them as much on land,

As when they leapt manfully onto horse-transport ships,

600 Purchasing drinking cups, others also garlic and onion.

Then grasping the oar handle just as we mortals do,

They set to pulling hard and neighed nice and loud,

    "Hippapai![123] Who'll put their shoulder to it?

Must take better hold! What're we doing? You aren't pulling,

    S-brand!"

They then leapt out at Corinth. The youngest

605 Made dugouts with their hooves and went to fetch blankets.[124]

They ate crabs instead of Medean grass,

If a crab should crawl out toward them, and they also hunted

    them from the depth of the sea.

Theorus[125] said as a result that a Corinthian crab said:

"It's a terrible thing, Poseidon, if I won't be able, even in the depth,

610 Either on land or at sea, to flee the horses!"

[*Sausage-Seller returns*]

---

122. Consider in this regard Nicias's recent victory over the Corinthians at Solygeia, where two hundred cavalry were brought by transport ships (Thucydides 4.42–44).

123. The equine equivalent of the (human) sailors' cry, *rhuppapai!* (consider *Wasps* 909 and *Frogs* 1073).

124. One MS reads, instead of "blankets" (or "bedding": *strōmata*), "food" or "fodder" (*brōmata*), perhaps rightly.

125. Presumably the associate of Cleon's attacked elsewhere by Aristophanes; see *Acharnians* 134 and following.

CHORUS

O Dearest of Men and Most Youthfully Vigorous!
How much worry you gave us while you were gone!
And now that you've come back again safe and sound,
Report to us how you did in contending the matter!

SAUSAGE-SELLER

What else other than that I became "Nicoboulus"![126]   615

CHORUS

Now *that* deserves a joyful shout from everyone!
O you who speak nobly, and carried out deeds much better still
Than the speeches,
Would that you might recount each and every point to me clearly.
I think that I'd   620
Traverse a long road
To hear it! For these reasons,
Best fellow, be bold and speak, since
We are all of us delighted by you!

SAUSAGE-SELLER

And indeed it *is* worthwhile to hear of what happened!
I sped off from here immediately, right behind him.   625
He was inside [the Council], breaking forth with thunder-hurling
    words.
He hurled astounding things against the Knights,
Hurling mountains of bombast and saying, very persuasively, that
    they're conspirators.
The whole Council was listening

---

126. That is, Victor-in-the-Council.

630 And became full of false-orach[127] because of him,
And they took on a mustardy look and knitted together their
brows.

And for my part, when I knew they were accepting his arguments
And being completely fooled by his bogus baloney,
I said, "Come now, Friskies and Fakers,
635 Knuckleheads and Imps and Impudent Ones,[128]
And Marketplace, where as a boy I was educated,
Let boldness be mine now and grant me a resourceful tongue
And a shameless voice!" As I was thinking on these things,
On the right[129] side a bugger of a man let out a fart!
640 And so I made obeisance. Then striking with my butt
The entry gate I broke it and, my mug gaping wide,
I cried out: "O Council, bearing a good word,[130]
I want to be the first to report the good news to you.
For from the time when the war first broke out for us,
645 Never have I seen sprats be a better deal!"
Right away their faces grew quite calm,
Then they crowned me with a wreath for my good news. And I at
once told them,

---

127. "The herb orach was thought to make the face grow pale . . . : the councilors are so alarmed by the alleged conspiracy that they go pale" (Sommerstein, *Knights* ad 629–30); the term "false-orach" (*pseudoatraphaxus*) suggests that there is no conspiracy in fact.

128. The meanings of most of the names the Sausage-Seller here calls on or invokes, as his special deities, are somewhat uncertain, although the gist seems clear.

129. The right side is always auspicious; the left, foreboding and "sinister." An eagle soaring on the right side is a very good sign (see, e.g., Xenophon, *The Education of Cyrus* 2.1.1).

130. Literally, "good speeches."

Making it a secret not to be repeated,
That in order to buy many sprats for an obol,
They must seize the bowls of the craftsmen.   650
They applauded and were all agape at me.
But *he* suspected, Paphlagon did, knowing
What phrases especially please the Council,
And so he stated his judgment: "Men, it seems best to me now
In light of the good turn of events just announced,   655
To sacrifice, for the good news, one hundred bulls to the
    goddess."131
The Council then nodded their head in his direction once
    again.
And for my part, when I knew I was being defeated by bull crap,
I overshot him with *two* hundred bulls!
And to [Artemis] the Wild One I advised them to make a vow   660
Of one thousand goats tomorrow,132
If anchovies should become a hundred an obol.
The Council then looked eagerly at me again.
But when he heard these things, he was dumbstruck and began to
    babble.
Then the Prytaneis and the police started to drag him off,   665
And the others got to their feet and began shouting about
    sprats.

---

131. That is, to Athena.

132. Prior to the battle of Marathon, the Greeks vowed to sacrifice to Artemis the same number of goats as of the Persians they might kill in battle. In the
event, the number of Persian dead was so high that the Greeks chose instead
to sacrifice five hundred goats a year to Artemis, a practice that continued
down to Xenophon's day (*Anabasis of Cyrus* 3.2.12). Thus the Sausage-Seller
suggests sacrificing one thousand goats in thanks for . . . cheap anchovies!

He was pleading with them to let him stay for a little while longer,
    saying,
"So that you might learn what the herald from Lacedaemon is
    saying—
For he's come concerning the treaty!"
670   But they *all*, with one voice, cried out:
"*Now?!?* About a treaty?!? Yeah right: only once, sir,
They learned that sprats are a bargain here with us!
We don't need a treaty! Let the war creep on!"
And they cried out to have the Prytaneis adjourn.
675   Then they leapt over the railings everywhere.
But I outran them and bought up the coriander
And all the onions there were in the marketplace.
Then I gave them out, gratis, as seasonings for the sprats
When they had no way of getting any, and I gratified them!
680   They all of them highly praised and acclaimed me
So much so that, as a result,
I've come back with the entire Council in the palm of my hand—
    for an obol's worth of coriander!

CHORUS

Well, you've done all the sorts of things a fortunate fellow should!
And that dirty crook found another fellow who surpasses him by far
685   In greater crookedness
And complicated snares
And wheedling words.
Just reflect on how you'll best contend
In what remains.
But that you have in us well-disposed allies,
690   This you've long known.

SAUSAGE-SELLER

And here's Paphlagon approaching,
Pushing along a cresting wave and stirring and mixing things up,
Like he's going to swallow me up! Mormo,[133] what boldness!

PAPHLAGON

Should I fail to destroy you, if I've still got some of the same lies
Within me—I'd fall to pieces entirely!   695

SAUSAGE-SELLER

[*Dancing in delight*] I'm pleased by your threats—laughing at your
    thunderous talk,
Dancing a crazy jig, crying "cuckoo" all round!

PAPHLAGON

By Demeter, I'll no longer go on living
If I don't devour you from this earth!

SAUSAGE-SELLER

If you don't devour?!? And [I won't go on living either] if I don't   700
    guzzle you down,
Even if, by swallowing you up, I myself may burst!

PAPHLAGON

I'll destroy you, [I swear,] by the front-row seat I got as a result of
    Pylos![134]

---

133. A terrifying she-monster invoked to frighten children; see also *Acharnians* 582.

134. Yet another reference to Pylos, the locale of Demosthenes' greatest military triumph, for which Cleon claimed credit. Free meals in the Prytaneum and front-row seats in the theater were evidently among Cleon's rewards; see also 575 above.

SAUSAGE-SELLER

"Front-row seat" my foot! How I'll look at you
When I'm seated in your front-row seat, as you watch from the
    very back!

PAPHLAGON

705   I'll put you in stocks, by the heaven!

SAUSAGE-SELLER

How sharp-spirited! Come now, what may I give you to eat?
What would you most delight in eating? A . . . wallet?

PAPHLAGON

I'll tear your guts out with my fingernails!

SAUSAGE-SELLER

I'll scratch out your [free] meals at the Prytaneum!

PAPHLAGON

710   I'll drag you before Demos[135] so you can pay me the just
    penalty!

SAUSAGE-SELLER

And I'll drag you and slander you more!

PAPHLAGON

But he won't be persuaded by *you* in anything, you bastard.
Whereas *I* can ridicule him as much as I want!

SAUSAGE-SELLER

How strongly you believe Demos is yours!

---

135. Or "the demos," i.e., the Athenian majority; Paphlagon does not
always observe the conceit that Demos is an individual (see, e.g., 764 below).

PAPHLAGON

For I know the tidbits of food he's hand-fed.   715

SAUSAGE-SELLER

So then you feed him badly, just like nannies!
You feed him a little after you've chewed it,
While you yourself gulp down three times as much!

PAPHLAGON

And, by Zeus, through my cleverness
I'm able to make Demos expand and contract.   720

SAUSAGE-SELLER

Even my butthole knows *that* sophistic trick!

PAPHLAGON

No, good fellow, you won't gain the reputation of treating me
   insolently in the Council.
Let's go before Demos.

SAUSAGE-SELLER

Nothing's preventing it.
See—walk on! Let nothing keep us!

PAPHLAGON

O Demos, come out here!

SAUSAGE-SELLER

Yes, by Zeus, O Father!   725
Do come out, darling Demos, dearest one!

PAPHLAGON

Come out, so you may know the sorts of outrageous insolence I
   suffer!

DEMOS

Who's shouting? Won't you get away from my door?!

[*Demos comes out of his house*] You've shredded my harvest-
   wreath![136]

Who, Paphlagon, is doing you an injustice?

PAPHLAGON

730   On your account I'm being beaten
By this guy here and the youths![137]

DEMOS

Why?

PAPHLAGON

Because I am your friend, O Demos, and because I am your lover.

DEMOS

[*Turning to Sausage-Seller*] And who indeed are you?

SAUSAGE-SELLER

This guy's rival in love!

I've loved you for a long time and want to benefit you,

735   As do many others, those who are noble and good gentlemen!
But we aren't able to do so, on account of *this* guy! For you
Are like boys who are the objects of love:
You don't accept those who are noble and good gentlemen
But give yourself to lamp-sellers[138] and shoe menders

740   And leatherworkers and hide-sellers.

---

136. A wreath hung on the front door in honor of Apollo every autumn.

137. That is, by the Knights, who would all be young men (consider 270 above).

138. Perhaps a reference to Hyperbolus, successor to Cleon as demagogue;
see 1300–1315 below.

PAPHLAGON

For I benefit Demos!

SAUSAGE-SELLER

Tell me, by doing what?

PAPHLAGON

What, you ask? I slipped in before the generals from Pylos,[139]
Having sailed there, and then led back the Laconians.[140]

SAUSAGE-SELLER

And I, while walking around, from a shop
I seized a pot that somebody else had on the boil!   745

PAPHLAGON

Convene an Assembly right now,
O Demos, so you may know which one of us
Is better disposed to you, and decide it, so you may befriend
    him.

SAUSAGE-SELLER

Yes, yes, decide indeed—just not on the Pnyx.

DEMOS

I wouldn't take up a seat in another place!   750
Just go on! Presence at the Pnyx required!

---

139. The text of this line is uncertain ("extremely difficult": Wilson ad loc.).
If the plural is to be read, with the majority of the MSS, Paphlagon would seem
to have in mind not only Demosthenes but also Eurymedon and Sophocles,
who were also serving as generals.

140. That is, the Spartan prisoners captured on Sphacteria, just off the
coast of Pylos.

SAUSAGE-SELLER

[*Aside*] Ah, wretched me, I'm a goner! For the old man
At home is the cleverest of men,
But whenever he sits on this rock here,
755   He gapes like a chewer of dried figs!

CHORUS

Now indeed you must let go all your own reefing rope
And bring an impetuous will and inescapable arguments,
With which you'll overthrow him. For the man is complex,
And from unmanageable circumstances he's good at managing to
        find ready resources.
760   So see to it that you'll unleash a great and keen [wind] against
        him!
But be on guard and, before he presses you hard, you first
Raise your dolphins[141] aloft and bring your boat alongside.

PAPHLAGON

[*Aside*] To Mistress Athena, Guardian of the city,
I pray that if, when it comes to the Athenian demos, I've been
765   The best of men (after Lysicles and Cynna and Salabaccho),[142]
Then I may dine in the Prytaneum, just as I do now, having done
        nothing for it.
[*To Demos*] But if I hate you and am not the sole person who
        stands firm in battling on your behalf,
May I perish and be sawn apart and cut up into leather straps!

---

141. Pieces of iron or other metal suspended from a ship and used as a
weapon against other vessels as they drew near; see, e.g., Thucydides 7.41.
142. For Lysicles, see n. 25 above. Cynna and Salabaccho were courtesans.

SAUSAGE-SELLER

And I, O Demos, if I'm not a friend and don't feel affection for
   you, then may I be cut up
And boiled in mincemeat! And if you're not persuaded by these   770
   things,
May I be grated on this [table] here for the savory stew with
   cheese,
And may I be dragged by the balls with a meat hook to
   Cerameicus!¹⁴³

PAPHLAGON

And how could there be a citizen, O Demos, who feels more
   friendship for you than I do?
First off, when I was on the Council, I made the most money for
   you
In the common account, by putting some people to the rack,   775
   squeezing others, demanding a cut from still others,
Not giving a thought to any private person, if I could gratify you!

SAUSAGE-SELLER

That, O Demos, is nothing grand, for I too will do this for you.
Snatching up the bread of others, I'll give it over to you.
I'll teach this very thing to you first—that he isn't your friend or
   well disposed,
Except for this reason, that he enjoys your fire.   780
For you fought to the end for the land against the Medes at
   Marathon
And in victory you gave over to us much to talk loudly of,
But he gives no thought to you seated here on such hard rocks—

---

143. The principal cemetery in Athens.

Unlike me, who bring you this that I've sewed [*holds up a cushion*].
Just sit up
785 And then sit down gently, so you don't chafe what was at Salamis.¹⁴⁴

DEMOS

Fellow,¹⁴⁵ who are you? Surely you're not someone born of that
illustrious line of Harmodius,¹⁴⁶ are you?
At any rate, this deed of yours truly is well-born and demos-
friendly!

PAPHLAGON

From such small little bits of flattery, you've come to be [seen as]
well disposed toward him!

SAUSAGE-SELLER

And you got your hooks into him with much smaller bait than this!

PAPHLAGON

790 Well, if some man has appeared somewhere who defends Demos
more
Or who is a better friend to you than I am—I'm willing to stake my
head!

SAUSAGE-SELLER

And how are you his friend, you who, though you see him living in
casks

144. Site of the great Athenian naval victory over the Persians in 480.

145. Literally, "Human being."

146. Harmodius, together with Aristogeiton, was popularly credited with
the assassination of Hipparchus, son of Peisistratus, and so with bringing to an
end the rule of tyranny in Athens.

And crannies and little towers, for seven years now,[147] you feel
    no pity,
But instead you've locked him in and take the honey? And when
    Archeptolemus[148] brought
Peace, you scattered it to the winds, and when it comes to the   795
    embassies
Proposing a treaty, you drive them out of the city with a slap on
    the backside!

PAPHLAGON

[Yes,] so he may rule all Greeks! For it's in the oracles
That he must at some point sit in court in Arcadia[149] for five obols
    a day,
If he is patient. At all events *I* will nourish and tend to him
By discovering sources, good or foul, from which he'll have his   800
    three obols.

SAUSAGE-SELLER

No, by Zeus, you aren't planning so that he may rule Arcadia, but
    so that
You may snatch up more and take bribes from the [subject] cities,
    and so that Demos
Not catch sight of you, on account of the war and its fog, as you
    do your crooked things,
But instead so he'll stand gaping before you, through necessity
    together with need and [the prospect of] pay.

---

147. Pericles' war strategy required the rural folk of Athens to abandon
their land to the depredations of the Spartans and come to live in cramped
quarters in the city proper; see also *Acharnians* 71.

148. An Athenian politician and son of Hippodamus; see 327 above.

149. That is, in the central part of the Peloponnese.

805 And if ever he goes back to the fields and spends his days at
    peace,
  And regains his spirit by eating groats and chatting with olive-
    cake,
  He'll know the sorts of goods you swindled him out of, by way of
    a public wage.[150]
  Then he, a fierce rustic fellow, will come to you and track down a
    ballot against you.
  Knowing this, you utterly deceive him and dream dreams about
    yourself.[151]

PAPHLAGON

810 Isn't it terrible that you say these things about me and
    slander me
  Before the Athenians and Demos, when I've done far more
    useful things
  For the city—yes, by Demeter—than Themistocles[152] ever did!

SAUSAGE-SELLER

"O City of Argos! Hearken to the sorts of things he says!"[153] You
  measure yourself against *Themistocles?!?*
Finding our city not quite full, he filled it right to the brim.

---

150. Thucydides suggests that Cleon was so adamantly in favor of war because "he thought that in peaceful times he would become more apparent as an evildoer and his slanders would be less trusted" (Thucydides 5.16).

151. The reading of the principal MSS. Most modern editors read, instead of "about yourself," "about him," taking the verb to mean "cheat or deceive by dreams."

152. See n. 18 above.

153. A fragment from Euripides' lost *Telephus*.

And, in addition to this, while the city was feasting midday, he   815
   kneaded the Piraeus¹⁵⁴ as well,
And though removing none of the old fish, he added new ones.
But you sought to make Athenians appear to be micro-citizens
By building walls and reciting oracles, you who measure yourself
   against Themistocles!
And he's exiled from the land, while you wipe your hands on
   Achilles' [cake].¹⁵⁵

PAPHLAGON

Isn't it terrible, O Demos, for me to hear these things from him,   820
Just because I feel friendly affection for you?

DEMOS

Stop, you, and don't utter foul abuse!
For much too much time now your underhanded dealings have
   gone undetected!

SAUSAGE-SELLER

It's the bloodiest bastard, O dearest little Demos, who's done the
   crookedest misdeeds!
When you stand agape,
He breaks off the stalks of officials undergoing an audit¹⁵⁶   825

---

154. Athens' port, whose fortification was completed at Themistocles' urging; see also 884–85 as well as Thucydides 1.93.

155. A cake or bread made from fine barley and served in the Prytaneum.
As a result of Pylos, Cleon was awarded free meals in the Prytaneum; see also
1404–5 below.

156. Public officials were subject to being audited upon completion of their
service. The suggestion is that Paphlagon takes bribes ("stalks") from public
officials on the promise that he will not harass them during their audits.

And gulps them down, and with both hands
He sops his bread in the public funds!

PAPHLAGON

You won't be so gratified: I'll
Convict you, for you're stealing
Thirty thousand!

SAUSAGE-SELLER

830   Why strike your oar on the sea and splash about,
Since you're the bloodiest bastard when it comes to
The Athenian demos? And I'll show,
By Demeter—or may I not go on living—
That you took as bribes from Mytilene[157]
835   More than forty minas!

CHORUS

O you who are manifest as the greatest benefit to all human beings,
I envy you the readiness of your tongue! For if you press on like this,
You'll be the greatest of Greeks, and you alone will be master
Of the city's allies and rule them while holding a trident,[158]

---

157. The nature of the alleged bribe is not certain, although one account has
it that "a bribe of ten talents was given to Cleon by Lesbians [i.e., citizens of Les-
bos] resident in Athens" (Neil ad loc.). Mytilene, on the island of Lesbos,
attempted to revolt from Athens in 428. The attempt failed badly, however, and
aroused the ire of the Athenians. Thucydides presents the debate between
Cleon—who argued for sticking to the previous day's resolution to kill all the men
and enslave all the women and children—and Diodotus—who argued for what
might be called greater leniency (3.36–49). See the appendix for a translation of
Cleon's speech; at 3.38.2 Cleon insinuates that his opponent has taken bribes.

158. The Chorus is thus comparing the Sausage-Seller to Poseidon; see also
559–64 above.

With which you'll make much money by shaking and stirring   840
    things up!
And don't let the man go, since he's given you a handhold,
For you'll easily finish him off, with a chest like yours!

PAPHLAGON

No, good men, things are not yet that way, no, by Poseidon!
For such is the deed I've done that
I put a bit in the mouth of my enemies all at once,   845
So long as something remains of the shields from Pylos!

SAUSAGE-SELLER

Hold on—those shields!—you've given *me* a handhold!
For if in fact you're a friend to Demos, you shouldn't have
    knowingly let
These [shields] be hung up with their handles [still on].[159]
But this, Demos, is a trick so that, if you want
To punish this man here, it won't be allowed you to do it.   850
For you see the sort of gang of young leather-sellers he has,
And dwelling around them are honey-sellers
And cheese-sellers. This gang has put their heads together for
    one thing:
So that if you should snort with anger and look toward ostraca,[160]   855
Then at night they might snatch down those shields and, at a run,
Seize the entry points for our barley!

---

159. The handles or armbands would normally be removed so that the shields could not be used—by slaves, for example—when in storage.

160. Shards of pottery used to record votes for "ostracizing" or banishing a citizen for a set time. Thus Sausage-Seller here refers to the possibility that Demos might wish to banish Cleon from Athens.

DEMOS

Ah, wretched me! They have handles?! [*To Paphlagon*] You dirty crook,

For such a long time you've been swindling me, cheating Demos in such things!

PAPHLAGON

860 Amazing fellow,[161] don't believe what's being said, or suppose

That you'll ever find a better friend than I am, I who, though one individual,

Put a stop to the conspirators, and nothing in the city

That's been contrived has escaped my notice, but instead I've immediately cried out about it!

SAUSAGE-SELLER

Which is just what happens to eel hunters:

865 Whenever the lake is calm, they gain nothing.

But if they stir the mud up and down,

They do catch something. And you too gain, if you mix up the city!

Just tell me this much, this one thing: selling so many hides as you do,

Have you ever given him leatherwork for his shoes from your own supply,

870 When you claim that you are his friend?

DEMOS

No indeed, by Apollo!

---

161. Literally, "O daemonic one" (*daimonie*), often said of one who has uttered something amazing—or crazy.

SAUSAGE-SELLER

So have you recognized by now what he's like? But me,
I bought for myself this pair of shoes here, and I give them to you
    to wear!

DEMOS

I judge you, of all those I know, to be the best man when it comes
    to Demos
And best disposed to the city and to my toes!

PAPHLAGON

Now isn't it terrible that shoes are able to do so much,   875
But you have no recollection of all the things I've done for you?
I put a stop to the buggers by removing Gryttus¹⁶² [from the
    citizen roll]!

SAUSAGE-SELLER

Well isn't it terrible that you keep a watch over buttholes
And put a stop to the buggers? And there's no way that you
Didn't put a stop to them out of envy—so they'd not become   880
    orators!
And though you see this fellow here without a cloak, at such an
    age,
You've never yet thought it worthwhile to clothe Demos,
Though it's winter. But I give him *this*. [*Hands him a garment*]

DEMOS

This sort of thing Themistocles never thought of!
Though that Piraeus thing¹⁶³ too was wise, and yet to me at least   885

---

162. Otherwise unknown. One source reads "Grypus."
163. See 815 above and the accompanying note.

It doesn't appear to be a greater invention than the cloak!

PAPHLAGON

Ah . . . wretched me . . . Such monkey-shenanigans you're
harassing me with!

SAUSAGE-SELLER

No, but I'm making use of ways that are *yours,* just as a man who's
drinking, when he wants to take a crap,
Uses another's slippers!

PAPHLAGON

890   But you won't outstrip me in flatteries. For I
Will clothe him in *this,* but you'll be saying "alas!" you bastard!

DEMOS

Yuck!
Won't you perish?!? To the crows with your very evil smelling
hide!

SAUSAGE-SELLER

And yet he put this around you for that express purpose, so he'd
suffocate you!
In fact he plotted this against you before, too! You know that
Silphium stalk,[164] when it was a good price?

DEMOS

895   I know it indeed.

SAUSAGE-SELLER

This guy on purpose went to great lengths to make it cheap

---

164. A now-extinct plant used widely in cooking and medicine.

So that people would buy it and eat it, and then in court
The jurors would fart and kill one another!

DEMOS

Yes, by Poseidon, and a man from Dungsville told me that too!

SAUSAGE-SELLER

Didn't you then fart yourselves brown?   900

DEMOS

Yes, by Zeus, that was a clever contrivance of Pyrrander!¹⁶⁵

PAPHLAGON

With such stupid tricks, you bastard, you're stirring things up
    for me!

SAUSAGE-SELLER

For the goddess ordered me to win a victory over you, by means
    of boasts!

PAPHLAGON

But you *won't* win! [*To Demos*] For I assert I'll supply you,
O Demos, with three obols to gulp down as pay for doing nothing!   905

SAUSAGE-SELLER

But I give you a little jar and some medicine
To smear on the little sores on your shins!

PAPHLAGON

And I'll make you young by picking out your gray hairs!

---

165. Although the name is attested, its main purpose here is to pun on the
same word translated in the previous line by "brown" (yellow or yellowish
brown, more precisely: *purroi*); hence a man (*-ander*) of that color.

SAUSAGE-SELLER

Here, take this rabbit's tail and wipe around your little eyes
with it.

PAPHLAGON

910　Wipe your nose, O Demos, and then wipe it off on my head!

SAUSAGE-SELLER

On mine!

PAPHLAGON

On mine!

[*To the Sausage-Seller*] I'll make you commander of a trireme,
spending

Your own money, with an ancient ship,

915　Which you'll never stop spending on and rebuilding![166]
And I'll contrive it that
You get a rotten sail!

SAUSAGE-SELLER

The man's at a boil—stop, stop!—

920　He's boiling over! You've got to take out some of the kindling
under there

And draw off the threats with this! [*Holds up a ladle*]

PAPHLAGON

You'll pay me a beautiful penalty,
Hard pressed by levies.[167]

---

166. It fell to wealthy citizens to pay for public works, including the outfitting and maintenance of triremes or warships—an expensive duty.

167. That is, taxes or levies raised by Athens to pay for the war.

For I'll bring it about   925
That you're enrolled among the rich!

SAUSAGE-SELLER

I'll threaten nothing,
But I pray for these things for you:
Your fry pan of squid is
Set out and sizzling, but you   930
Are about to render your judgment [in the Assembly] about
The Milesians, and make as a profit
A talent, if you can pull it off.[168]
Hurrying to fill yourself full of squid   935
So you might still get to the Assembly in time,
Then the man comes for you before you've eaten,
And, wanting to get that talent,
You choke [on the squid] as you're eating it!   940

CHORUS

Well done, by Zeus and Apollo and Demeter!

DEMOS

That's my opinion as well! And in other respects, too, it's plain
He's a good citizen to the obol-many, such as no man has been
For a long time.   945
But you, Paphlagon, though you claim to be my friend, you just
      feed me garlic.
And now take off your ring, since
You'll no longer be my steward.

168. See also 361 above for another reference to the Milesians, although
here as there the precise nature of the profit is unclear.

PAPHLAGON

Hold on! Know this much, that
If you won't allow me to oversee things, another, in turn,
950 More crooked than I am, will appear.

DEMOS

There's no way that this ring here
Is mine. At any rate, the signet appears different.
[*Showing it to the Sausage-Seller*] Am I just not seeing it?!?

SAUSAGE-SELLER

Let's see . . . what was your signet?

DEMOS

Cow's fat wrapped in a fig leaf that's been well baked.[169]

SAUSAGE-SELLER

It isn't there.

DEMOS

955 Not the fig leaf? What is it then?

SAUSAGE-SELLER

A seagull all agape, haranguing[170] (the) Demos on the rocks.

DEMOS

Ah, wretched me!

SAUSAGE-SELLER

What is it?!?

---

169. The word for "fat" differs only in accent from that for "demos."
170. The word is *dēmēgorōn,* related to "demagogue."

DEMOS

Take it away!

He didn't have mine, but Cleonymus's![171]

[*To the Sausage-Seller*] Take this one here from me and be my
steward!

PAPHLAGON

No, not *yet,* Master, I beseech you!   960

Not before you hear the oracles I have!

SAUSAGE-SELLER

And mine too now!

PAPHLAGON

But if you're persuaded by this guy,

You'll have to become a wineskin![172]

SAUSAGE-SELLER

And if you're persuaded by *this* guy,

Your foreskin will be pulled back right to the shaft!

PAPHLAGON

But [the oracles] say to me that you must rule   965

Over quite all the land, crowned with roses!

SAUSAGE-SELLER

While mine, in turn, say that, wearing an embroidered purple robe

---

171. A minor Athenian politician routinely lampooned by Aristophanes for
both his gluttony (*Acharnians* 88) and his cowardice; see also 1290–99 below.

172. Presumably this means that he'll be flayed alive. There may also be an
allusion here to a famous oracle pertaining to Athens, according to which the
city might be tossed about but, like a wineskin, it would never sink.

And a wreath on a golden chariot,
You'll pursue[173] Smicythe[174] and the master of the house!

DEMOS

970 [*To the Sausage-Seller*] Well, go and bring them, so this fellow here
May hear them.

SAUSAGE-SELLER

Certainly!

DEMOS

And you, you bring yours now too.

PAPHLAGON

Okay.

SAUSAGE-SELLER

Okay, by Zeus! Nothing prevents it!

[*Exit both the Sausage-Seller and Paphlagon*]

CHORUS

Most pleasant will be the light of day
For those here present and
975 For those who here arrive,
If Cleon perishes.
Yet there were certain
Quite troublesome elders
In the bazaar of the courts
980 I heard gainsaying this—

---

173. The verb can also mean "prosecute."
174. Identity uncertain. Some suggest that this feminine name may make
fun of an effeminate man actually named Smicythus.

On the grounds that if he had not become great
In the city, there'd never have been
Those two useful implements:
A pestle and a ladle.
But I for my part also wonder at this,   985
At the swinishness of his Music education.
For the boys who went to school
With him assert that
Often he would tune his lyre
Only to the Dorian[175] mode   990
And that he was unwilling to learn another.
And then the cithara teacher,
In his anger, ordered him to be led away
On the grounds that "this boy is incapable of learning   995
Anything except the Dorian!"

PAPHLAGON

There, look! And I'm not even bringing them *all* out!

SAUSAGE-SELLER

[*Carrying a heavy load*] Oh boy, how I want to take a crap! And I'm
    not even bringing them *all* out!

DEMOS

What are these here?

---

175. Spartans were Dorians and not known for their refined education in or
appreciation of the things of the Muses. Consider Aristotle, *Politics* 1342b13–14,
where he recommends that younger people learn the Dorian mode—at least
with a view to inculcating steadfastness and courage.

PAPHLAGON

Prophecies.

DEMOS

All of these?!

PAPHLAGON

Are you amazed?

1000   Yes, by Zeus, and I have a chest full of still more!

SAUSAGE-SELLER

I've got an attic and two lean-tos full!

DEMOS

Come now, whose oracles are these?

PAPHLAGON

Mine are from Bacis.

DEMOS

And whose are yours?

SAUSAGE-SELLER

They're Glanis's,[176] the older brother of Bacis.

DEMOS

[*To Paphlagon*] And what are they about?

PAPHLAGON

1005   About Athens, about Pylos,
About you, about me, about *all* matters!

------

176. A made-up name.

DEMOS

And what are *yours* about?

SAUSAGE-SELLER

About Athens, about lentil stew,
About Lacedaemonians, about fresh mackerel,
About those who do a bad job of measuring out barley in the
    marketplace,
About you, about me—[*gesturing to Paphlagon*] this guy, he can   1010
    bite the dick!

DEMOS

Well now, see that you read them to me,
In particular that one about me, which pleases me—
That I'll become an "eagle in the clouds."[177]

PAPHLAGON

Just listen, now, and pay heed to me.
"Show forth, Son of Erechtheus,[178] the path of the prophecies   1015
    that Apollo
Proclaimed to you from the innermost sanctuary through his
    much-prized tripods.
He bade you to keep safe the sacred, saw-toothed dog,
Who is open-jawed before you and barks frighteningly in your
    behalf

---

177. The oracle has been preserved in the scholium to this passage:

"Happy city of Athena, driver of spoils,
Having seen many things and suffered many things and toiled over many
    things,
An eagle in the clouds will it become for all the days."

See also *Birds* 978.
178. The name of an early king of Athens.

And will supply you with pay. And if he[179] should not do so, he'll
   perish.

1020 For many jackdaws croak in hatred against him."

DEMOS

As for these things, by Demeter, I don't know what they mean!
For what's with Erechtheus and jackdaws and a dog?

PAPHLAGON

Well, I am the dog, since I speak in your interest.
And Phoebus [Apollo] says to you to keep me safe, the dog.

SAUSAGE-SELLER

1025 The oracle doesn't say this. But this dog here
Gnaws away at your oracles as if they were doors.[180]
My [reading] is the correct one when it comes to this dog.

DEMOS

You now have your say. But first I'll get a stone
So the oracle about the dog doesn't bite me!

SAUSAGE-SELLER

1030 "Take heed,[181] son of Erechtheus, of Cerberus,[182] a slave-dealing
   dog,

---

179. The Budé reads, "if you should not do so," but without evident MS
support.

180. The Budé follows the suggestion of a modern scholar and reads,
instead of "doors" (*thuras*) with the MSS, "porridge" (*atharēs*). Wilson (ad loc.)
defends the reading of the MSS.

181. The Sausage-Seller's prophecy begins with the same word (*phradzeu*),
as does Paphlagon's at 1015; the word has a range of meanings.

182. The terrifying, multiheaded guard dog in Hades; see, e.g., *Frogs* 467 as
well as Hesiod, *Theogony* 310–12.

Who wags his tail whenever you're dining, and, keeping a
    close watch,
He'll devour your fine food, whenever you gape in another
    direction.
And often visiting the kitchen, he'll go undetected, like
    a dog
At night, licking clean the dishes and the islands."

DEMOS

By Poseidon, that's much better, O Glanis!   1035

PAPHLAGON

O Sir, listen to this, *then* form a judgment:
"There is a woman who will bear a lion in sacred Athens,
A lion who will do battle for Demos against many gnats,
As steadfastly as for his cubs. Guard him,
Building a wooden wall[183] and iron towers."   1040
Do you know what these things mean?

DEMOS

By Apollo, I don't!

PAPHLAGON

The god was clearly indicating to you to keep me safe.
For I correspond to the lion for you.

---

183. Herodotus reports (7.141) an oracle of Apollo, prior to the Persian
War of 480, that the whole land of Athens would be conquered except a
"wooden wall." This encouraged the Athenians to put complete confidence in
their navy.

DEMOS

And how did you escape my notice, having become Antileon?[184]

SAUSAGE-SELLER

1045   There's one of the prophecies he isn't explaining on purpose—
What the "wall of iron and of wood" is,
Where Loxias[185] ordered him to keep you safe.

DEMOS

So how *did* the god mean that?!?

SAUSAGE-SELLER

This guy here
He ordered you to lock up in a five-holed wooden pillory!

DEMOS

1050   *These* prophecies will soon be fulfilled, seems to me!

PAPHLAGON

Don't be persuaded by him! For "envious are the crows that
    caw"!
But "be a friend to the hawk, remembering him in your heart," he
    who
Brought back for you young Lacedaemonian ravens[186] in
    fetters!

---

184. At 1044, Paphlagon says that he "corresponds to the lion" (*anti tou leontos*); Demos now wonders how Paphlagon became Antileon (*Antileōn*), also the name of a tyrant of Chalcis.

185. That is, Apollo.

186. The word (*korakinous*) can also refer to a kind of fish, so called because of its black color. Paphlagon is once again referring to the Spartans captured on Sphacteria.

SAUSAGE-SELLER

Paphlagon took *that* risk when he was drunk![187]

"Son of Cecrops, ill-advised, why do you hold this to be a great   1055
    deed?

A woman, too, might bear a weight, should a man place it on
    her.[188]

But she couldn't fight. For she'd crap herself, should she fight."

PAPHLAGON

But take heed of this, "before Pylos, Pylos," which [the god]
    declared to you:

"There is a Pylos before Pylos."[189]

DEMOS

What does this mean, "before Pylos"?

SAUSAGE-SELLER

He contends that he'll seize a pile of tubs in the bathhouse![190]   1060

DEMOS

And I'll be unwashed today?!?

---

187. Consider Thucydides 4.27–28 and 39.2 (and context).

188. The words for "woman" and "man" in this line can also mean "wife"
and "husband," respectively.

189. The full verse, which may have been a proverb rather than an oracle,
reads: "There is a Pylos before Pylos, and there is another Pylos besides." This
is said to refer to "the dispute among three places in the western Peloponnese,
all bearing the name Pylos and all claiming to be the Pylos where Nestor had
ruled" (Sommerstein, *Knights* ad loc.).

190. The word for "tubs" (*pyelous*) suggests "Pylos."

SAUSAGE-SELLER

For this guy'll snatch up our pile of tubs![191]
But *this* oracle here concerns the navy,
To which you ought to pay very close attention.

DEMOS

1065 I am—but read first how
My sailors will receive their pay.

SAUSAGE-SELLER

"Son of Aegeus, take heed of the dog-fox, lest he trick you,
Biting-without-barking, swift-footed, a wily trickster, highly
   shrewd."
Do you know what this is?

DEMOS

Philostratus[192] the dog-fox!

SAUSAGE-SELLER

1070 It doesn't say that, but the swift, revenue-collecting
Ships this guy here is always asking for:
Loxias is forbidding you to give these to him.

DEMOS

So how is a trireme a dog-fox?

SAUSAGE-SELLER

How, you ask?
Well, the trireme and the dog are both swift.

---

191. This line is missing in two MSS. Sommerstein, *Knights,* among other
modern editors, rejects it as a gloss, although Neil and Wilson read it.
192. A pimp (see also *Lysistrate* 957).

DEMOS

How is it, then, that the "fox" was added to the "dog"?   1075

SAUSAGE-SELLER

It drew a likeness between soldiers and foxes
Because they nibble grapes in the fields.

DEMOS

Well then—
Where's the pay for these foxes?

SAUSAGE-SELLER

I'll supply it, and that within three days.[193]
But listen closely to this too, to the oracle of the Son of Leto[194]   1080
That said to you "Beware Crooked Harbor,[195]
Lest it trick you."

DEMOS

What "Crooked"?!?

SAUSAGE-SELLER

[The oracle] correctly has it that this guy's hand
Is Crooked, because he says, "Throw [a little something] in my
     crooked hand."[196]

---

193. This alludes to Cleon's evidently crazy vow to kill or capture the Spartan soldiers on Sphacteria "within twenty days" (Thucydides 4.27-28 and
context).

194. That is, Apollo.

195. Literally, Cyllene (harbor)—the name of the harbor in Elis, but used
here because it begins with the same syllable as does the adjective "crooked"
or "twisted" (*kyll-*).

196. The cry of alms-seeking beggars.

PAPHLAGON

He's explaining it incorrectly. For when it comes to "Crooked,"
1085   The correct thing is that Phoebus [Apollo] enigmatically spoke of
the hand of Diopeithes.[197]
But I have an oracle concerning you, a winged one,
How you'll become an eagle and rule as king over every land.

SAUSAGE-SELLER

I do too! Over land and the Red Sea[198] too,
And you'll judge cases in Ecbatana, licking up cake-and-sauce!

PAPHLAGON

1090   But I had a dream, and the goddess herself[199] seemed to me
To be pouring health-and-wealth over Demos with a pail!

SAUSAGE-SELLER

By Zeus, I had one too! And the goddess herself seemed to me
To come from the Acropolis, an owl perched upon her.
Then with a flask she poured over your head a libation of
1095   Ambrosia—but over *this* guy, garlic brine!

DEMOS

Oh! Oh!

---

197. An expert in oracles, prosecutor of atheists, apparently possessed of a misshapen hand or hands, and "widely regarded as not quite sane" (Sommerstein, *Knights* ad loc.).

198. "This meant in the classical period not only the modern Red Sea south of the Suez Canal but also our Persian Gulf and Arabian Sea." Hence this would suggest for Aristophanes and his audience "a spot on the farthest shores of the Persian Empire." Nan Dunbar, *Aristophanes: Birds* (Oxford: Clarendon Press, 1995), 180.

199. That is, Athena.

Nobody's wiser than Glanis!
And now I turn myself over to you here
"To guide me in my old age and to educate me afresh once
   again"![200]

PAPHLAGON

Not yet, I beseech you, just wait a bit, since   1100
I'll supply you with barley and your daily sustenance!

DEMOS

I can't tolerate hearing about barley! Often
I was deceived by you and Thuphanes![201]

PAPHLAGON

But I already supply you with prepared barley groats!

SAUSAGE-SELLER

But I'll supply nicely baked barley biscuits   1105
And the relish for them too: there's nothing to do but eat!

DEMOS

You two now hurry and do whatever it is you're going to do.
   Because
Whichever one of you now benefits me more,
To him I'll give over the reins of the Pnyx!

PAPHLAGON

I'm going to run inside first!

SAUSAGE-SELLER

No, but I will!   1110

---

200. A fragment from Sophocles' lost *Peleus*.
201. Apparently a public official and partisan of Cleon.

[Exit Paphlagon and the Sausage-Seller]

CHORUS

O Demos, noble
Is your rule,[202]
Since all human beings fear you
As they would a man who's tyrant.[203]
1115 But you are easily led astray:
You delight in being flattered
And utterly deceived,
Gaping before whoever happens
To be speaking. And your mind,
1120 Though it's around, is on vacation.

DEMOS

There's no mind in that long hair
Of yours, since you believe that I'm not sensible.
But I voluntarily
Say such foolish things.
1125 For I myself take pleasure
In my daily feeding,
And I want to raise up
One thief as leader.
But when he's full,
1130 Having raised him up, I knock him down.

CHORUS

That way you would do well,

---

202. The same word for "rule" (*archē*) can mean "empire."
203. For Athens as a tyrant, or like one, consider Thucydides 2.63 (Pericles) and 3.37 (Cleon).

If there is sagacity
In this character of yours, as you say,
Very great sagacity indeed,
If on purpose you raise up these   1135
Like public property,
On the Pnyx, and then whenever
You happen not to have any fine food,
Whoever among these is plump
You sacrifice and dine on!   1140

DEMOS

Examine me, as to whether I wisely
Outmaneuver them,
They who suppose they're sensible
And utterly fool me.
For I keep a constant watch over them   1145
Even though I *seem* not to see them
Stealing. Then I force them
To vomit up again
Whatever they've stolen from me,
Using the funnel of the voting urn as a probe.[204]   1150

[*Paphlagon and the Sausage-Seller return*]

PAPHLAGON
Get out of the blessed bloody way!

---

204. The suggestion is that sooner or later Demos forces the democratic
leaders to give back their ill-gotten gains as the result of being found guilty by
a jury.

SAUSAGE-SELLER

You, you pest!

PAPHLAGON

O Demos, I've been sitting here
For a long, long time, all ready and willing to benefit you!

SAUSAGE-SELLER

And *I've* been here for ten long and twelve long
1155 And a thousand long, long-long-long times!

DEMOS

And I, expecting [you] for thirty thousand long times,
I'm revolted by you both—and for a long-long-long time!

SAUSAGE-SELLER

So do you know what to do?

DEMOS

I will know, if you tell me.

SAUSAGE-SELLER

Let us go, me and this guy, from the starting line
So we can benefit you from an equal start.

DEMOS

1160 That's what must be done.
Off you two go [to the starting line]!

SAUSAGE-SELLER AND PAPHLAGON

There!

DEMOS

Run!

SAUSAGE-SELLER

[*To Paphlagon*] No cutting in allowed!

DEMOS

Well, either I'll be made greatly happy today
By these lovers, by Zeus, or else I'll play hard to get!

PAPHLAGON

See? I'm bringing out the seat for you first!

SAUSAGE-SELLER

But not a table! I brought that out firster! 1165

PAPHLAGON

Look, I'm bringing you this here barley biscuit
Kneaded from the grain from Pylos!

SAUSAGE-SELLER

And I've got breads scooped out to ladle the soup,
Made by the ivory hand of the goddess![205]

DEMOS

How big your finger is, O Mistress! 1170

PAPHLAGON

And I've got pea soup, fresh and beautiful,
That Pallas [Athena] herself, Pylisades-Fighter,[206] stirred!

---

205. The loaves must very large, since the Parthenon's statue of Athena
was said to be nearly seven times life size. See also Carl A. Anderson, "Athena's
Big Finger: An Unnoticed Sexual Joke in Aristophanes' *Knights*," *Classical Phi-
lology* 103:2 (2008): 175–81.

206. A genuine epithet of Athena (*pylaimachos*), "Fighter at the Gates," but
its first syllable brings to mind "Pylos."

SAUSAGE-SELLER

O Demos, plainly the goddess is watching over you!
In fact right now she is holding over you a pot full of broth!

DEMOS

1175 Yes, for do you suppose that this city would still be inhabited
If she did not manifestly hold over us her . . . pot?[207]

PAPHLAGON

This slice of fish here the Terrifier of Armies[208] has given you!

SAUSAGE-SELLER

And the Daughter of the Mighty Father [has given you] meat
    boiled in broth
And a slice of tripe and stomach and belly!

DEMOS

1180 A fine thing she did, in remembering the Robe [I gave her]![209]

PAPHLAGON

The Gorgon-Crested One[210] bade you to eat this
Flat cake, so that we may row our ships finely.

SAUSAGE-SELLER

Now take these things here too.

---

207. According to a famous verse of the Athenian statesman Solon, Athena
held her hands over Athens in protection of it.

208. Epithet of Athena.

209. See 566 above.

210. Presumably an epithet of Athena. In its masculine form, it is applied
to Lamachus in the *Acharnians*.

DEMOS

And what use will I make
Of these innards?

SAUSAGE-SELLER

She sent them to you expressly
To use as belly-timber for the triremes, the goddess did!   1185
For she's obviously keeping a watch on the navy.
Take this too and drink it, mixed three [parts wine] to two [of water].

DEMOS

How sweet, O Zeus, and finely does it take the three parts!

SAUSAGE-SELLER

Yes, for Tritogenes [Athena] made it tripartite![211]

PAPHLAGON

And now take from me a slice of rich cake!   1190

SAUSAGE-SELLER

From me this whole cake!

PAPHLAGON

But you won't have anything from which you can give him hare's
    meat.[212] But I do!

SAUSAGE-SELLER

Oh boy . . . where'll I get hare's meat?
O Spirit, now discover some beggarly trick!

---

211. Athena's epithet suggests her connection to Lake Tritonis in Libya, but
here the Sausage-Seller puns on the prefix *tri-* (three).

212. Hares were rare in Attica, especially so in wartime; see Sommerstein,
Knights ad loc.

PAPHLAGON

[*Brings hare out of his sack*] See *that*, you wretch?

SAUSAGE-SELLER

1195 Matters little to me!
For there are some ambassadors coming over to me,
With bags of silver!

PAPHLAGON

Where?!? Where?!?

SAUSAGE-SELLER

But what's that to you? Won't you leave the foreigners alone?
[*Snatches up Paphlagon's meat*] O little Demos! Do you see the
hares I'm bringing you?

PAPHLAGON

1200 Oh, wretched me! You've snatched up my things unjustly!

SAUSAGE-SELLER

Yes, by Poseidon, just as you did with the men from Pylos!

DEMOS

[*To the Sausage-Seller*] Tell me, I beseech you, how did you think
of snatching them?

SAUSAGE-SELLER

The thought belongs to the goddess, the theft was mine.
But I ran the risk![213]

PAPHLAGON

But *I* roasted it!

---

213. Some editors give this line to Paphlagon.

DEMOS

Go away—for the thanks go only to the person who served   1205
   it up!

PAPHLAGON

Oh unhappy me! I'm going to be outdone in shamelessness!

SAUSAGE-SELLER

Why don't you judge, Demos, which of the two of us
Is the better man when it comes to you and your stomach?

DEMOS

But by using what evidence
Might I seem to the audience to judge wisely?   1210

SAUSAGE-SELLER

I'll tell you. Go get
My basket, in silence, and examine what's in it,
And Paphlagon's too. Not to worry, you'll make a fine
   decision!

DEMOS

Well now, what's in here?

SAUSAGE-SELLER

Don't you see it's empty,   1215
Dear Grampa? For I served up *everything* for you!

DEMOS

This basket is taking thought for what concerns Demos!

SAUSAGE-SELLER

Now stroll over there to Paphlagon's.
Do you see?

DEMOS

Oh! How many goods it's full of!

How big that cake is he put aside for himself!

1220 But for *me* he sliced off just this little bit!

SAUSAGE-SELLER

Yet he was doing that sort of thing to you before too—

Giving over to you a little of what he got,

While putting aside for himself the greater share!

DEMOS

You bloody bastard! You deceived me by stealing these things?!?

1225 But I "crowned you and bestowed gifts upon you"![214]

PAPHLAGON

But I was stealing for the good of the city!

DEMOS

Put down your wreath immediately, so I

May put it on this fellow here!

SAUSAGE-SELLER

Take it off immediately, you fit-to-be-whipped-crook!

PAPHLAGON

No! For I have a Pythian oracle

1230 That indicates the only one by whom I ought to be defeated!

SAUSAGE-SELLER

Indicating my name—and perfectly clearly!

---

214. This line, in Doric dialect, is of uncertain origin. Sommerstein suggests that it comes from the comic poet Eupolis.

PAPHLAGON

Well, I want to test you by means of the evidence,
If you'll turn out to accord with the things decreed by the god.
And first I'll put you to this much of a test:
When you were a boy, what school did you attend? 1235

SAUSAGE-SELLER

I was disciplined in the slaughterhouses, with knuckles!

PAPHLAGON

What's that you said?! [*Aside*] How the oracle grips my heart!
Well then . . .
What wrestling moves did you learn from the trainer?

SAUSAGE-SELLER

When stealing, to swear a false oath while looking 'em straight in
the face!

PAPHLAGON

"O Phoebus Apollo of Lycia, whatever will you do to me?"[215] 1240
And whatever was the art you gained when you reached manhood?

SAUSAGE-SELLER

Selling sausages and . . . getting screwed some!

PAPHLAGON

[*Aside*] Oh, wretched me! I'm no longer anything!
There's *some* hope remaining to which we hold fast . . .
[*To the Sausage-Seller*] And tell me this much: was it in the 1245
marketplace
Or at the city gates that you usually sold your sausages?

---

215. A fragment of Euripides' *Telephus*.

SAUSAGE-SELLER

At the gates, where they sell salt-fish.

PAPHLAGON

Ah! What's decreed by the god has been fulfilled!
"Roll me inside, this ill-starred fellow!"²¹⁶
1250 O Wreath, fare-thee-well, unwillingly
Do I leave you. But someone else, taking you up, will possess
    you,
One who's not more of a thief than I am . . . but maybe luckier.

SAUSAGE-SELLER

Zeus of the Greeks, the victory prize is yours!

DEMOSTHENES²¹⁷

O Gracious Noble Victor! And remember that
1255 You've become a real man through me! And in brief I ask you
That I'll be your Phanus,²¹⁸ clerk of lawsuits!

[*Exit Demosthenes*]

DEMOS

Tell me, what is your name?

SAUSAGE-SELLER

Agoracritus.
For I was raised disputing things in the marketplace.²¹⁹

---

216. Parody of a line from Euripides' *Bellerophon.*

217. Some MSS give these lines to the Chorus, although both the Budé and the OCT give it to Demosthenes.

218. Mentioned also at *Wasps* 1220, in a list that includes Theorus and Cleon.

219. Agoracritus's name is ambiguous. Neil (ad loc.) suggests that *-critus* means "approved by" and hence "Marketplace-approved." Yet the Sausage-

DEMOS

To Agoracritus, then, I entrust myself,
And I hand over this Paphlagon here.   1260

SAUSAGE-SELLER

And I, O Demos, will take fine care of you,
So you'll agree that you see no human being
Better than I am, for this city of Gaping-thenians!

CHORUS

"What finer thing is there for those beginning
Or ending [a song] than for drivers of swift horses not to sing   1265
    of . . ."220
Anything against Lysistratus
Nor with a willing heart
To cause the homeless Thumantis any further pain?221
For he, O Dear Apollo, is ever   1270
Hungry, and with abundant tears
Touches your quiver [in supplication],
In divine Pytho, so that he not be badly impoverished.
There is nothing invidious in reviling those who are dirty
    crooks;

Seller's own, presumably comic explanation of his name is different, the parti-
ciple in the next line connected with it (*krinomenos*) meaning "one who judges"
or "one who is judged" but also "disputing." Mitchell (ad loc.) calls this a "difficult verse" and suggests as a translation "quarrelling, battling, litigating":
perhaps "marketplace-wrangler."

220. A parody of lines of Pindar (fr. 89).

221. Lysistratus was an Athenian mentioned elsewhere by Aristophanes
(*Acharnians* 855–56, *Wasps* 1311–13) as being impoverished. Nothing certain is
known of Thumantis, although one source reports that he was very thin.

1275   Rather, [doing so amounts to] an honor paid to the upstanding,
        for whoever reckons well.

      If, then, the human being who ought to hear many bad things said
        of him,

      Were himself well known, I would not have mentioned a man
        who's a friend.

      Now there's nobody who does not know Arignotus,[222] at least not
        anybody who knows white from . . . the Orthion tune.[223]

1280   Yet he has a brother whose characteristic ways are not akin to his
        own,

      Ariphrades, a dirty crook.[224] But this he even *wants* to be!

      But he's not only a crook—I wouldn't even have noticed him in
        that case,

      Not even if he were entirely crooked. But in fact, he's devised
        something on top of that!

      For he treats his own tongue outrageously with shameful
        pleasures:

1285   In whorehouses he licks the abominable dew,

      Both soiling his mustache and stirring up their hearths,[225]

      Acting like Polymnestus and associating with Oeonichus.[226]

---

222. A famous lyre player (*Wasps* 1277–78).

223. In place of the usual "white from black," Aristophanes substitutes "Orthion tune," which was "one of the most famous Greek melodies" (Sommerstein, *Knights* ad loc.); see also *Acharnians* 16.

224. See also *Wasps* 1280–83 and *Peace* 883–85, where the man is mentioned again.

225. "Hearths" is a euphemism for the female genitalia also at *Thesmophoriazusae* 912.

226. Polymnestus was a seventh-century musician, Oeonichus evidently a musician or poet. "Associating with" can also mean "having intercourse with."

Whoever, then, does not intensely loathe such a man
Will never drink from the same cup with us.
Many times in the night   1290
I've been together with my thoughts
And inquired however in the world it is that
Cleonymus eats so easily.[227]
For they assert that he, feeding on
What belongs to wealthy men,   1295
Wouldn't leave the trough,
But they all alike would beseech him,
"Come now, O Lord, by your knees,
Leave—have some sympathy for the table!"
They contend that the triremes gathered with one another for a   1300
    parley,
And a certain one of them, who was older, said:
"You don't even inquire, Maidens,[228] about these things
    pertaining to the city?!
They say that somebody is requesting one hundred of us for
    Carthage,
A man who's a base citizen, that sour Hyperbolus."[229]
Now this was in their opinion terrible and not to be tolerated,   1305
And someone, who had never come near men,[230] said,

---

227. With so great an appetite as he has; see also 958 above.

228. "Trireme" (a fast-sailing warship) is feminine in Greek, and so the
ships are personified as women.

229. An ambitious Athenian politician, a lamp-seller by trade, frequently
mocked by Aristophanes (*Acharnians* 846–47, *Clouds* 1065, *Peace* 690). After
Cleon's death, Hyperbolus rose to take his place as demagogue. See also 739
above.

230. That is, had never been boarded by men, a "virginal" ship.

"Averter!²³¹ [Hyperbolus] will never rule over *me*, but if I have to,
I'll grow old right here, rotting away with wormwood!"
"Nor over Nauphantes, daughter of Nauson, no indeed, O Gods!

1310   If in fact I was built from pine and timbers!

If these things are to the Athenians' liking, I think it best that,
Sailing to the Theseum²³² or to [the shrine] of the August
    Goddesses,²³³ we take sanctuary.

For he won't make a mockery of the city by being our general!
Just let him sail by himself—to the crows with him!—if he wants
    to,

1315   Launching the trays on which he used to sell his lamps!"

SAUSAGE-SELLER

One must speak good omens and close one's mouth and abstain
    from calling witnesses
And close up the law courts, in which this city has taken such
    delight,
But given our novel good fortune, let the theater sing a paean.

CHORUS

O Light of sacred Athens and helpmate to the islands,

1320   With what good report have you come, for which we fill with
    sacrificial smoke our streets?

SAUSAGE-SELLER

Having boiled Demos for you, I've made him, once ugly, now
    beautiful!

---

231. Epithet of Apollo, who averted evils for human beings.

232. The shrine to Theseus, legendary founder of Athens as a unified
whole; see Thucydides 2.15 and context.

233. That is, the Furies.

CHORUS

And where is he now, O you who've discovered wondrous
   notions?

SAUSAGE-SELLER

He dwells in the violet-crowned[234] Athens of olden times!

CHORUS

How might we see him? What sort of outfit is he wearing? What
   sort of fellow has he become?

SAUSAGE-SELLER

Such as he was previously when he shared a mess with Aristides   1325
   and Miltiades.[235]
But you will see. For . . . there now is the sound of the Propylaea[236]
   being opened!
Just give a joyful shout for the Athens of old as it comes into
   sight,
Both wondrous and much-hymned, where famed Demos dwells!

CHORUS

O Athens—Gleaming and Violet-Crowned and Much-Envied!
Show us the monarch of Greece and of this land!   1330

---

234. An epithet of Athens in the poetry of Pindar; see also *Acharnians*
637-38.

235. Aristides, nicknamed "The Just," was an Athenian general and statesman who served during the Persian War, including at the battle of Marathon.
Miltiades was from a distinguished Athenian family, and he too served as a
general at Marathon.

236. The western entrance of the Acropolis; Demos emerges from the *skēnē*
at the back of the stage in his new garb.

SAUSAGE-SELLER

There he is to see, wearing a golden grasshopper,[237] gleaming in
    his garb of old,
Smelling not of seashells[238] but of treaties, anointed with myrrh.

CHORUS

Greetings, O King of the Greeks! We share in your joy as well!
For you carry out deeds worthy of the city and of the trophy
    erected at Marathon.

DEMOS

1335   O Dearest of Men, come here, Agoracritus!
So many are the goods you've done me, by boiling me!

SAUSAGE-SELLER

Me?
Well, my fellow, you don't know what sort of fellow you really
    were before,
Or the sorts of things you used to do! For [if you did know] you'd
    believe me to be a god!

DEMOS

What did I do before, tell me, and what sort was I?

SAUSAGE-SELLER

1340   First, whenever somebody should say in the Assembly,
"O Demos, I am your lover and I am your friend[239]
And I care for you and deliberate for you, I alone"—

---

237. An old-fashioned and aristocratic adornment characteristic of pre-
democratic Athens; see Thucydides 1.6.

238. Athenian jurors used seashells or mussel shells to cast votes.

239. Consider Paphlagon's remark at 732.

Whenever somebody should use these preludes,
You'd flap your wings and toss your horns!

DEMOS

I *did?*

SAUSAGE-SELLER

Then, in exchange for these things, he'd go off, having completely   1345
   fooled you.

DEMOS

What are you saying?!?
They used to say these things to me, and I didn't perceive it?

SAUSAGE-SELLER

Because your ears, by Zeus, would spread open
Just like a parasol and then close up again.

DEMOS

Had I become so thoughtless and old?

SAUSAGE-SELLER

Yes, by Zeus, and if two orators should speak,   1350
The one in favor of making long ships, the other one, in turn,
For using this for public pay, the guy talking about pay
Would run right over the one talking triremes.
[*Pauses*] You there . . . why are you bowing your head? Won't you
   remain as you were?

DEMOS

I'm ashamed, you know, at my former mistakes.   1355

SAUSAGE-SELLER

But you're not responsible for these things, don't fret.

Rather it's those who deceived you in this. So now tell me:
If some tricky beggar of an advocate says:
"There's no barley for your jurors,
1360 Unless you pronounce a guilty verdict in this case,"
What, tell me, will you do to that advocate?

DEMOS

Tossing him in the air I'll throw him into the pit,
With Hyperbolus hanging from his neck!

SAUSAGE-SELLER

Now there you're speaking correctly and prudently!
1365 But as for the rest, come now, how will you govern? Tell me.

DEMOS

First, all those who row the long ships
I'll pay in full when they put in to shore.

SAUSAGE-SELLER

You just gratified many flat-bottomed little butts!

DEMOS

Then no hoplite, once placed on a roll,
1370 Will, by going to great lengths, get himself moved to a different
        one,
But instead he'll stay where he was registered from the first.

SAUSAGE-SELLER

That bites Cleonymus's shield handle!

DEMOS

Nor will anyone without a beard speak out publicly in the
        marketplace.

SAUSAGE-SELLER

So where will Cleisthenes and Straton speak out?!?[240]

DEMOS

I mean those lads in the perfume market   1375
Who chatter away like this while seated there:
"Wise Phaeax cleverly didn't die.[241]
For he's argumentatively aggressive and conclusive
And maxim-coining-clever and clear and striking,
Best at being able to check the uproarious."   1380

SAUSAGE-SELLER

Aren't you skilled at flipping-off-with-the-finger whoever
    chatters away?

DEMOS

By Zeus, no! Instead I'll compel them all to go hunting,
Putting a stop to their decree-making!

[*A servant holding a folding chair enters*]

SAUSAGE-SELLER

Now in that case take hold of this folding chair here
And the boy, balls and all, who'll bring it to you.   1385
And if it seems at all best to you, use *him* as a chair to sit on!

---

240. Two beardless, or perhaps clean-shaven, men mocked for their effeminacy; see also *Acharnians* 122 and context.

241. That is, he was acquitted on a capital charge. Phaeax was a prominent Athenian politician around the time of the Peace of Nicias, although it is not known what charge is here at issue.

DEMOS

Blessed I am to be again in the ancient ways!

SAUSAGE-SELLER

You will indeed assert it, when
I give over to you the thirty-year peace treaty! Come here, Treaty,
    quick!

[*A beautiful girl appears*]

DEMOS

1390   O Much-Honored Zeus! How beautiful! In the name of
        the gods,
Is it permissible to thirty-year-icize her?!?²⁴²
Wherever did you get her?

SAUSAGE-SELLER

Wasn't Paphlagon
Hiding her away inside, so you wouldn't get her?
So now I hand her over to you
To take her and go off to your fields.

DEMOS

1395   That Paphlagon,
Who did this—I hope you'll do something bad to him!

SAUSAGE-SELLER

Nothing big—he'll just take over my art.

---

242. Aristophanes coins a term (*katatriakontoutisai*) that bears a resemblance to "thirty year" (*triakontoutidas*) but can also be taken to mean "'to pierce them (*outasi*) three times (*tria*) with a long pole (*kontos*) from below (*kata-*)'" (Sommerstein, *Knights* ad loc.).

He alone will sell sausages at the gates,
Mixing up dog meat with donkey . . . affairs.
Getting drunk he'll talk trash with the whores   1400
And drink the water from the bathhouses.

DEMOS

You've thought out well what he deserves!
To have a shouting match with whores and bath men!
And you I invite, in return for these things, to the Prytaneum
And to the seating there, where that poisoner used to be.   1405
Take this frog-green robe and follow along
And let someone carry off *that* guy to his art
So the foreigners whom he used to mistreat may see him!

On the *Knights*

The *Knights* was performed at the Lenaea of 424 B.C.E., where (like its immediate predecessor, the *Acharnians*) it was awarded first place.[1] The most obvious theme of the *Knights* is altogether political: the restoration of Athenian democracy such that it will once again be what it was during the glory days of Marathon and Salamis, when Athens fought off the aggression of the barbarian Medes (781–85, 1334). One might suppose, it is true, that the play abstracts from politics entirely on account of the comic conceit at its center. For rather than depicting the city of Athens and its people, the demos, who constitute the city's majority and hold its power, Aristophanes instead portrays the city as a single household headed by a certain (Mr.) Demos and run by three "servants": the newly purchased Paphlagon ("Blusterer"),[2] the stand-in for the notorious demagogue Cleon; the great general Demosthenes; and Nicias, also a prominent general. But what is the upshot of that portrayal? By making the polis equivalent to a single household, the people to a single person, Aristophanes in effect removes not politics but family life from the *Knights*. In contrast to the *Lysistrate*, *Assembly of Women*, and *Peace*, for example, no women or children are featured in the play; the woman and the boy who appear very briefly at the play's end point only to erotic delights and not at all to family life. The *Knights*, then (in contrast to, say, the *Acharnians* or

---

1. See, e.g., the Budé, 69; and Sommerstein, *Knights*, 2.

2. See n. 2 to the translation.

Wasps), does not include within its purview the possible tension between city and family. The theme of the tension between city and family is replaced by that of the cleavages between or among the political classes: the poor majority, who cannot be equated with the city entire;[3] the ambitious few who seek to lead them; and the wealthy upper classes, to which the very title of the play draws our attention. (Knights had to supply their own equipment and horses, and, then as now, horses are a very expensive affair.)[4] Moreover, although the play will feature the political use of allegedly divine oracles, no god appears on stage. Nothing that might transcend the world of Demos, of the Athenian demos understood as a political class, is permitted to appear there.[5] The *Knights,* to repeat, is an altogether political play.[6]

The political restoration of Athens is brought about by two key events: first, the rise of a hand-picked sausage-seller, Agoracritus by name (1258), who proves instrumental in the fall of Cleon and even becomes the sole servant of Demos; and, second, the Sausage-

---

3. Consider "O City and Demos!" (273) and "Before the Athenians and Demos" (811): the demos may be the single largest class in the city, but it remains only one of the classes.

4. Consider Aristotle, *Politics* 1289b33–36: "We see that the demos is in part farming, in part of the marketplace, in part laboring. And among the notables there are also differences in point of wealth and the size of the property—for example, in horse breeding, for this is not easy to do for those who are not wealthy."

5. Gods and demigods appear in *Acharnians* (Amphitheus), *Clouds* (Hermes), *Peace* (Polemos, Hermes, perhaps Peace), *Birds* (Iris, Prometheus, Poseidon, the Triballian, Heracles), *Frogs* (Dionysus, Heracles, Pluto), and *Wealth* (Plutus, Penia, Hermes).

6. Consider Leo Strauss, *Socrates and Aristophanes* (Chicago: University of Chicago Press, 1966), 108 and context.

Seller's rejuvenation of the elderly and befuddled Demos by way of a miraculous "boiling" that renders him young and beautiful—and sensible—once again. These two events lead inevitably to a joyful ending in which the Sausage-Seller receives his just reward, Paphlagon his just punishment, and the household of Demos is set aright top to bottom. All will now be well with Demos and hence with the Athenian democracy. Both the leadership of the city and its people are, in the world of the comedy, vastly improved, and even the Peloponnesian War is brought to an end in its seventh year (793). The obvious message of the play, then, is that Athens must finally flush Cleon out of its political system. He is a dangerous and self-serving demagogue who only makes the demos worse and lines his own pockets all the while. In addition, since the removal of Cleon from public life requires (as we will see) the cooperation of a lowly sausage-seller, the distinguished general Demosthenes, and the wealthy Knights, Aristophanes seems to imply that a mixed regime, encompassing the poor but with the active cooperation of the upper classes, would be better than a pure democracy, prone as it always is to demagogic manipulation.

Before turning to the *Knights,* we should sketch some of the most important political facts that inform it. In 428 B.C.E., the city of Mytilene (consider 834), on the island of Lesbos, revolted from Athens in the hope that it could unite the whole island and rule it, urged on in this by the Spartans. The Athenians found this act of rebellion particularly galling because they had always treated the city with consideration, allowing it to maintain its own defensive walls, for example, and fleet of triremes or warships (Thucydides 3.39.2). In their anger, the Athenians initially voted to kill all the Mytilenean adult males and to enslave the women and children. Soon gripped, however, by misgivings over the harshness of their own decree, the Athenians convened a second assembly to reconsider their decision. Here Cleon, "the most violent of the citizens and much the most persuasive with the demos at that time" (Thucydides 3.36.6), rose to speak with fiery indignation in favor of maintaining the preceding day's decision: kill or enslave them all. The speech as recorded by Thucydides is a decidedly noncomic presentation of the character of Athens' leading demagogue of the period and so is useful in bringing to life the words and deeds of "Paphlagon."[7]

Infinitely more attractive, in both Thucydides and the *Knights,* is Cleon's counterpart, Demosthenes. Thucydides first mentions him in connection with naval operations in the summer of 426 (3.91). Subsequently, Demosthenes on his own initiative undertook to subdue part of Aetolia. As a result not least of his own error or impatience, however, he suffered a terrible loss there, one that led to the death of "the best men from the city of Athens who perished in this war," according to Thucydides (3.98.4). So terrible was his defeat, in fact, that Demosthenes declined to return to Athens for fear of its angry retribution. He eventually redeemed himself, more than redeemed himself, first by gaining a signal victory over the Ambraciots (3.105–14), then by taking advantage of a chance storm to implement a plan he had conceived: to put in at the small town of Pylos, on the coast of the Peloponnese, and fortify it. This move permitted Demosthenes to launch a surprise attack on the adjacent island of Sphacteria and eventually surround the 420 Spartan hoplites stationed there. This stunning turn brought Sparta to the peace table—and Cleon again or still more to the fore. Convincing the Athenians to reject Spartan peace overtures and

---

7. For the text of Cleon's speech, see the appendix.

mocking Nicias and the other generals for their failure to have settled the matter by immediately bringing the Spartans back to
Athens as prisoners, Cleon contended that if "real men" (*andres:*
4.27.5) were in command—like him—the thing could be done forth-
with. Nicias called his bluff; Cleon balked; the crowd gleefully
goaded him on "as it is wont to do" (4.28.3); and in the end he was
forced to accept the command—adding, with entirely unearned
bravado, that he would carry the whole thing off in under twenty
days. But Cleon was no fool. His first act as commander was to
select Demosthenes as his colleague. Led by Demosthenes in fact,
the Athenians did capture the Spartan soldiers, who astonished the
Greek world by surrendering, and Cleon's seemingly crazy boast
(*Knights* 1054) was in this way vindicated. Thus he was riding high
in the wake of the Pylos affair and at the time of the *Knights*' performance. So it is, too, that the play refers to Pylos some fourteen
times; Demosthenes himself is made to complain that, "the other
day," while he "was kneading a Laconian barley-cake at Pylos, /
How very much like the dirtiest crook did [Paphlagon] run around
me and snatch it up, / And he himself served the cake *I'd* kneaded!"
(54–57).

Finally, the pairing of Demosthenes and Nicias at the play's
beginning is compatible with the fact that, of the ten elected generals in Athens, they were the most prominent by far. And although
Aristophanes could not have known it when he composed the
Knights, it would eventually fall to the same pair to try to save the
Sicilian expedition (415–413 B.C.E.), Athens' ultimately ruinous
attempt to subjugate the whole of that distant island. Even in the
brief opening scene of the play, Aristophanes captures well the
characteristic traits of the two generals, Demosthenes with his
clever inventiveness, especially when in a tight spot, and Nicias's

far more cautious outlook: he lacked boldness (17), was reluctant to fight (consider 13), and was deeply pious (30–35). With this much as preparation we may turn to that opening scene.

Demosthenes and Nicias begin by lamenting their current plight. Each is suffering daily at the hands of the newly acquired Paphlagon, who in short order has wheedled his way into Demos's good graces and so taken over the running of the entire household. After the duo sings in unison a pitiable lament, in a moment constituting their greatest comity, it falls to Demosthenes to take the initiative and "seek out some salvation for the two of us" (12). He compels Nicias to make the first suggestion, which proves to be escape or desertion from the household. When Demosthenes demurs, Nicias can think of no better alternative than to "prostrate ourselves before images of the gods" (31). Demosthenes' blunt statement of incredulity at this ("do you really believe in gods?" 32) makes plain how great the gulf is between them, although Demosthenes is not entirely unimpressed by Nicias's proof of the existence of gods, namely . . . their manifest hatred of Nicias! After Demosthenes, who is clearly the better speaker, explains to the audience the affair that concerns them, Nicias can but repeat his suggestion that they escape. This Demosthenes takes somewhat more seriously than before, at least inasmuch as he now demonstrates more clearly its impossibility (compare 74–78 with 29). There seems to be nothing for it; in the judgment of Nicias, "the most excellent thing for us both would be to die!" (79). Nicias's deliberations thus follow a path from human calculation to dependence on the divine to utter despair or resignation. Soldier that he is, Demosthenes is not concerned by the prospect of death but is concerned only that their death be as courageous as possible. When Nicias suggests that they adopt the means of suicide of that great

Athenian statesman Themistocles (84; also 812–13, 818, 884)—drinking bull's blood—the mere mention of drinking has something of the good effect on Demosthenes' spirits, on his hopefulness, that wine drinking will very soon have on him in fact and in spades: an altogether human deliberation may save them yet! Not the gods, then, but wine may bring their salvation. The abstemious Nicias cannot approve of this proposition. Still, demonstrating that he too is not without physical courage, Nicias ventures back into Demos's house to snatch the wine from a slumbering Paphlagon. And the wine soon has its hoped-for effect. In his new state Demosthenes conceives the idea of stealing the oracles known to be in Paphlagon's possession, an idea that this unbeliever attributes, presumably for Nicias's benefit, not now to the wine but to the "Good Divinity" (107). In the case of Nicias the apparent futility of human deliberation or action led first to the idea of gods and then to the embrace of death; in the case of the much more agile Demosthenes, the apparent futility of human deliberation or action also led to the idea of gods—or rather to the entirely human idea that the belief in oracles may be of great political use. The play as a whole underscores the soundness of that idea. The brief unity in song between the two servant-generals is in a manner restored now, for only when Demosthenes is drunk can he take seriously what Nicias takes seriously when sober.[8]

It again falls to Nicias to steal from Paphlagon, this time the oracles. According to Demosthenes' report or paraphrase of the oracle that Paphlagon was guarding especially closely, which paraphrase we and Nicias must rely on (compare 197–201), the prophet Bacis foretold of both the succession of democratic leaders in

8. Consider Strauss, *Socrates and Aristophanes*, 82.

Athens and the eventual fall of Paphlagon. First must come a dealer in oakum (Eucrates), then a dealer in sheep (Lysicles), and then "another man, more loathsome / Than he is" will take the helm: Paphlagon the leather-seller. Thus the prophecy foretells of the rise of the rule of "sellers" and hence of the lower classes in Athens, and at least in the change from sheep-seller to leather-seller, the prophecy speaks explicitly of a decline. (Paphlagon himself will later grant the point at 765.) Athens would seem to be going from bad to worse. Nicias infers from the pattern thus established that another seller will be required to oust Paphlagon, although Demosthenes' report of the oracle does not quite dictate this; it seems to be Demosthenes who suggests that the one to destroy Paphlagon will be "possessed of an extraordinary art" (is this necessarily a worse art?): a sausage-seller! And when Nicias wonders where they might find such a fellow, he himself announces in his very next breath the good news: "But here's one coming over / Into the marketplace, as if divinely!" (146–47) The appearance of not just any sausage-seller but of what proves to be *the* sausage-seller could well seem to be a stroke of great good luck, but Nicias of course attributes it to the divine. (Perhaps in his view the gods do not hate Athens, or they do hate Cleon.) It is not impossible, however, that Demosthenes the atheist worked backward, so to speak, from his happening to spot a sausage-seller approaching them to the particulars of the "prophecy": the very thing we need to get us out of our fix is . . . a seller of sausages!

Demosthenes' announcement to the sausage-seller of the astounding future awaiting him is understandably greeted by that fellow with disbelief: "Why, good fellow, don't you let me wash my tripe / And sell my sausages, rather than ridicule me?" (160–61). In this way the Sausage-Seller first comes into sight as a rather modest fellow and, in his readiness to make obeisance "to the earth and the gods," also a pious one (155–57 and 640; consider 193). It is easy to share the Seller's disbelief. For Demosthenes promises him not only complete supremacy in Athens over demos, Council, Assembly, and generals—hence over Demosthenes and Nicias— but also the control of Athens' navy and therewith of the empire. In short, Demosthenes promises the Sausage-Seller that he is about to become "a real man" (177–79). It turns out that the qualities the Sausage-Seller thinks will preclude him from such greatness are the very ones most needed to assure it: he is low-class, of the marketplace, bold, and all but uneducated in the things of the Muses. "For demagoguery no longer belongs to a man acquainted with the things of the Muses," Demosthenes says, "or to one whose ways are upright, / But to one who is unlearned and loathsome" (191–92). That the Sausage-Seller can barely read and write *is* cause for concern: if only he were illiterate! Demosthenes' thought, which one can arrive at without recourse to an oracle, seems to be that only a man at least as crude as Cleon is or pretends to be can dislodge him from the favor he enjoys with the demos. Demosthenes must out-Cleon Cleon. He cannot do so himself. Therefore he needs a proxy. But to what end exactly, once Cleon is gone?

Demosthenes makes good use of the oracle or oracles in his possession to convince the Sausage-Seller that the grand future thus sketched will necessarily be his (193–210). The Seller then raises a sensible concern: "But I wonder how / I can govern the demos" (211–12). Demosthenes assures him that he need only be who and what he already is ("Brutal voice, bad lineage, marketplace made. / You have *everything* needed for political governance!" 218–19) and do the sorts of things he already does. Hence the Sausage-Seller is truly a born leader of the demos, a natural. At this point in the play, Demosthenes cannot know just how true this is. Yet the Sausage-Seller remains uncertain: "And what ally / Will I have? / For the wealthy / Are afraid of him, and the crowd of the poor is petrified!" (223–24). Here Demosthenes speaks for the first time of the group of wealthy young men (731; consider 270), the cavalry or knights, who give to our play both its title and its Chorus. "But there are knights—one thousand good men / Who hate him—they'll come to your aid." In fact the anti-Cleon coalition is broader than this, for it includes also "the noble and good gentlemen among the citizenry / And whoever is clever among the spectators. / And I, together with them, as well as the god, will assist!" (225–29). If all the knights must be assumed to be among the gentlemen, not all gentlemen are of course knights; and "the clever" among the audience of Athenians is clearly intended as a term of distinction (consider, e.g., 264, with the MSS). The coalition against Cleon consists of strange bedfellows, the lowest of the demos together with the elite, whether an elite by nature or upbringing or both. One might say that the sensible or moderate (*sōphrones*) as such are opposed to Cleon (consider Thucydides 4.28.5). But it would be more precise to say that that coalition consists only of members of the elite, who agree to make use of the Sausage-Seller (or someone of his ilk) as their blunt instrument; the Knights will soon say to Paphlagon, but in the presence of the Sausage-Seller, that a man "more of a reprobate [*miarōteros*] than you" has appeared, who will "outdo you, that's clear, on the spot, / In crookedness and boldness and duping-with-stupid-tricks!" (329–31; consider also 684–86). That the Knights and the Sausage-Seller cannot be considered as anything more than temporary allies of convenience is clear enough from their exhortation to him to "demonstrate now that being raised in a moderate way [*sōphronōs*] means nothing!" (333).

At Demosthenes' summons, the chorus of Knights appears and exhorts the Seller to attack Paphlagon, the Chorus that knows nothing of the oracles of which Demosthenes has made so much to both Nicias and the Sausage-Seller. The importance of the Knights to the whole scheme becomes clear immediately. As soon as the blustering Paphlagon first appears, in advance of the Knights, the Sausage-Seller starts to leave in fear; his confidence or courage returns to him only once the Knights appear and begin to assault Paphlagon (compare 240–41 with 271–72). Yet the change in Athenian politics the elite have in mind cannot be accomplished by brute force alone, for in that case recourse to the Sausage-Seller would be unnecessary; and neither does it aim at replacing the democracy with an oligarchy or aristocracy or, still less, tyranny (consider the mention of the tyrant Hippias at 447–49). Instead, Demosthenes and the Knights seem to have in mind the installation of a new leader of the demos and hence of the democracy, but a leader with two outstanding qualifications from their point of view: one who can exceed even Paphlagon in "shamelessness" in speech and deed,[9] a man who looks fondly on the gutter as a familiar haunt; and one who will pay heed to his betters or defer to them. The Sausage-Seller gives every evidence of such deference thus far, and he will very soon demonstrate beyond all doubt his "shamelessness."

In fact there prove to be three main contests between Paphlagon and the Sausage-Seller that eventually decide the fates of each, contests that are variously described as a cock fight, a naval battle, and a wrestling match: the initial skirmish just alluded to concerning superior shamelessness, which Demos does not witness (271–

_____

9. Consider 277, 324, 385, 398, 409, 638, and 1206.

494); the contest before the Athenian Council, which takes place offstage while the first parabasis is performed (compare 482–487 with 611–15 and context); and the climactic contest before Demos himself (722–972) that includes among other things the presentation of competing oracles (997–1110) and the final showdown involving benefactions performed or promised (1151–1228).

Of the first contest we note only a few things. Paphlagon initially expresses surprise at the hostility of the Knights, and his paper-thin attempt to win them over by flattery is brusquely rejected by them (266–70). However lowly his family's source of income in the leather trade—a point Aristophanes hammers away at here and elsewhere—Paphlagon does not consider himself of the demos or multitude (consider 346); he boasts of mocking Demos behind his back even as he curries favor with him (713). Paphlagon considers himself, if anything, a father to Demos, whereas the Sausage-Seller considers himself a son to Demos, "O Father . . . dearest one," and he never mocks him (compare the implication of 1037–39 with 725–26; also 1216). Paphlagon, then, is between two chairs. He is a lowly seller who nonetheless despises Demos and yet must fawn over him for ends of his own; and he is in his turn despised by the Knights and the wealthy more generally. If the Knights have only contempt for Paphlagon, they take pleasure in and then evince something approaching respect for the Sausage-Seller, as he stands toe to toe with Paphlagon in the delivery of eye-watering abuse and tit-for-tat vulgarities; their praise of him advances from "O Most Clever Flesh!" to "O Most Noble Flesh and Best in Soul of All!" to "the greatest benefit to all human beings" (421, 457, 836). The Knights surely see in his unflinching feistiness, in his utter shamelessness, the means to their own de facto victory (consider 277).

The end of the first contest prepares the way for the second, in front of the Council. Before that can occur, or as it occurs, the Chorus must sing its "anapests," in what constitutes the first parabasis. In doing so, however, the Chorus does not "strip" (compare *Acharnians* 627) but instead remains in character as knights. Their first task is to sing in praise of Aristophanes. They have agreed to do so, as they would not readily have done in the case of any old-fashioned comic poet, "because [Aristophanes] hates the same people we do and dares to say the just things" (510). An alliance is possible, then, between the Knights and the poet. The Knights manifest no interest in poetry, but then again Aristophanes is a most political poet; their shared hatred of Paphlagon and their shared interest in the just cause supply common ground enough for the purpose at hand.

We are somewhat surprised to see that the Chorus turns next to explain on behalf of the poet what "many of you" have been asking him, namely, "how it is that long ago he didn't ask for a chorus of his own," but instead delayed putting forth plays under his own name. This is surprising because—if Aristophanes did not himself produce his first three plays, as the record suggests[10]—he was still young, perhaps even in his early twenties, when he stepped forward with the *Knights* to make his debut as a writer-producer ("teacher": *didaskalos*). Apparently this struck "many" as constituting a "delay"![11] At any rate, the wisdom of that "delay," if such it was, is demonstrated

10. See, e.g., the list of Aristophanes' plays, complete with producers' names, in Henderson (Loeb), 4–5.

11. This statement may be of a piece with the report here that Aristophanes regards being a comic producer as "the most difficult task of them all" (515-16)—more difficult than being, say, a knight? Aristophanes' dates are quite uncertain, his birth being assigned anywhere from 457 to 445 B.C.E.

by the fates of three comic predecessors or older contemporaries (Magnes, Cratinus, and Crates), to whom Aristophanes here doffs his hat: all of them knew considerable and justified success, only to be set aside by the fickle Athenians as they aged. This fate Aristophanes apparently wished to put off (by a few years at most). What is more convincing and probably more important, Aristophanes also acknowledges that he needed time to perfect his craft, as a ship's pilot must first become a rower before taking the rudder in hand and then commanding the bow (541–45). In contrast to the Sausage-Seller, then, whose untutored nature is sufficient to rise to democratic prominence, Aristophanes himself must undergo a rigorous training or apprenticeship; serving or wooing the comic Muse (517) is more intellectually demanding than is serving or wooing the demos. Still, Aristophanes, too, is concerned with winning the favor of the demos; the Knights conclude their discussion of Aristophanes by urging the audience to raise a great round of applause for him, "a fine, Lenaean clamor," which would amount to giving him back-to-back victory prizes (545–47). (Here the Knights acknowledge the fact that they are in play, which means that they come very close indeed to "stripping.")

Just as in the *Acharnians*, so also in the *Knights*, Aristophanes "interrupts" the overwhelmingly political proceedings of the comedy to comment or have commented on his own doings as a poet. We note that, in the earlier play, Cleon proved to be the link between politics and poetry (consider *Acharnians* 628–64); in the present play, the Knights more obviously supply that link (consider above all 507–10 and context). And if the earlier play stressed the great risk that Aristophanes ran in fighting Cleon, the present play stresses instead the powerful alliance that Aristophanes, and of course the Sausage-Seller, can rely on now in that same fight: the Knights.

Aristophanes, then, has something in common, not only with the Knights, or with the noble and good gentlemen more broadly, but also with the Sausage-Seller. More precisely, Aristophanes must fall somewhere between the upper-class loathers of Cleon and the low-class man who will displace him; Aristophanes can speak the language—can anyone doubt that he has mastered the language?—of both the justice-loving Knights and the vulgarity-spewing Seller. But this is to say that he cannot be equated with either, even as he somehow encompasses them both.

The Knights then turn to speak of what is most important to them as distinguished from Aristophanes. They call upon or praise (1) Poseidon, god of horses; (2) their fathers, who fought bravely on behalf of the city and (in contrast to too many today) expected no special recompense for so doing; (3) Athena, "city defender," together with her companion Nike (Victory); and, most charmingly, (4) their noble horses. It should be noted that the Knights do not praise themselves, and they request no special honor for their deeds, alluding to a recent victory of theirs over Corinth only in order to lavish praise on their equine comrades (595–607). Aristophanes both praises himself (he is after all the author of this parabasis) and requests special honor for his poetry. He is not as noble as the Knights, then, to say nothing of their fathers. To repeat, the alliance between Aristophanes and the Knights is a strictly political one and so has its limits.

With the conclusion of the parabasis, the Sausage-Seller returns from the Council. He gives an animated account of the proceedings. By the time he arrived there, we learn, Paphlagon was already unleashing "thunder-hurling words" and uttering amazing things "against the Knights" (626–27): Paphlagon is silent about the Sausage-Seller because he does not yet take seriously the threat he poses. After calling on the patron saints that are his and making obeisance in response to what he is sure is a sign of divine favor (640; recall 156), the Sausage-Seller addresses the Council. He gains their favor first with the news that since the war broke out, sprats have never been cheaper. He thus appeals to their economic interests. Paphlagon does not dispute the news but appeals instead to their higher concerns by suggesting that they sacrifice "one hundred bulls to the goddess" in thanks (656). The Sausage-Seller does him one, or two, better. He proposes that they sacrifice *two* hundred bulls in thanks—at a cost that would far outstrip their savings in sprats—and, if anchovies go for a hundred an obol, that they add to the sacrifice one thousand goats. The combination of economic benefit (and delicious food) with ostentatious piety proves irresistible to the Council; the Council rejects out of hand Paphlagon's attempt to regain their favor by suggesting that they listen to a Spartan herald who has come to negotiate a peace treaty. Why agree to peace when things are going so well?! This plea for peace is an astonishing about-face for Paphlagon, the most vocal proponent of the war or the most vigorous opponent of peace (794–96). Yet it would be wrong to accuse him of operating here without principle; the clear principle that guides Paphlagon in everything is his own advancement. Questions of policy, even of war and peace, amount to mere details by comparison.

The Chorus is of course delighted by the Sausage-Seller's speeches and deeds (617–18 and 683–87), but, veterans of battle as they are, they warn him that more is still to come. Right on cue—Nicias would say "as if divinely"—Paphlagon appears in a rage. In the brief interlude before the first appearance of Demos, each man trades insults and threats in a manner we have almost become accustomed to, although the Sausage-Seller, fresh from victory before the Council, seems more emboldened than before. When the old curmudgeon Demos appears, both men vie for his favor by appealing to the friendship and indeed the love each feels for him. Here Paphlagon has the advantage because he can appeal to past deeds done in his capacity as household servant or—forgetting for a moment the comic conceit of the whole play—as a commander who sailed to Pylos (see 743). The Sausage-Seller, by contrast, shows his love by venturing what is (if I am not mistaken) the only criticism of Demos stated to his face in the play, at least prior to his miraculous rejuvenation (1340–55): "For you / Are like boys who are the objects of love: / You don't accept those who are noble and good gentlemen / But give yourself to lamp-sellers and shoe menders / And leatherworkers and hide-sellers" (736–40). Here, at any rate, the Sausage-Seller seeks not to flatter but to improve Demos. Striking too is the fact that the Seller does not make the case for himself but rather for "the noble and good gentlemen" as potential allies of Demos. The Sausage-Seller remembers his betters.

Still, the contest between these two lovers of Demos will mostly revolve around flattery and the performance of benefactions past, present, and future. There is no limit to the promises that democratic politicians must make to curry favor with the electorate, who individually may be quite sensible but, en masse, tend to be remarkably foolish (consider especially 752–55). In short order, the Sausage-Seller produces a cushion for Demos's behind—the very behind that sat on the benches of the ships at Salamis!—shoes for his feet, a warm winter cloak, medicine for his shins, and a soft rabbit's tail with which to daub his eyes. The concern for bodily health and comfort constitutes a great part of democratic politics, then and now, and since Paphlagon matches him in none of these, his descent begins. Demos's initial criticism of Paphlagon (822–23) is extended or amplified in the course of these exchanges (858–59, 892, 946–48) while also being punctuated by growing praise of the Sausage-Seller (786–87, 873–74, 884–86, 943–45). The change in favor thus begun first culminates in Demos taking his signet ring from Paphlagon and giving it to the Sausage-Seller. Accordingly, Paphlagon must now rely on the heavy artillery: he begs Demos ("Master": 960) to listen to the oracles and prophecies in his possession. (Nicias's theft of Paphlagon's oracle or oracles, it turns out, left him with a great many more; there is no shortage of oracles in Athens.) Not to be outdone, the Sausage-Seller too claims to have a vast store of them, these from Bacis's older and hence better brother Glanis. Here Aristophanes mocks both the proliferation of oracles and the notorious ambiguity of them. Demos cannot make head or tail of Paphlagon's oracles; Paphlagon's interpretation of them always redounds to his own benefit, the Sausage-Seller's always to Paphlagon's detriment. Paphlagon sees only himself, of course, in the oracles' references to a lion, a hawk, and a "sacred, saw-toothed dog"—he who had earlier heaped contempt on dogs (415–16). The culmination of this competition in oracles and prophecies (and dreams: 1090–95) is Demos's preference for Glanis over Bacis and hence for the Sausage-Seller over Paphlagon (1096–99).

As Paphlagon and the Sausage-Seller prepare offstage for one last competition in the proffering of benefits, the Knights and Demos have a remarkably frank conversation (1111–50). The Knights follow the example of Pericles and Cleon by comparing Demos's rule or empire to a "tyranny" feared by all human beings,[12] foolish or mindless in other respects though Demos may be. For his part, Demos contends that he voluntarily says the fool-

---

12. Compare 1111–14 with Thucydides 2.63 and 3.37.

ish things he does and that he knowingly raises up a leader for a time, only to swat him down again at will when the flow of benefits ceases. Demos, in other words, is not quite the old fool he seems to be and is certainly taken to be by Paphlagon. In keeping with this revelation, Demos expresses annoyance at both Paphlagon and the Sausage-Seller for the first time (1157; consider also 1163). The transition from the leadership of Paphlagon to that of the Sausage-Seller is complete when Demos sees that the basket of the former is still full of goods, that of the latter empty. That transition is sanctioned even by "a Pythian oracle / That indicates the only one by whom I ought to be defeated!" (1229-30). For when the Sausage-Seller gives the correct reply to each of Paphlagon's four questions based on that oracle, Paphlagon himself concludes that he is doomed. This is so despite the fact that the Sausage-Seller here overstates somewhat his lack of education (compare 1235-36 with 189); and his claim to have sold his sausages at the city gates, as distinguished from the marketplace, is at least surprising, since he has never spoken of the former but only, and repeatedly, of the latter.[13] If, in addition, Paphlagon is still in possession of this oracle predicting the manner of his demise, Demosthenes must not be (compare his mention of a Pythian oracle at 220). Was he ever in possession of it? And speaking of Demosthenes, he here puts in one last appearance: he comes to the Sausage-Seller, hat in hand, asking to be the equivalent of a law clerk in the new order. The Sausage-Seller never replies in speech or in deed to this request. It would seem that the Sausage-Seller no longer defers to his betters or is in the process of forgetting them.

---

13. Consider 180, 218, 293, 410, and 636, as well as Strauss, *Socrates and Aristophanes*, 102-3.

Of the second and very late parabasis (1264–1315), we note only a few things. First, it is not quite as clear in the second parabasis as it was in the first that it is the Knights who address us, although Aristophanes himself does not explicitly do so. Two badly impoverished fellows are mentioned (Lysistratus and Thumantis), against whom singers should say nothing; this is followed by the mention of two fellows fully deserving of much censure (Ariphrades and Cleonymus), each licentious in his own way. And just as the first parabasis ended with a personification of Athenian horses, so the second ends with a personification of Athenian ships. These lady ships protest the request of Hyperbolus, a leading Athenian demagogue and the man who will succeed Cleon, for a hundred of them to head to Carthage. This they refuse to do and resolve instead to seek sanctuary by sailing to the (landlocked) Theseum or to the shrine of the Furies.

Enter now the Sausage-Seller. He is a new man, fully in command of Demos and the household. He soon presents to us the miracle at which he has been laboring, a feat belonging more to a god than to a mere man (compare 1335 with 1338; recall 177–79): Demos having been boiled so as to be rendered beautiful and young once again, just as he was some sixty years ago in the days of Aristides and Miltiades. And as the Sausage-Seller had ventured to do once before, so now he again criticizes Demos to his face, informing him of how foolish he used to be in his senescence; Demos's profession of shame at hearing this undercuts his earlier contention that he knew full well what he was doing (compare 1121–50 with 1355). Aristophanes, we note, is somewhat less daring here than is the Sausage-Seller, for the poet offers what amounts to a tough criticism of the present-day behavior of the current demos—well represented in the theater (consider 1318)—but he does so only in the guise of a comic critique of the past behavior of a fellow named Demos.

We learn now how the new-old Athens will be governed or how Demos will conduct himself in his vigorous youth, freshly decked out in the garb of an earlier and finer epoch. The first matters he and the Sausage-Seller take up concern the military. The navy must be maintained, and no delay in paying the sailors, that is, the poorest citizens, will be allowed; hoplites—the middle class—will not be permitted to alter their registration once made. (No mention is made of the upper-class knights.) In addition, no beardless youths will be allowed to speak in public, "those lads in the perfume market / Who chatter away . . . while seated there" (1375–80). The remedy that Demos proposes for such chattering youths will be hunting, *the* preparation for warfare. And, just as in the good old days, pederasty will be prevalent. A personified thirty-year peace treaty now appears, and the end of the war thus allows Demos to return "to [the] fields" (1394; 805). It remains only to punish Paphlagon, and this the Sausage-Seller does with remarkable gentleness: Paphlagon need only take up the art of sausage-selling at the city gates!

The new-old Athens, then, will remain a democracy. The temporary cooperation of Demosthenes, the Knights, "the noble and good gentlemen," and the Sausage-Seller does not result in a mixed regime, contrary to our initial expectation and whatever Aristophanes himself might have thought of such an arrangement. For the Sausage-Seller here reigns supreme and alone; he is at least as much in charge of the city as was Paphlagon, although he is surely a better man by nature than is Paphlagon. Demosthenes' rather humble request to become a law clerk is, as we saw, met with perfect silence. There is no obvious place for the Knights in the new order. We are struck now by their passing note of hesitation or concern in the midst of heated exchanges between Paphlagon and the Sausage-Seller: "The rest that you [i.e., the Sausage-Seller] say I found pleasing, but one thing doesn't agree with me: / That you alone will drink down the gravy from the [political] affairs" (359–60). Democratic Athens will in addition be largely rural once again, founded on the mostly conservative agricultural or farming populace that shuns the city and its modish ways (consider *Assembly of Women* 431–32). Of course, if the demos returns to the fields, it will only occasionally take a hand in the governance of the city; the day-to-day governance will be left to the Sausage-Seller. Athens will surely maintain its martial excellence and be as brave in the defense of itself and of Greece as it was in its golden age; less clear is the fate of the empire in the new dispensation, although the maintenance of the navy is certainly compatible with the maintenance of the empire. Finally, Athens will shed its notoriously litigious ways: closing up the law courts is in fact the first order of business announced by the Sausage-Seller (1316–18).

Thus the new-old Athens will make possible for the bulk of its citizens a peaceful, bucolic way of life under the remarkably capable administration of the Sausage-Seller. According to Demosthenes, we remember, the Sausage-Seller is particularly well suited to his new task because of his all but nonexistent education. He utterly lacks refinement or "culture." Yet we can now say that the man is certainly clever or cagey, not without courage or at least boldness, and possessed of a native intelligence. He is well informed of Paphlagon's doings, both at home and abroad.[14] Paphlagon

---

14. Consider 316–18, 391–94, 438 (Potidaea), 465–67 (Argos and Sparta), 469 (the Spartan prisoners), 480 (Boeotia), 792–96 (Archeptolemus's offer of peace), 801–9, 813–19 (Themistocles), and 834 (Mytilene).

naturally rises to the top when given the opportunity to do so. And this despite the fact that he is wholly without political ambition: he was twice told—once in his youth (425–26) and once in his maturity—that he would one day rule the demos, but neither prediction fired his ambition. He rules and rules well without seeking to rule; this accords with the adage that those hungriest to rule are for that very reason the least fit to rule. The Sausage-Seller comes into view here as the natural leader of a democracy: devoted to the demos as to its father, eager to aid it in all things but also willing to criticize it when criticism is due, not clamoring for rule but willing to take it on when called to do so.

There is just one massive problem with this otherwise pleasing spectacle. The transformation of Demos and all that goes together with it depend on things either impossible or highly unlikely: (1) the comic impossibility that is boiling Demos, and (2) the chance discovery of so naturally gifted a ruler as the Sausage-Seller. And so we must ask: is a return to the golden age of Athenian democracy really possible according to Aristophanes? The answer to this question must be no. For that age—if in fact it *was* a golden one—is gone and gone for good. There is no real world, noncomic equivalent of boiling the demos. Civic virtues once lost cannot be regained.

Yet this thought need not lead one simply to despair over the fate of Athenian democracy or of democracy as such. This is so because what we have called the obvious message of the *Knights* remains: Athens should rid itself of Cleon and guard against taking on another of his kind. That step is possible and worth taking. By ridiculing Cleon mercilessly and repeatedly, Aristophanes does all he can to strip the luster off Cleon, to defang him, to puncture his bluster and bravado. In this respect Aristophanes does dare to teach "the just things." And to that end Aristophanes can be at least as vulgar as the Sausage-Seller; and, again like the Sausage-Seller, he evinces no interest in ruling Athens himself. Yet he is surely also wiser than the Sausage-Seller. Aristophanes, one might say, is a sort of super Sausage-Seller who tries in his comedies to effect a "boiling" of the Athenian demos, even as he remains entirely sober about the prospect of a genuine return to any allegedly golden age.

In the *Knights* we are witnesses to both the decline of Athens and its wonderful restoration. This restoration, to repeat, belongs in a comedy because it is comically impossible. It is outlandish. "All things by nature also decline," as Pericles himself once went so far as to say publicly (Thucydides 2.64.3). Within the confines of the comedy, we witness this succession of democratic leaders: Eucrates, Lysicles, Cleon, the Sausage-Seller. Hence the decline is stopped and indeed reversed. But the play itself points us in the direction of the truth. Cleon is followed in fact, not by the Sausage-Seller, but by Hyperbolus, waiting in the wings (1304 and context; 1363). If political decline is inevitable, then, are we compelled at best or at most simply to accept that harsh fact? Is political decline always and in every respect to be lamented? Much depends on the standard or standards in the light of which one judges the decline in question. In this connection we note that for all the abuse Cleon suffers in the play, the Chorus is permitted to report a certain praise of him (973–84):

> Most pleasant will be the light of day
> For those here present and
> For those who here arrive,
> If Cleon perishes.
> Yet there were certain
> Quite troublesome elders
> In the bazaar of the courts

I heard gainsaying this—
On the grounds that if he had not become great
In the city, there'd never have been
Those two useful implements:
A pestle and a ladle.

In the only passage of the play in which the name Cleon appears, Aristophanes conveys the judgment of certain "elders"—they could well be from the vaunted generation of those who fought against the Medes—that in fact Cleon was instrumental in attacking Athens' enemies (the pestle) and adding to its coffers (the ladle; consider 774–76). In other words, from a strictly political point of view, Cleon is not so easily to be condemned or is even to be praised. A majority of Athenians, after all, found him very much to their liking for a good number of years.

Immediately following the lines quoted, the Chorus (again speaking in the first person singular) criticizes Cleon on somewhat strange or at any rate surprising grounds (985–96):

But I for my part also wonder at this,
At the swinishness of his Music education.
For the boys who went to school
With him assert that
Often he would tune his lyre
Only to the Dorian mode
And that he was unwilling to learn another.
And then the cithara teacher,
In his anger, ordered him to be led away
On the grounds that "this boy is incapable of learning
Anything except the Dorian!"

Thus Cleon is contemptible on account of the poverty of his youthful education in things Musical. This criticism has nothing whatever to do with politics. We discern the following range of educations on display in the *Knights:* from one who is all but ignorant of the Muses (the Sausage-Seller) to one who knows only the Dorian mode (Cleon) to Aristophanes' audience, who, officially at least, are "by yourselves already experienced / In all manner of Muse" (505). Whether this characterization really applies to the whole of Aristophanes' audience or only to its most serious part (those possessed of a "mind": 503) is less important than seeing that it undeniably applies to the poet himself. The difference in the two standards of judging is connected with the two peaks of which human beings are capable, as members of a political community and as individuals concerned with "the Muses," for example, or with the truth. To put this in Aristotelian terms, the two peaks of human life are acting and thinking, action and contemplation. The olden times officially celebrated here include Miltiades, Aristides, and, one might add, Aeschylus; the debased present includes Cleon, the Sausage-Seller, and Euripides (18). And Aristophanes. Would the very comedy we have been enjoying and learning from be possible in times of the strictest public rectitude? A highly developed education in the things of the Muses is possible in at least some decadent times, decadent judged from the point of view of an altogether political—and martial ("Dorian")—excellence. In the first parabasis, we remember, the Knights praise not only Poseidon, "Lord of Horses," but also Athena, "city defender," to be sure, but also the goddess of wisdom: we are told there that Athens surpasses all other cities in "war and poets and power" (585). This praise of the city captures beautifully the difference in the standards under discussion, for Athens is impressive for its "power" but also for its "poets." Cleon can thus be praised for giving to his city a pestle and a ladle; and he can be condemned for the swinishness of his education in the things of the Muses. The latter, alas, in no way precludes the former, just as a city of great power may be without great poets. Athens, to its credit, had both for a time. With this consideration in mind, we note that it is not so clear that Aristophanes would condemn those youths chattering away in the perfume markets (recall 1375–80). At any rate, if those youths need improvement, as they surely do, it would likely come not from hunting (1382) but from an education deserving of the name. The *Knights* is indeed a most political play. But Aristophanes cannot treat politics in his manner without at least pointing toward what in his view transcends politics and so permits one to understand it in its proper perspective.

Cleon's Speech to the Athenian Assembly

Thucydides, *War of the Peloponnesians and Athenians* 3.37–40

In 428 B.C.E., the city of Mytilene, on the island of Lesbos, revolted from Athens in the hope that it could unite the whole island and rule it, urged on in this by the Spartans. The Athenians found this act of rebellion particularly galling because they had always treated the city with consideration, allowing it to maintain its own defensive walls, for example, and fleet of triremes or warships. In their anger, the Athenians initially voted to kill all the Mytilenean adult males and to enslave the women and children. Soon gripped, however, by misgivings over the harshness of their own decree, the Athenians convened a second assembly to reconsider their decision. Here Cleon, "the most violent of the citizens and much the most persuasive with the demos at that time" (Thucydides 3.36.6), rose to speak in favor of maintaining the previous day's decision: kill all the men and enslave the women and children.[1]

3.37 [1] "On many other occasions before now, I for my part judged democracy to be incapable of ruling others, and especially at present in your change of heart concerning the Mytileneans. [2] For on account of your day-to-day freedom from fear and the absence of any plotting in your relations with one another, you are of the same disposition also as regards the allies; and you believe that your softness does not bring you into danger when either you make

---

1. I have used the text of Thucydides, *Historia*, ed. Henry Stuart Jones, Oxford Classical Texts (Oxford: Clarendon Press, 1942).

mistakes, being persuaded by an argument of theirs, or you give in through pity—without, however, gaining the gratitude of the allies thereby. For you fail to examine the fact that the empire you hold is a tyranny imposed on those who are plotting against you and who are ruled involuntarily, they who heed you not as a result of favors you do them to your own detriment, but rather as a result of your superiority in strength and not their goodwill. [3] But the most terrible thing of all is this: if nothing will be firmly fixed for us concerning whatever resolutions seem best, and if we will not recognize that a city using inferior but unaltered laws is stronger than one that uses fine laws lacking authority; that ignorance accompanied by moderation is more beneficial than is cleverness accompanied by license; and that more ordinary human beings for the most part manage cities better than do those who are more intelligent. [4] For the latter wish to appear wiser than the laws and to prevail over whatever may be said at a given time bearing on the commonweal, on the grounds that there could not be any other, greater matters in which they could make clear their judgment; and it is a result of some such thing that they most often cause cities to falter. But the former types, mistrusting their own intelligence, deem themselves to be more ignorant than the laws and less capable of censuring the argument of a fine speaker; and, being impartial judges rather than competitors in a contest, they mostly proceed correctly. [5] We, too, then, ought so to act and not be carried away by cleverness or by a contest in intelligence such that we advise your assembly contrary to the resolution that seemed best to it.

38 [1] "Now as for me, I am of the same judgment; and I wonder at those who are proposing to speak about the Mytileneans again and who have thus fostered a delay, which is more to the advantage of those who have committed injustice. For in that case he who suffers something proceeds against the doer of it with a duller anger, whereas the vengeance that lies as close as possible to the suffering obtains the punishment that is particularly fitting. And I wonder, too, at anyone who will speak against this and deem it worthwhile to contend that the injustices of the Mytileneans are advantageous for us, whereas our misfortunes have become harmful to the allies. [2] In fact it is clear that either he, trusting in his ability to speak, would strive to show that the resolution that seemed altogether best was not in fact pronounced, or else, being carried away by profit, he will attempt to mislead by working out a specious argument.

[3] But the city, as a result of such contests, grants the prizes to others while it itself takes on the dangers. [4] And you are to blame in that you conduct contests badly, you who are accustomed to being spectators of speeches, on the one hand, and listeners to deeds, on the other, examining how future deeds will come to pass on the basis of those who speak well about them but, as for actions already undertaken, you regard as more trustworthy not what you actually see of the action done but rather what you hear about it, relying on those who utter fine rebukes of the relevant speech. [5] You are best at being deceived by a speech marked by novelty and at being unwilling to go along with the tried and tested, slaves that you are to whatever is newfangled at a given moment but despisers of whatever is usual or customary. [6] And each person especially wants to be able to speak himself but, failing that, then, in competing with those who do state such things, you want not to be held to be slow in following the judgment rendered, instead anticipating with praise any sharp remark made and being eager to perceive in advance the points stated—but slow to understand in advance what will result from them, [7] since you examine anything else, so to speak, other than the actual circumstances in which we are living and give no adequate thought at all to what is present to hand. You are simply overcome by the pleasure involved in hearing and resemble more spectators seated before sophists than those who are deliberating about a city.

39 [1] "In my attempt to turn you from this, I declare that Mytilene is the single city that has done you the greatest injustice. [2] For I—when it comes to those who cannot bear your rule² or who revolted because they were compelled to do so by enemies—I have sympathy for them. But those who are in possession of an island equipped with walls and who were afraid of our enemies only by sea, where they themselves, outfitted with triremes, were not defenseless against them; and who dwell there autonomously and receive from us preeminent honors: it was they who did such things. What else did they do except plot against us and rebel, rather than revolt—for "revolt" belongs to those who have suffered something violent—and seek to destroy us by standing with our worst enemies? And that is more terrible than if, having come into possession of their own power, they had waged war against us. [3] Moreover, the disasters suffered by

_____

2. Or "empire."

their neighbors did not serve as an example to them, when all those who revolted from us were subdued, and neither did their present prosperity prompt them to hesitate to enter into terrible dangers. But being bold about the future and filled with hopes greater than their power but less than what they wished for, they declared war, deeming it right to set strength before justice. In so doing they supposed that they would prevail and hence attacked us, and not because they are victims of injustice. [4] Those cities whose faring particularly well comes quite unexpectedly usually turn toward insolence, whereas for the most part the good fortune that befalls human beings in accord with their calculation is safer than that which is contrary to their expectation; and it is easier for them to keep faring badly at bay, so to speak, than it is for them to preserve prosperity. [5] The Mytileneans long ago should not have received any different honors from us than did the rest, and in that case they would not have proceeded to this height of insolence. For it is natural in other cases, too, for a human being to feel contempt for that which caters to him but to admire that which does not yield.

[6] "And let them be punished even now as the injustice at issue deserves, and do not attach blame only to the few while you absolve the demos. For all alike attacked you,[3] they who could have turned to us and so been in [charge of their] city right now. But in their conviction that the risk run in conjunction with the few was a surer thing, they joined in the revolt. [7] And consider: if you will assign the same penalties to those of the allies who are compelled by the enemies to revolt as you do to those who revolt voluntarily, who is there who will not revolt on the slightest pretext, given that, when they succeed, they gain their freedom and, when they falter, they suffer nothing fatal? [8] Our money and our lives[4] will in that case be subjected to the utmost risk against each city. And upon winning you take over a ruined city and henceforth will be deprived of the revenue from which we derive our strength, but when we falter, we will add enemies to the ones we already have; and the time that we ought to spend opposing those who are at present hostile to us, we will spend waging war against our own allies.

40 [1] "Hope, then—whether won by persuasive argument or purchased with cash—ought not to be held out, on the supposition that they will attain some

---

3. One MS reads "us."
4. Literally, "our souls."

sympathetic forgiveness for having erred in a manner that is only human. For the harm they did was not involuntary; they hatched a plot knowingly; and it is the *involuntary* that is forgivable. [2] So I insist now, just as I did at first as well, that you not change your mind about your prior resolutions and that you not make a mistake traceable to the three greatest disasters for the empire: pity; and pleasure in speeches; and equitable treatment.[5] [3] For it is just to grant compassion to those who are similar, but not to those who will not pity us in return and who are necessarily such as always to be our enemies. As for the orators who bring delight through their speeches, let them have a contest that involves other, lesser matters and not one in which the city, while enjoying a momentary pleasure, will suffer a great penalty, whereas they themselves will gain, in return for a good speech, good treatment. And equity is granted to those who will henceforth remain friendly associates rather than to those who continue to be such as they are, our enemies no less.

[4] "I make one point by way of summary: in being persuaded by me, you will do simultaneously what is just in regard to the Mytileneans and what is advantageous, whereas if you judge otherwise, you will not gratify them but *will* exact a penalty against yourselves. For if they were correct to revolt, you ought not to rule. And if indeed you nonetheless deem it worthwhile to rule, even though it is not appropriate, then you must punish them to your advantage, contrary to what is fitting though it be, or put a halt to the empire and act as upright men instead. [5] Deem it right to defend yourselves by means of the same penalty and to disallow those who have managed to survive the plot from coming to sight as less aggrieved than the very plotters; reflect on the things it is only likely they would do were they in a position of superiority over you, especially since they were first in committing injustices. [6] It is particularly those who do someone some harm without pretext who attack even so as to destroy him, eyeing warily the danger of an enemy who remains. For he who suffers something not demanded by necessity is harsher when he survives than is an enemy who [gives and receives] equally.

[7] "Do not become traitors to your own cause, then, but, bringing yourselves as close as possible to the judgment you held when you suffered and to the estimation you made to crush them above all else, pay them back now.

---

5. Or "equity," "fairness" (*epieikeia*).

Do not grow soft before the present case or forget the terrible danger that once hung over you. Punish them as they deserve and make of them a clear example to the other allies—that he who revolts will suffer the penalty of death. For if they know this, you will battle your own allies, and thus neglect your enemies, less."

Further Reading

Aristophanes. *Acharnians, Knights.* Ed. and trans. Jeffrey Henderson. Loeb
Classical Library. Cambridge, MA: Harvard University Press, 1998. A
relatively recent Greek-English edition, with helpful notes, by a leading
scholar of Aristophanes.

Aristophanes. *The Comedies of Aristophanes.* Vols. 1–2, *Acharnians, Knights.*
Ed. A. H. Sommerstein. Warminster: Aris & Phillips, 1980–81. These
volumes contain lively translations of the *Acharnians* and *Knights* with
thoughtful commentary keyed to the Greek text.

Dover, K. J. *Aristophanic Comedy.* Berkeley: University of California Press,
1972. A classic study by a leading classical scholar. Particularly helpful for
those seeking to understand the conventions of Greek comedy in
performance as well as Aristophanes' predecessors and contemporaries.
Also contains interpretations of the extant plays.

MacDowell, Douglas M. *Aristophanes and Athens: An Introduction to the Plays.*
Oxford: Oxford University Press, 1995. Contains general information
about Aristophanes and Greek comedy, together with discussions of each
of the eleven extant plays.

Mhire, Jeremy J., and Bryan-Paul Frost, eds. *The Political Theory of Aristophanes: Explorations in Poetic Wisdom.* Albany: SUNY Press, 2014. An
interesting and diverse collection of essays focused on the political
features of Aristophanes' comedies.

Olson, S. Douglas. *Acharnians.* Oxford: Oxford University Press, 2002. An
edition of the Greek text accompanied by very detailed commentary. For

those seeking to explore historical, literary, and political allusions or references in the plays.

Strauss, Leo. *Socrates and Aristophanes.* Chicago: University of Chicago Press, 1966. Extraordinarily detailed interpretations of all eleven plays, guided by the question of Aristophanes' critique of Socrates in the *Clouds*.

Founded in 1893,
UNIVERSITY OF CALIFORNIA PRESS
publishes bold, progressive books and journals
on topics in the arts, humanities, social sciences,
and natural sciences—with a focus on social
justice issues—that inspire thought and action
among readers worldwide.

The UC PRESS FOUNDATION
raises funds to uphold the press's vital role
as an independent, nonprofit publisher, and
receives philanthropic support from a wide
range of individuals and institutions—and from
committed readers like you. To learn more, visit
ucpress.edu/supportus.